TALES OF A SMALL-TOWN KING

Antony Takis Tsegellis

First published by Dog Ear Publishing
4011 Vincennes Road
Indianapolis, IN 46268
www.dogearpublishing.net

dog ear
PUBLISHING

ISBN: 978-145756-715-5

For Antony and Andromahi,
who have shared all my journeys,
and always love me anyway.

1

ONE LAST DRIVE

THIS MORNING, 8:00A.M.

"*Dig!*" I had to remind myself to work even as distracted as I was by my grandmother's gravestone just a few feet away. The same gravestone I had helped set in place twenty years ago. The same grandmother I had helped lay to rest.

What the hell am I doing HERE? I muttered inside my mind. Here—in middle of our family cemetery disturbing my sweet grandmother's corpse, out back behind her old house that I had grown to love, in the middle of the small town I had loved but had now grown to hate.

How the hell *did* my life get to this point? This desperate…this lost on what to do…when just two days ago I had been just a few loose ends from being clean, from finally reaching the shore after years of treading the sea of life just trying to get to the next buoy in sight. There was always another buoy to reach, another disappointing road sign pointing to my *real* destination—always still up ahead.

But this felt like something different, like something beyond another line or another hurdle. It felt more like a wall. I guess there really are moments that split life in two—into a life before and a life after. I had heard and discarded that idea offered by wannabe wise men or as a clever saying quoted in a movie. But now here was my own defining moment. Color me a naysayer now converted.

My whole life up to that point had been one job, one move, one stepping-stone to another, hoping always that temporary sweat or aggravation

1

would pay dividends leading to something "better"—though I never really had a clear view of what that would actually be. And when I had returned to my hometown for my uncle's funeral less than a week ago, I had no doubt it would bring yet another hassle to dance through, another finish line pulled yet a few days further out of reach. I would have to make small talk with family and friends I barely knew and show up with free legal documents in a small-town courthouse I despised. Dip myself back into a swamp I had gladly left behind six years ago. The dread was worthy of actual nausea, but I would do my duty as the "family attorney." No matter what they say or how gracious they seem, every lawyer or doctor hates the obligatory family favors they must perform. I promise you. Still, like a good nephew, I would appear at the funeral and get my uncle's will on the docket and probated within a week—I guess there were some benefits to small-town life—and then I would file a final inventory in six months based upon what my aunt Ellen sent me at that time.

And then I could say I was finally all but done with the town of Shiloh. My parents had passed away within six months of each other the year before. Both of my kids had already left for college, with our family home sold and my former wife relocated. Uncle Miklos, his wife, Ellen, and his son, Paris, were all that remained of the "family," which at one time had been a fairly popular, albeit unusual group of eight Greeks tucked away in a crater among the Appalachian Mountains in southeastern Kentucky. Our family photo was a clear picture of fish that had been caught in the wrong stream. Sure, a few extended relatives on my mother's side remained, but none I had seen in years, even when I was living just down the road. So, nothing to see here. Wrap up Miklos's affairs, and yet another hurdle would be cleared—and although I had said this many times before, perhaps it would be the last in putting my former life to bed.

But that was seven days ago, back when I thought I understood the course my life had taken. Pick a movie—*The Matrix, The Truman Show, Shutter Island*—or a mix of all three perhaps, any script in which the protagonist learns that his world is not what it seemed. Perhaps a "mystery wrapped in a riddle inside an enigma," if you prefer *JFK*. I had slowly unraveled all of it in the past week, most of it even in just the past day, unveiling a true puppet master with strings attached to my entire forty years spent in this place. I had cycled through amazement, anger, and now fear, all of it wholly justified.

In fact, just seven hours ago, in perhaps my final drive from Pittsburgh to Shiloh, I was forced to confront a *Neo*-like decision on what to do with my revelation—as in, I was forced to take the blue pill or the red pill without truly knowing whether Morpheus was my friend or foe. I had mindlessly made the very same drive twice a month over the past two years to visit my daughter in her last years of high school, but this time my path was consumed with a decision that would determine the rest of my life—both its course and its duration. And neither would be what I had imagined.

It was laughable, really. I had become horrible at even the most mundane life decisions. I could spend two hours picking out a pair of shoes. That's what happens when OCD meets law school. I was trained to see, argue, and believe both sides. Paralysis by analysis. While seeing and anticipating all the angles proved an admirable trait in the legal profession, some would say a constant maze of choices had wreaked havoc with my life. And after making all of those agonizing decisions, nothing in that past life even mattered now. None of my accrued wisdom and experience could help at all. I had exited the Fort Pitt Tunnel last night near midnight, and as I hit I-79 South toward Morgantown, I realized that I was truly alone. I had only my wandering thoughts and memories of Shiloh, none of which seemed applicable to the current mess I was in. If he were still around, Miklos would have been the obvious choice for advice on such life-altering matters. The obvious choice, that was, before bridges had been burned. I had severed the bulk of that relationship along with many others in Shiloh, most happily by design, but some, like my relationship with Miklos, through inertia.

1997

The phone rang just after 2 a.m. Waking up had never been an issue. I usually slept in no more than two- or three-hour chunks…two chunks a night if I was lucky. So, there was no anger at the ringing phone, just some anxiety at the timing of the call. I experienced the American Dream at times, caged monotony at others, but excitement or a 2 a.m. disruption was rarely a part of either. The typical lawyer like me in the Eastern Kentucky coal fields practiced disability law, an unglamorous exercise of sifting through opposing medical opinions to evaluate the jobs a person could or could no longer do. No fancy courtroom antics. No heated debates, smoking guns, or tearful confessions. My first job out of law school had actually been defending those claims, nothing more than a glorified insurance adjuster working against my friends, neighbors, and their families. So, I had the added stress of tiptoeing through depositions and hearings without offending anyone; I was a smiling assailant carving up a claim one sweet, innocent question at a time. My only challenge was whether I could develop the tact to deliver bad news while diverting blame to others—like the big, stingy insurance company —before the job overcame our "good guy" family reputation. That skill would become my one true superpower.

On the bright side, the pay was decent for a rookie, the cost of living was well below average, and I was home in plenty of time to see the kids on most days—my main priority in returning home after law school. I honestly wanted to be a good dad. Money was a distant second priority, other than having what I needed to provide for them, and legal fame was completely irrelevant. Six years and two kids in, mission accomplished on all counts.

However, ego also dictated some hope for myself, a desire that while creating a comfortable family life, the small-town sacrifice would also afford me a better chance to become "more"—not in the legal community, of course. From day one, I had no stomach for the nonsense there. Most of my fellow law students seemed generally petty, arrogant, and hypocritical, and most law school graduates are the same brand of sandwich, just with a heavy spread of greed on top. I know that's a broad brush to stroke across a whole profession, and maybe I was lying to myself and projecting my own issues onto others. But at least I was genuine in the hope that in a small-town country law firm, I would have the time to actually help the predominantly blue-collar folks around me, something I had yet to see from the law. Maybe this kind of life would even allow for some type of opportunity for community service or public office. There lay the perpetual struggle, though: Despite endless effort or thought, I always faced an inability to precisely define the "more" for which I had hoped, essentially any path that could combine upward mobility and social significance.

You always remember your first boss, and mine, Mr. Griffin as I would always call him, had been one of my Little League coaches when I was a kid, and he knew me and my family well. We met in his office on a Saturday morning, and dressed in hospital scrubs while slouched back in his chair behind an avalanche of case files, he asked, "Would you want the job?" That was the extent of the interview. The macroeconomic cycle in southeastern Kentucky rarely changes. If the Democrats take over Washington, coal regulation and cost of production generally go up. That equates to fewer jobs and more layoffs, which in turn spikes disability claims. So, in 1994, in the middle of the Clinton era, the workers' comp biz was booming. As the only defense lawyer in town, Mr. Griffin was as excited to have help as I was to have a job, and he wrongfully presumed I was debating between several offers. My wife, Annie, and I were so excited that I got home with no answer to her first question: "How much is he paying you?" Like I said, cash was generally a distant second priority to me.

But the job really was a good fit. The work was easy to learn, and Mr. Griffin could cut me loose with my own cases right away. Juggling numerous cases at once, trying to keep the clients updated and billed, and swapping pleasantries with the judges and opposing lawyers—to get favors when needed—fit both my OCD tendencies and my avoidance of confrontation. I had always caught more flies with honey than vinegar throughout my life, a personality trait that my new boss shared, and that could have easily been our firm's billboard slogan. Still, though I had mastered the work, it soon grew stale. And despite the free time, the inconsistent raises had stopped outright two years ago. By 1998, nearing the end of two Democratic terms, the plaintiffs' lawyers had actually mined most all of the coal of comp claims from the locals that they could. You have to actually work at some point to get injured. And since the work was drying up, so were the claims.

The writing on the wall—a decelerating law firm—actually accelerated my discontent. I had already been pining for over a year, contemplating various other jobs. Yeah, money was a distant second, but it was still second. And I had no interest in any other local firm—I was not that desperate, and any non-legal work in town would never pay enough. Despite countless hours spent scheming and wasted stamps sending out letters and résumés all over the country, not wanting to uproot the kids from school would always end any discussion inside my head about moving anywhere else.

There were still months of oxygen left at the firm, and Mr. Griffin would let me go last—and only then if he had to close the doors entirely. Not only from sentiment, but also by virtue of my being his only buffer from a return to a full slate of daily trial work and social interaction, both of which he had written off to "burnout" when I walked in the door. For proof, I needed only to remember our first trial together, just three weeks into the job. It was scheduled over in Cameron County, just across the Rupp County line, and he was going to "show me the ropes." We stopped for drive-thru drinks at a Dairy Queen on the way out of town—coffee for me, Diet Coke for him. I watched him take a sip, then proceed around the restaurant and get back into the drive-thru line, wait his turn, and then hurl his incorrect order through the window, splashing everything in sight. He drove off without a word, and I sat in fear beside him the rest of the trip. That wasn't the real him, but it was very real stress for us all.

Though I was clearly not facing burnout myself, the now-visible sight of the dead end I had always felt on the horizon had forced my own tailspin. Whether I was faced with too many choices or none at all, I could always conjure the same panic, uncertainty, and despair. *"Surely I am meant for "more,"* I would think, even as the face in the mirror whispered back, *Count your blessings.* At least I managed to fight it inside my head. For the most part, I tried to protect my loved ones from worry, and a smile and a full daily routine made a great shield, so long as no one noticed my sleep habits.

The phone rang a third time, and speaking of protecting loved ones, I realized that I had to answer it before it woke them up. "Yeah?" I mustered.

"Takie, this is Miklos. I'm really sorry to wake you. Nothing is wrong, so please don't worry. But if you have a minute, I would like to talk to you, and if you are interested, it is something you may need to hear before you go to court tomorrow."

"Okay." My mind was searching its card catalog for what Uncle Miklos could possibly mean.

"Would you be able to leave the house? Maybe for about thirty minutes? I could meet you at Huddle House for coffee. I would rather not wake up either family."

"No worries." I spouted the usual lie told by anyone taking a call at 2 a.m. "Will be right there"—I fumbled for my glasses beside the bed—"just need shoes."

And so began the first of many times Uncle Miklos went out of his way to look out for me, to show me opportunities I would have never seen on my own.

2

BLESSING IN DISGUISE

Miklos had always been fun to be around while I was growing up. The oldest of three children raised by Papa Deo to work and not be heard, even at the dinner table, Miklos managed to grow into a jolly soul. He would arrive unexpectedly with a fruit tray, a cake, and noisemakers on New Year's Eve, and he would routinely open the chocolate chip cookies and play Nintendo with me and Paris for hours during our middle school years. You can imagine how a kid would much rather hang out with Miklos than at his own house, and I lost many weekends watching football and shooting pool in his basement office, which he had transformed from a garage. I vividly remember the small work station covered in Post-it Notes, the dim parlor lighting, the filing cabinet exploding with invoices, the mixed scent of oil, grease, and hand cleaner, and the five-foot stack of legal pads in the corner. And there would be Miklos on his stool, usually in a visor or a newsboy cap on top of mechanic's pants and shirt, work boots, and suspenders—the latter of which was his trademark. His five-foot-five-inch frame was always springing with energy and he always wore a smile when I arrived, offering a drink or snack much like his mother, my Mamaw Mikey, always had. He was proof that despite Deo's stranglehold on the family business and household, her spirit had survived. Miklos combined an adorable appearance with an infectious personality, as if a sarcastic, experienced Danny DeVito and the "can do" smile and optimism of Super Nintendo's Luigi had had a child.

The short story of Miklos and the only Greeks in Shiloh, or any of the surrounding counties for that matter, had started in 1956. Picture a four-foot-ten-inch, thirty-four-year-old widow coming through Ellis Island with three kids in tow, ages thirteen, eleven, and nine, and not a word of English spoken among any of them. Deo Sideris, Miklos's stepfather, had already come to America, earning money driving a car service for the wealthy in Pittsburgh, and he had earned enough money to send back for the family's passage. Andromahi Laskaris, maiden name Tsegellis, would come from Athens and settle with Deo to form a new life not in Pittsburgh, but in small-town Kentucky, where Deo had decided he could make his fortune buying and reselling scrap metal and machinery coming out of the booming coal industry. It was there that she would grow into her role as Mamaw Mikey.

Mikey's prior husband and Miklos's father, Parisi Laskaris, had died at sea while serving in the Greek Navy after World War II, as she would tearfully tell me as a child. Through Deo, she had a chance to give Miklos, Dimi, and Terez—all listed as "John Mike Sideris" on the ship manifest since the crew could not make out their names—a better life.

Whether in Greece, Pittsburgh, or Shiloh, Deo's life was simple and constant. Like most people from the "old country," he had grown up in survival mode, so he put work first and everything else second. Miklos and my dad, Terez, were carrying cinder blocks and driving trucks by the age of thirteen, and they did not go to school until fifteen, still without knowing a word of English, and only then upon threats of truancy charges. Deo accumulated money and a few properties, expected his dinner on time, and did not care for small talk. I was four when he died of cancer in the early 1970s, and my only fleeting memory of him was one of fear and not wanting to disturb him as he sat at the kitchen table by Mikey's back door.

After that, despite her broken English, odd superstitions, and fear of most new things, Mamaw Mikey, as the kids called her, survived by salting away the money he left behind. Sure, she took forever in a grocery store matching old food can labels from her purse to those on the shelves—her idea of a grocery list since she couldn't read English—but for a child who had hidden in the bushes to spy stray food dropped from passing trucks during Mussolini's invasion of Greece in the 1940s, single motherhood in rural America was a piece of cake. She liked 7-Up, Reese's Peanut Butter Cups, and dancing to Barry Manilow, and she'd offer them up by imploring you to "Catch you some!" She held the family together as our grand matriarch, and she was the toughest person I knew until I gave her eulogy in the spring of 1998, about six months after Miklos's late-night phone call.

1997

Miklos had unnecessarily grabbed a corner booth for privacy at the Huddle House. As it was nearing 3 a.m., we were alone, and I smiled inside that there could be any Shiloh news worthy of such secrecy. Cups of coffee were already on the table, and he put down a newspaper with a smile, standing to shake my hand.

"Hey, good to see you. Take a seat."

He had the Dick Clark gene of aging; he had looked exactly the same at my high school, college, and law school graduations. Always happily social, he would never have missed such an event, and he basked in the attention that his accent and being "Greek" brought from the locals. I had seen him much less frequently since I had gone away to school, but he had made his presence and pride in my accomplishments known.

Any pride and admiration was mutual. Miklos had done rather well with the family scrap metal and recycling business, which he had turned over to Paris before getting into politics. He had also famously won one million dollars in the lottery on two different tickets in a two-month span, getting laughs and no resentment from the locals for his crazy luck followed by well-deserved pats on the back for giving generously of his newfound wealth to those in need. He was a jack-of-all-trades with chameleon-like charisma, a true blue-collar millionaire who could blend in with both rich and poor. This made Miklos the perfect asset as Rupp County's Deputy County Judge Executive, so much so that when the Democratic candidate defeated Miklos's Republican boss in the 1988 election, Miklos had simply switched parties and managed to keep his job with the newcomer. He had negotiated twenty years in politics without ever holding office himself, slowly evolving into the "guy behind the scenes" who knew everything, everyone, and how to get things done. Picture Red in *The Shawshank Redemption*.

"Big news tonight, Takie. You know Donnie Bell, don't you?"

"Of course. 'Skinny' Don, right?" (Believe it or not, Shiloh also had a larger Donnie Bell, also an attorney, whom we affectionately called "Heavy D".

"Yes. He just turned himself in to local police about an hour ago, Takie. Apparently, he drove to Louisville and killed two clients last night. It looks bad."

I raised my eyebrows and sat up straight. "Say what?"

Skinny Don had been the assistant county attorney at least since I had returned to town five years before. He kept his distance but was always cordial. He was known for his role as the delinquent tax collector, for helping with the local high school wrestling team, and for the dip of snuff always under his lip. Long before I ever knew him as an attorney, he had helped me and many a high school athlete score beer from Shiloh's most famous career bootlegger—and perhaps the only ninety-year-old female in her field—Cass O'Malley. More time for playtime memories later, though. This was business.

"Really?" I wanted details, but I also wanted to know how this connected to me.

"Don's family had called us to the parish to pray. Apparently, he had called his wife on the way home. She was hysterical. I think they had found Yancey [Yancey Danforth, the richest lawyer in town and most likely to lie in any given sentence] to get him cleaned up and discuss his options."

Miklos was relatively calm for describing such an outlandish event, though I must admit I had never really seen him at "work," his wheels spinning as a politician. Still, a local lawyer and fellow church member with a good reputation in jail for double murder?

"Do you think it's *true*? There has to be another story, right?"

"May have been an affair gone wrong...or maybe a financial disagreement. No one knows for sure yet." Miklos spoke deliberately, with his tight lips and heavy accent. Again, I had never seen him on alert or in crisis mode. He made you wonder whether he lacked the words he needed or just could not decide on those he wanted.

"The reason I called you"—Uncle Miklos cleared his throat—"is that they are going to need a replacement for him. Part-time to start and then full-time in the event he never makes it back. The offer may not come for a few days, or maybe even a couple of weeks, but they will make the decision quickly...maybe even tomorrow. So, if you have any interest in leaving Mr. Griffin and getting into the courthouse scene, you need to have your answer ready."

"Really? And you think they would want *me*?" I drowned out the gleeful music in my head.

"No reason they wouldn't, Takie. You've worked hard. You're raising a good family. You have a good reputation. We are always looking for good people to help us in politics, especially since most of us are getting on the older side. You could be part of the new guard."

He had made it simple, even for me. Right place, right time, right relative. "I don't have much to think about, Miklos. I have to make sure that Mr. Griffin would allow me to work part-time somewhere else, but it should be okay. And it would give me a gradual, graceful way out that I definitely need."

"I had hoped it would fit what you want. I know you feel like you are... maybe not reaching your full potential there. Don't burn any bridges yet, but I will pass along your interest, and you will likely get a call later today." He wiped his mouth neatly, then started to stand, dropping a five-dollar bill on the table. "Here's money for the coffee. I need to get back, else Ellen will start to think I'm up to no good." He chuckled.

With that, he was gone. And all he left behind was new hope for a new plan for my life.

3

LOST AND FOUND

LAST NIGHT, 1:00 A.M.

The gas warning *ding* brought me out of my Huddle House daydream. Stopping somewhere in upper West Virginia, at what resembled virtually any rural Kentucky interstate exit, the only thing that mattered was whether there was a twenty-four-hour place open for gas. Coffee and fuel actually seemed petty at this point. I ignored the usual small talk from the truckers in line at the counter, as it was hard to imagine that the weather, the traffic, or whether the coffee was freshly made still mattered in some parts of the world. The typical fight sprang from the voices in my head—one anxiously thumped to get back on the road, as if Shiloh would close its doors if I didn't arrive by morning; another remembered the unresolved issue at hand and urged me to make this stop, however trivial, last as long as possible.

Those competing characters in my head, one bold and ambitious, the other ever fearful of rocking the status quo, had tugged my life into an oddly misshapen path, at least from the rearview mirror. Along the way, the path of least resistance had guided most decisions. I had never grown comfortable with being a true shyster, say, the characters in *The Lincoln Lawyer* or *Better Call Saul*, for example—an attorney who could stretch the rules and dodge the raindrops all while lining his pockets. So, I lived with equal doses of disdain and envy of Shiloh's equivalent attorneys such as Yancey Danforth or his partner, Sean Dixon—aggravation with their moral flexibility balanced by aggravation with my own financial instability.

I had taken the initial job with Mr. Griffin over and against the risk and turmoil of a big firm in a larger town, and I had stayed there seven years, unwilling to leap into solo practice. Instead, I would come home railing on Yancey and Sean as they had ranted and raved during hearings, all a show for their injured client, before later sharing coffee with me and accepting the settlement offer I had placed on the table even before their shenanigans began. Of course, the client would thank them profusely for their wizardry, without which, they were led to believe, their claim was destined for failure. Rarely, the approach would fail—either an unreasonable client or an insurance adjuster would prevent the acceptance of a "reasonable" value— but even then, a good "show" would end with Yancey and Sean able to blame the immoral, corporate-financed defense attorney, the unethical "hired gun" medical expert, or even politics itself that made the law so difficult for the hardworking injured guy to get the money he deserved. For the most part, though, clients would typically sign off for any settlement amount that covered their desired mortgage, credit cards, bass boat, pickup truck, or at least their unpaid fines and child support. And more importantly, the amount would always be high enough to max out the attorney fees.

Meanwhile, I toiled in monotony, with the same cases, the same results, and the same biweekly paycheck. When opportunity knocked—such as in the case of a wealthy, grieving widow in need of estate work—I would waive the fee out of sympathy. Their thankful Christmas cards and hugs didn't buy many presents. I hated the thought of the slick life of my colleagues, yet I failed to love mine without the financial comfort, vacation homes, and notoriety. I felt relatively smart, I worked hard, and I tried to do the right thing—all the things blue-collar parents tell you to do—but I seemed destined for the "gray line of mediocrity," to quote my son on what he most wanted to avoid when he graduated from college. I was learning the hard way that there was no "success" for someone who had yet to define it for himself, no matter how hard he worked. And even if he were to ever see what he wanted, and know it, there was little reward if he insisted on taking little risk. Meanwhile, what is the constant collateral damage from someone who is both ambitious and afraid? From someone who constantly sees what appears to be greener grass but who is unwilling to jump the fence to get it? *Misery.* Including for anyone close or caring enough to listen to him. I drove Annie half-crazy over the years before ultimately driving the relationship into the dirt. She would deny it out of love for me, and I would deflect it and avoid it out of guilt, but 'twas true. Bless her heart.

The one silver lining of such a life? Motivation. When channeled in the right direction, the perpetual desire to do and to be "more" ended up helping a lot of people in that small town. While I was pining for a more significant career during my time with Mr. Griffin, I used my free time to coach youth sports with the energy and passion few people have for anything in their lives. I loved sports, I loved kids, and I was void of the purpose at work that needed such emotion. Maybe such an opportunity was truly the reason my decisions had led me down such a path toward Shiloh, or maybe it was just a perfectly timed and fitting distraction. No matter. Life became full of daily practices, weekend trips. Sweat, dirt, sun, and fun. Purpose and meaning, as teams turned into leagues, and leagues turned into activities beyond just sports for over a thousand kids in need. By late 1998, that momentum turned into money, local political support, and—four years later—the founding of a local Boys & Girls Club, an actual self-sustaining, fully staffed after-school facility for local kids. There would be tutoring, mentoring, meals, and fun and games, and it was the only club at that time in such a small town like Shiloh. For now, the growing groundswell of goodwill offered plenty of bait to attract local big fish.

1998

The same motivation that prompted the coaching and eventual founding of the Boys & Girls Club also left me perfectly dehydrated for the fountain of Miklos's late-night revelation. In hindsight, high desperation was necessary to offset my customary reluctance to change. A few days had passed since the Huddle House meet, and pretty much every coffee shop, gas station, or post office conversation involved theories on what had happened with Donnie Bell. In fact, rumors had metastasized to the current county attorney, Jay Curry, who might have helped Don stash or destroy some of the evidence as he had returned home from the scene that night. Apparently, the police had never recovered the gun or Don's bloody shirt, both of which could have been discarded at any point along the two-hour stretch of highway between Louisville and Shiloh.

Enter Frank Coxton. In the colorful history of Shiloh, which included wars between the coal mines and the unions (like those in our neighboring *Bloody Harlan*), family violence and rivalries similar to the Hatfields and the McCoys, and a long line of bootleggers, marijuana farmers, and corrupt politicians, there might never have been a more colorful character. Who could ever forget a conversation starting by him banging on and then yelling out the window of his third-story office as I walked into the post office on the sidewalk below? Frank had made his fortune as "the" local insurance agent—

granted, not much competition in Shiloh—and now he sought to lend his talents to help his hometown as the Rupp County judge executive. He was a great mix of generosity and ego—part Santa and Satan—honestly believing he was the best thing for the town while downplaying his knowledge that running the town would be the best thing for him.

His flattery appealed to me. Everyone knew Frank, and his enormous combination of resources and personality gave him a lot of momentum for the upcoming election. It was hard to be in a room with him and not truly believe he could improve things in Shiloh, even though no one had halted the steady dwindling of the coal mine economy and the surrounding population since the mid-1970s. A stagnant town with a lot of desperate people looking for change meant that Trump-like charisma and promises could buy a lot of votes, especially when it was intertwined with Frank's genuinely good intentions.

"C'mon in! Sit down!" said Frank.

He wasn't yelling, but his natural volume was that of a megaphone. It literally echoed around what was the nicest office I had ever seen, and surely permeated the walls of every other office on the third floor. He kicked back in his leather chair to show his perfectly polished teeth, his smooth ebony skin, his hulking forearms, and his customary unlit Cuban cigar, all part of his persona. I had seen Frank my whole life, as he had long been a member and a regular attendee of our local Catholic parish, usually sitting in one of the rear pews and always bending Miklos's ear for far too long after the mass while we waited to eat. He was ten years older than me, but he had always had a robust word of encouragement for me and my family, always projecting "Shrangri-La" instead of "Shiloh." But he had never cast his shine and true power toward me until right then.

"You know why I called you up, don't you?"

My mouth opened to say I had no idea, but you had to be fast when Frank was on a roll.

"Of course you do! I know Miklos filled you in. Look, the only thing we need from you right now is patience and a 'yes.' I'll do all the rest. It's already in motion."

"Well…I'm appreciative. Please know that. Miklos said I would be contacted, and I think Don's ACA position would fit me well. Already gave him my 'yes' with the same smile you see now."

He leaned in over his desk, supporting his widening grin over with his massive shoulders and forearms.

"Takie, honey! Don't play coy with me, son! You know I'm running for county judge, right?"

Another breath spent trying to chime in was wasted as he continued.

"Well, I want you as *the* county attorney. Not as an assistant. You're a perfect for it, I tell you. I know you and your family, and this stuff you're doing with the kids all over town, it's politically priceless. You can't buy support like that. And besides, all us Cardinal boys [referring to the neighborhood where we both grew up] stick together. I know I can trust you!"

My mouth was open now out of astonishment, not in an attempt to speak, but he held silent with his never-ending smile, waiting for my response. My mind raced through two dozen thoughts, all of which boiled down to the usual *ambition versus fear*. The thought of campaigning made me ill, as I had no experience, no money, and even less desire to be exposed to the public. But the thought of missing the only such opportunity—perhaps past, present, or future in this town—was equally sickening.

Didn't matter. Frank injected too much enthusiasm for any negative virus to take hold.

"Of course I'd be interested, but—"

"I know you don't have a clue what you're in for…let me deal with that. For now, go home and talk to your wife about it, but keep it in house otherwise. Call me back by the end of the week, and I'll tell you what to do from there. As long as you file for the ballot by the deadline in two weeks, you'll be on for the May primary. Curry will be easy to beat anyway, but with all this Donnie Bell stuff, he may not get a vote!" I could see him mentally patting himself on the back. "There are no Republicans expected to run, so you win in May and you're done!"

He was already walking me toward the door, one arm around me. It had the feel of Willy Wonka showing me the inner workings of the factory, and just a smidge of Jim Jones telling me about a great new flavor of Kool-Aid. But as I left his office and bounded down the stairs, excitement prevailed over uncertainty. I guess Frank had a superpower, too.

4

THE NEW DEAL

The tornado of politics I had just stepped into would not wait until Friday. As I walked to my car after work the next day, Miklos's pickup—its exterior typically dirty from his recycling work and its interior typically cluttered with receipts, ledger books, and Post-It Notes—pulled up alongside me.

"Ride with me around the block?" he offered as he reached to manually roll down the passenger-side window while literally shoveling two handfuls of paperwork from the passenger seat to the floor.

"So…have you thought any more about what we discussed?"

I hesitated. Did Miklos not know about Frank's plan? I was clueless, perhaps naïve, and tired from the day, but I could always trust Miklos.

I quickly spit out what Frank had said. "You know, my situation…my life. You think that's a good idea? No riddles today, please…"

Miklos pulled in and parked behind the post office, which was always empty and secluded once the outgoing trucks left by 5:30 p.m.

"Politics is a shifting, murky cloud, Takie. It's like a wheel with spokes in all directions, each spoke connected to several others. We have to figure out where you fit on that wheel, and it's hard when we don't know where the center is. The entire courthouse could be in for big change this election cycle, and we have to align ourselves with the right group—the winning group—and that group could change between now and the election."

Sitting there knowing I could not afford to run for office, much less spend money on a campaign and lose, the only comfort I felt was in his use of the word *We*. Otherwise, I was feeling no guarantees that I would be able to parlay politics into a career move. I wanted assurances, but Miklos failed to give them and did his best to explain why. What he did give out was an itinerary of five people across the five Rupp County voting districts whom I would need to see quickly. As he described it, I would introduce myself as Miklos's nephew, express my interest in running for county attorney, and then state a desire for their support. Make a little small talk—the usual Kentucky basketball or whatnot—and then move along.

"Be sure to tell them you've got several other people to see," said Miklos. "That will perk their ears up. These are a few of the gatekeepers for certain precincts. They control large families or groups of voters. They know the deadline to file is coming, and they will start calling each other. Some will call me. I will be able to read the chatter about you and see where we stand."

Miklos picked up his car phone—as in the large box with the "old school" '80s receiver straight out of *Wall Street*. The call lasted only a couple of sentences, then he proclaimed, "Mr. Vinchi will be ready for you in the morning. Start there." As usual, I couldn't help but be both amazed and humored by his skills. He could simultaneously evoke supreme confidence and confusion, so he was always great fuel for the fire of my indecisions.

I followed his directions, no matter how uneasy it felt. Literally, I could just as well have walked on the moon. There was Mr. Vinchi, the wealthy, well-dressed funeral director in South Fork; Mr. Helmsley, the arrogant school board member from Poor Fork; Mr. Jensen, the unassuming florist from "downtown" Shiloh; Mr. Leddington, the grimy junk car lot owner from Pups Branch; and Mr. Wheaton, the seemingly hurried and disinterested sign maker from Sugar Creek. I covered all five areas in half a day—not an easy feat—and still got all my usual work done for Mr. Griffin. I would still need to find the only woman he assigned, none other than the bootlegger Cass O'Malley herself, but I'd have to see her at sundown, lest any of the church crowd peg me buying booze during work hours and spread gossip against me.

Driving back to the office, it was incredible to think that this cross-section of oddballs had anything to do with power, politics, or government anywhere. The only common thread was that I recognized all of them from church growing up. With only one Catholic church in the entire county, I guessed everyone had gone at least once…even Cass.

More incredible was how fast they worked. By nightfall, Miklos had called to say we were likely a go, but that there was just one more person to meet. Bud Keegan, one of the more respectable attorneys in town, would be on waiting on the bench on the courthouse lawn in the morning.

"You know Bud, don't you?"

"Of course," I said. Bud was also about ten years older, in the same ballpark as Frank Coxton. Bud had grown up an altar boy at the church, excelled in school, and graduated at the top of his law school class. I had seen him intermittently at the barbershop on any given Saturday morning. By all accounts, Bud was an actual craftsman at the law, rare in that town, someone who you could actually trust to know what the law said, as opposed to what the locals believed on the street corner from Yancey. He could have gone anywhere, but he chased his future wife back to Shiloh. She would never leave town, and he would never leave her, or so the story went.

"Bud is very smart and a lot like you, Takie. He's looking to make more of his career here and has thoughts of running, too. But because he's smart, he won't run if he sees you've already lined up support from the same people he would need. You just need to reinforce the fact that you are already invested…already in the race, okay?"

I was waiting on the bench at 7 a.m. as Bud came down the steps of the courthouse from inside, already hard at work. He was an early riser and, as arguably the best real estate attorney in town, had sweet-talked the clerk to predawn access to all the deed books he could handle. The conversation was surprisingly short and contentious. No salutations.

"You're not serious, are you?" he asked, but it was more condescension mixed with anger on his face. I was still cautiously treading water and just learning to swim, but Bud's feel was definitely foe, not friend.

"Uh…yeah. I've given my word to several guys who have promised their support. No way to turn back now," I said, trying to sound resolved but also blaming it on someone else.

"Let me guess. Frank Coxton approached you? You realize he said all the same things to me two months ago? Already had me fund-raising and doing social events." He paused, spit harshly, and rubbed the back of his neck the way Mr. Griffin might have before slinging his drink through the Dairy

Queen window. I expected him to curse me, or maybe punch me, but he either didn't know me well enough or didn't blame me for his predicament.

"So, you're definitely running?" he asked again.

"Not sure what else I can say," I replied. And he looked me hard in the eyes for a couple of seconds, then walked back into the deed room.

THE PREVIOUS NIGHT, 1:15 A.M.

The *click* of the gas pump brought me back to reality. In hindsight, it all made simple sense, kind of like seeing how you lost a hand of poker after the fact, à la Mike McD knowing he's broke before KGB flipped his cards in *Rounders*. If you play poker like my son, you get that reference, but if not, just know that by Friday, Miklos had explained to me how this was my first appearance in the political game, and while some people hit a home run their first time up to bat, most had to work their way up around the bases one at a time. At least that was the best analogy Miklos could give. Frank had wanted Bud's action, or loyalty, on a certain matter, and he had used me as a bargaining chip against Bud, as a threat to pull his support and jump to another candidate. Frank and Bud had reunited, but not to worry, Miklos reassured, our moves had given us enough leverage to still work the process to our advantage.

"It speaks volumes that a wild horse like Bud would get in line a little over you," Miklos started. "There's some fear there. If you still want to be assistant county attorney in Don's slot when Bud takes over, tell me now."

"You actually think Bud will want me in his office after all this?"

"Let me deal with that and plant the necessary seeds," Miklos said. "You've already taken a major step the last two days, and we have until the end of the year now. They will need favors from me along the way. Bud will win in May, and then win unopposed in November. Just be ready after that."

Thoughts of the whole process that led me into the courthouse almost left me a little proud. I was completely out of my depth, but I still navigated things best I could. Granted, I caved and took the "deal" at the hands of some small-town wannabe puppeteers, but I had never wanted to run for office or deal with all of the political drama necessary to stay in office anyway. Conflict avoidance was my thing, remember? First mate had always been fine with me, and the next seven years in the courthouse would leave me happy on most days, even grateful. As I pulled back on the interstate near Morgantown, though, I grew painfully aware that my current mess left no means of conflict avoidance. And after years of watching the true shysters from the sidelines, and with Miklos now gone, I was ill-equipped for the battle at hand. I could use a Yancey or a television *Saul* character, but whether trying to buy drugs, find a hooker, hire a hitman, or in this case, escape a directive from the Mob, I realized I had no one to call.

5

COACHING 'EM UP

The present plea for help notwithstanding, I knew that not having a "fixer" or being in a position to "call my lawyer" was by my own design. Two decades of attorneys and not one real friend in the bunch, likely because I painted the whole profession with the same broad brush of distaste and distrust. It was nothing anyone ever really did to me on the job (although there are a few of them we'd all like to punch in the throat), but I just never really wanted any part of them. Even back before law school, I had no real interest...I just also happened to have no clear vision of anything else to do, either. I had hopscotched across six different majors in undergrad, ultimately ending up in economics, but nothing about that field really excited me or felt "right." I would tackle a new topic of study until the excitement wore off, or until I saw parts of the subject I didn't like, then I'd change it. That was my pattern all four years. None of the majors really were "wrong," per se, and I could likely have made a go of it in any field, but I failed to see a path to "more," even back then. Maybe the normal twenty-one-year-old was floundering and lost like that, or maybe I was just too weak and afraid to pick something and stick to it, but my penchant for indecision had clearly started early. At least I'm consistently inconsistent.

I bounced around outside of the classroom, too, building a résumé of widely varied part-time jobs between the ages of fourteen and twenty. There were stints as a radio disc jockey, a newspaper reporter, an assistant librarian, a UPS truck unloader, a mechanic's helper at a strip mine, a personal trainer at a gym, and even a postal carrier, among others. Dad started me early, like Deo did to him, so working hard was never the issue. Questioning what work I should be doing and why was more my struggle. Maybe that burden comes with more awareness, more opportunity, than Dad ever got to see.

Maybe it was easier for him to just put his head down and work. Regardless, I could extend a résumé to five pages by my junior year of college, but I still didn't have a clue what I actually wanted to do.

Fortunately, or pathetically, depending on your view, my college soccer teammates changed all that. You can picture me as a decent, albeit not spectacular athlete throughout high school and college. I was about five-foot-ten, 200 pounds, always in good condition but more of a genetic plow horse than a thoroughbred. I was never the superstar on any team, as even with the talent, I would have lacked the comfort of such responsibility. There's *always* room on a team for an extremely hard worker who would prefer to defer to others, so you could always pencil me in as a starter, a well-liked teammate, and a coach's favorite, but you might find very little of me in any given box score or stat sheet. Of course, I bounced around in sports, too, playing high school basketball, football, and baseball; the latter two I even tried briefly in college. But by my junior year, I actually latched on as a soccer goalkeeper, even though I had no prior experience beyond my own backyard.

The soccer guys readily accepted me as a sort of comic relief considering my background, but I learned quickly and earned the starting role, and as we started off 5-0, they chalked it up to my Greek pedigree. In any event, it was at one of the team's post-game parties that I—only partially inebriated—was dared to take the LSAT in hopes of outscoring another player who had irritated the crowd by bragging and boasting about his test results and his assuredly wealthy legal future. Fast-forward three months, and I had registered, taken the test, and earned a score not just worthy of admission, but of a scholarship to law school. So, when you've gone only straight from school to school your whole life, always doing what you're told without developing your own path, what do you do when everyone is congratulating you on possibly becoming a lawyer? You stay in school. It's safe. It's what you know. And it pleases others. *Ding, ding, ding.*

So, in some ways, one half-drunken decision at a college soccer party hatched an entire career for which I had no preparation or understanding. At law school, I felt more like a fish out of water than the Greeks among the rednecks in Shiloh. This led to a lack of confidence, a sense of inferiority among my classmates who all appeared to know where they were headed. Sure, I did just fine in class with decent grades, and I could always offer polite small talk as needed, but I dodged most social settings or study groups with people whom I began to see as arrogant and entitled. Truth in hindsight? I never really gave them a chance. I spent my spare time with more "noble" people and pursuits, or so I told myself, working out with inner city kids at the YMCA and volunteering legal work for indigent disability claimants. Thus, the die was cast for my future.

Fast-forward another frenetic three years, past the bar exam, marriage, our first child, and into my first job with Mr. Griffin, and those layers of life still lay forever uncomfortably on a shaky foundation. Before returning to Shiloh in 1994, the only courtroom experience I had was watching the O.J. trial that summer, so I brought all that same level of inner discomfort with the local attorneys. As always, I thrived in my work for Mr. Griffin, earning a good living for our family and professional respect among my peers, but personally I disliked my colleagues—both collectively and some individually—and thereby I disliked myself as a part of their group.

Call it weakness or wisdom, immaturity or indignation, either way I tried to escape my law persona afterhours, or at least try to turn it into something more worthwhile. Again, there's the ever-elusive word "more." And, similar to my life in law school, that inner friction provided energy for good works, this time helping local kids through coaching. It really was a good match of enthusiasms. A small town like Shiloh adores its local sports heroes and teams, perhaps a testament to a need for distraction from hard living or a lack of other forms of entertainment. And I was born and raised to coach, plain and simple. If I got one mulligan, it would be that I was mis-careered.

Coaching sports of any kind—basketball, baseball, football, track, soccer, anything—was a natural passion of mine, going back to being called on the carpet of a parent-teacher conference at the age of ten after refusing to stop sketching out football plays instead of doing my schoolwork. The chess match, the strategy, the "Xs" and Os," all of it, could occupy my mind for hours on end, and after volunteering for my first team at the local elementary school in the summer of 1994—when I got to add in the actual teaching and motivation of kids—I was hooked.

I coached year-round, from one sports season to the next, any team elementary through high school. It was a true addiction, but without the stigma of a vice. I was serving others, doing what I enjoyed, and I was actually good at it, that is, if you find value in the number of trophies collected, and especially if you count the number of parents who wanted their children on my teams. More important than the success, though…I was proud of it. No uncomfortable downplaying of my job, no self-deprecating joke about my profession, no regret or angst going to work—all things I experienced in my life as an attorney. As a coach, I could let out my true self, all my passion, all my joy, all my experiences… I could pour them all out over those kids and know they were better for it. That we all were. My own kids, though they were just toddlers when I started, got to see and hear all those lessons, to learn from their dad at his best, and I'm ever grateful for that.

Speaking of speeches, I was consistently amazed how during the height of an emotional pregame speech or timeout, some clever line or quote from one of my former coaches would come pouring out, words I had long since forgotten or tucked away in my youth, but yet words that instantly conjured up a specific memory of the locker room or field where I had heard them. Looking back, it is easy to see why so many coaches took a shine to me growing up, coaches *love* to talk, and I absorbed every word. After all, I was one of them.

Being "one of them" carries considerable weight. Like I said, Shiloh worshiped its sports heroes, and the little town was blessed with a long line of all-time greats. Best example, since Kentucky is generally known for basketball and thoroughbred horses above all else, one of the winningest high school basketball coaches in state history, Bobby Keith, coached a team from right there in nearby Manchester to a state title in 1987. Another, John D. Wilson in Loyall, amassed over five hundred career wins and was featured in an *ESPN* documentary. Though I never played for him, Wilson did leave behind a protégé, Earl Starks, who later mentored me—first as coach to player, then later as coach to coach and father to father.

Never has there been a better master of his own domain than Earl Dee Starks. About ten years older than me, Earl managed to navigate life simply and fiercely. He made a decision, went after it with all his might—whether in his personal life or in basketball—and then was truly content at the end of a hard day talking over a beer, playing a set of tennis, or his favorite—fishing off of the old Cardinal Bridge. He was the polar opposite of me, and I admired him instantly. The jokes, the crazy sports stories, and the coaching experiences are too numerous to recount, but somehow, when a similar play flashes across a television screen, or like now, when I am scrolling across his name among the contacts in my phone, a quote of his will come to mind.

I remember one mindless Saturday afternoon, not long after returning to Shiloh, I found him kicked back in a lawn chair on that old bridge, hat down over his nose, half-asleep, a cooler of beer alongside and the fishing pole awaiting a bite far too long. I stood a second, watching the ripples flow downstream, and ol' Earl said, "Takie, you always seem stressed, son. Don't you think it's time you figured this life thing out?" He always spoke with an exaggerated country drawl, so that you expected a chuckle at any moment, even when he was serious. You never knew whether to expect Confucius or a Bill Murray punchline, though based on past experience, you leaned toward Murray. Still, the nugget that day was worth holding on to. "Just make sure you do what's right, do your best at what you do, and try to help people whenever you can. If you do just those three things, life turns out alright. It's not that complicated."

Of course, I've long since learned that all coaches are copycats, and that the wise Earl had paraphrased that from Lou Holtz or maybe a dozen other famous coaches, but that doesn't diminish its impact on the listener. I'd learned that when I used copycat comments in my coaching speeches, too. It was such wisdom and experience that helped me stay sane navigating my life and career, particularly in light of my inner inability to pull the trigger on tough decisions. This particular comment, which Earl might not even remember saying, helped me resolve my will to take the job with Bud at the courthouse. Yeah, Frank had used me. Yeah, Bud might not truly want me. But it was the right thing to do…for my career, for my impact on others, and most importantly, for my family. I would do my best, just like always, and be the best first mate he'd ever seen. Never had I failed to please a coach or teacher or boss, and Bud would be no different. I would keep helping all the players I coached and all the people I saw at the courthouse, in every way I could.

In the absence of my own working compass, I had used Earl's—then and on many other occasions. I really could use his simple wisdom now, on the current and more pressing matter that I'm trying to avoid thinking about, but at 1:15 a.m., he'd answer the phone with a gruff, "Go to hell!" Yes, such was the makeup of the few friends I had. Guys I had coached with or against like Earl or Walt Isaacs, Andy Madsen, or Willie Marr. Guys who did other jobs by day like me and who spent their evenings and weekends just trying to help some kids. Yeah, it was fun, too…I'm not gonna lie…but they'd give you the shirt off their backs. Not perfect men, promise, but not lawyers. I was lucky in that regard.

6

GREASING THE WHEELS

1999–2007

No matter when or where thoughts of Bud arose, reflections on my seven-year run in the courthouse—and the whole process of small town justice—prove equal parts bitter and sweet.

On the one hand, it remains the most interesting of my varied career stops and hops, whether disability lawyer, prosecutor, nonprofit director, banker, government administrator, or now federal judge, that generally arose about every seven years. Yes, I had meandered to my mid-forties trying to strike a balance between ambition and income, prestige and significance, and family and inner peace. You think that's easy to find in a town of 3,500 surrounded by a dwindling coal mining economy during a prescription drug epidemic? You try it. Whatever. No time to reopen wounds lashing myself for life decisions now. I had eventually landed my judgeship two years ago, thankfully prior to my parents' deaths so they could appreciate it, and I had finally found some semblance of self-worth mixed with financial freedom that none of my other jobs had ever seemed to give at the same time. Still, nothing compares to the variety—the outright hilarity—of a typical day in the Rupp County courthouse.

You could walk into Wendy, Bud's slightly overpaid cousin and office social director (her full-time duties as receptionist were always optional). Her résumé revealed a high school diploma and immediate employment at Bud's law office thereafter, both clearly the result of her small-town charm and family connections. Of course, some might say the same about my job there, too. Wendy's "talents" were now on full display after following Bud into the courthouse, and her warmth proved handy in stalling or delivering rejection to precinct protectors who came in to bend Bud's ear for favors. On the downside, her personality also included part "gray god syndrome," our term for women who turned into giggling, swooning teenage piles of mush whenever a Kentucky State trooper came by for a warrant.

There was also Chase Cordon, or "Chaser" as we called him, a name that linked to his success as a cross-country runner during our high school days. Chaser was whippet-thin and squeaky clean on the surface, and his lack of political baggage mixed with a bit of his own family clout had earned him the nod for Bud's other assistant post. He matched me on confrontation avoidance, so he was never destined for riches in private practice, and he was actually nice to a fault, even running in circles around Bud and me on postwork jogs just so he could stay in the conversation and not go insane from our plow horse pace. Chaser was not without some ambition, stemming primarily from a spouse who had married an attorney and expected all of the stereotypical amenities supposedly attached, but in general, Bud had hired two competent, eager-to-please assistants who would never cross him politically. Bud always, *always*, saw such angles far in advance.

And daily, this army of four would tackle all of the arrest warrants, misdemeanor crime, delinquent child support, juvenile court, and tax collection that wayward county of 30,000 could muster. Chaser had child support and misdemeanors. I had juvenile court and tax collection. We tag-teamed the warrants as they came in. Bud weighed in on the higher-profile complaints, but he shrewdly insulated himself from the front lines of complaints from unhappy voters. Bud also handled any legal memos or opinions requested by local government, as this kept him in the political loop of information and readily available for any front-page credit or notoriety.

If you picture the average local resident as having dropped out of high school, lacking a job or income, disabled from injury in the coal mines, or having turned to the drug trade—or some combination of all four—you can see how the town provided ample caseload. The only way for our office, or any overburdened system, to survive this routine, and that's why most areas of law had grown into an assembly line of often melodic, often comedic ritual. The goal was always to fit every person through the door into the same case outline; you just needed to push play on the prerecorded cassette tape in your head.

Take a typical tax collection case, for example.

Citizen gets tax commissioner's notice of auction regarding their home due to delinquent property taxes.

Citizen comes into complain.

"You cannot sell my home for taxes!"

Show printout and explain law granting government first lien on property.

"But I don't even own this property!"

Show deed and tax assessor map tracking property to their name.

"But I already paid these taxes!"

Show clerk and sheriff records of those years paid and those years outstanding.

"But these taxes are outrageously too high!"

Show tax assessment and often a home mortgage at an even higher amount (thank you to those predatory lenders).

"But I just found out about these when I got the complaint! I shouldn't have to pay the penalties and interest!"

Really? This was the worst of the ridiculous. Show all they had already received—the original bill, the first notice of lien, the second notice of lien, the public advertisement of the tax bills, the first warning of foreclosure, the second warning of foreclosure, the complaint (which was served by the sheriff), the motion setting a court date to get a date for the auction, the order setting the date for the auction, the report of the appraisers, the auction posting in the paper for three straight weeks...

"Alright, alright! But I don't have the money! Can I make payments?"

Bingo.

Crank out the agreement. Stop the auction. Collect the payments. Pay the tax bills. And part of that included covered attorney fees for me. Sadly, they could have set up payments at any point, but their avoidance forced the lawsuit, upped their bill, and allowed me to earn a decent living.

I never dabbled much on the child support side, but Chaser reported a similar script when defusing the excuses of a guy about to go to jail for not paying as ordered. Just add in the usual emotional excuses such as, "My ex does not deserve the money!" or, "The kids do not see a dime!" or, "My divorce lawyer railroaded me with this agreement!" and change loss of liberty (jail) for loss of property (foreclosure) as the ultimate threat to make them pay. Again, the lack of ability or willingness to cooperate brings the legal action and a similar finder's fee for Chaser.

If the daily, repetitive grind of tax collection provided the meat of my paycheck, our juvenile court dockets every Wednesday added a whole mess of side dishes and seasoning to the courthouse gig. Though not nearly as lucrative, with just a small stipend paid by the county, the juvenile work supplied opportunity to and fulfillment of actually making a difference— that, and large doses of sobering reality and incredulity, often mixed equally, even in the same case.

A soft-spoken, experienced father figure, Judge Newberry presided over a courtroom that resembled an outdated small-town bus station. Envision six rows of pews, all historically carved with graffiti over the past thirty years, and twelve worn-out swiveling juror chairs, each with the stuffing exposed. Behind His Honor, a dilapidated, paneled wall minus the two-foot-wide hole created as the judge would routinely rock his chair back hard against the wall while conjuring up his Solomon-like wisdom. Matching such a glamorous courtroom, Judge Newberry, now thirty-plus years on the bench and over forty years from law school, had long since released any sense of pride in his personal appearance—he was unshaven, with a slack and unbuttoned shirt under his robe, unkempt bedhead, and absent false teeth. Think Otis Campbell on *The Andy Griffith Show*.

Still, the setting undervalued Judge Newberry's admirable legal skill and, more importantly, his keen sense of empathy for those walking through the door. Unlike most lawyers, Judge Newberry never lost his firm grasp on the true victims of the legal system—essentially everyone who had to deal with it.

I cut my teeth in trials as a prosecutor and learned much under Judge Newberry, who took care to protect me and all members of the local bar from missteps wherever he could. But beyond the courtroom fireworks, Judge Newberry's advancing case of burnout (did I mention thirty-plus years? That's seven election cycles to you and me) helped hone my best skill from my years from Mr. Griffin. Remember? The art of giving people crap news and having them go away happy...or at least not blaming the appropriate source and still voting for Bud. Fancy folks call this "building consensus" or "achieving strategic goals," or even *The Art of the Deal*. Others may call it *bullshit*. Either way, thankfully it paid the bills.

Facing a docket of twenty-five cases at 8 a.m. Judge Newberry would sigh and hand me the files. With that, he was asking me to get the cases settled through plea negotiations, and you wanted to please him, not out of fear but compassion. He (we) had neither the time nor energy to litigate routine, smaller juvenile matters, but that didn't make it easy.

Painting the picture of a sample case:

Child comes into court for truancy and theft charge after he stole a bicycle (obviously while skipping school).

Child: "I didn't do it, and I want to go home." (Even though he is lying, at least his motivation for self-preservation was the truest in the room.)

Public Defender: "My client is innocent, and it is my duty to get him cleared of all charges." (Best interest of the child always a distant second.)

Parents: "We cannot control him. The school will not help him, and we can't make him go. We have no idea about any bicycle." (In other words, do not hold us accountable for any jail time or restitution; feel free to take him off our hands...of course, this slant would always change once they learned that any disability check linked to the child ends when the child is removed.)

School Counselor: "His absences are killing our state funding, which is based on attendance, but if you make him attend now, he's so far behind that his year-end test scores will be terrible and hurt our state funding even further. Could you get him to drop out?" (Yes, they actually encouraged this, until so many quit that they blamed Bud's office publicly for reduced enrollment and—you guessed it—a loss of funding.)

Social Service Caseworker: "The home situation is a mess, and the child should be removed." (This opinion often ignored the law written to hold removal as a last resort after exhaustion of available services, and the fact that no services were available. I at least respected the fact that they were more underfunded than our office.)

Juvenile Justice Caseworker: "We have a spot at our detention facility ready and recommend that we use it." (This leaves out the cost to the county for lodging, meals, and transportation, and the caseworker's quota to have so many detention center beds filled at all times.)

Victim: "We want our child's bicycle back, or at least restitution…and the crime in our town is getting ridiculous." (Of course, the bicycle was typically long gone, the juvenile has no income to pay restitution, and they would have to sue the parents to collect from them.)

Magistrate 1: "This *kid's* family is a major part of my district. We need them to get full consideration." (Translation: Lot of votes at stake here.)

Magistrate 2: "This *victim's* family is a major part of my district. We need them to get full consideration." (Translation: Lot of votes at stake here.)

County Judge-Executive/Mayor: "We don't care what you do, but we have to get this crime stopped, though we have no budget for detention." (Feel free to chop down all the trees you want, but use no hands, no feet, and no tools.)

Amazing to remember, really, but this went on every day for over seven years. Throw all these competing parties in a room and get a solution everyone can live with. In the twenty minutes before we call the next case, if you can. *Good luck.* But I was eager for the change and I learned fast. After a year in, we could wrap up twenty-five cases and be done in time for lunch.

7

DROPPING LIKE FLIES

LAST NIGHT, 2:00 A.M.

The West Virginia interstate exits clicked by…Lost Creek…Big Otter…all the way south to Big Chimney. I'd always wondered how such little towns—towns just like Shiloh—got such names. Was there *really* a house with an extra-large chimney so high that they'd named the town after it? I could see where maybe a river had dried up or was diverted by coal-mining activity, thus naming the town "Lost Creek," but I highly doubt there's ever been an actual otter wandering around lost in West Virginia.

No matter. My mind was racing with such small talk, when I really needed to figure out a plan before I got back to Shiloh, now less than five hours away. Three times I had reached for my phone, but I still could not find a name in my mental Rolodex to call. Funny, there was no phone signal in those rural mountain areas anyway. I would need a place to hide and to think, and maybe some money if things went sideways. My true coaching friends like Earl and Walt could give me all their advice, but this was real—life-or-death real. I wasn't sure they would grasp that fact, if they'd even have anything helpful to offer, or even if I wanted to endanger them with any kind of involvement. Bud's name kept popping onto the screen in my mind. With Miklos gone, Bud might be the only one who would understand the dilemma, the players who were involved, and have the resources to help. But I was uncertain whether he would have the actual desire to help. Dealing with Bud, like everything else about Shiloh, had always been a mixed bag of good and bad. I'd get a step ahead, only to land in manure. Beautiful mountains, but no cell phone service, for example. As I said before, *bittersweet*.

1999

Yes, I had taken the "deal" with Bud, as approved by his supporters like Frank and brokered by Miklos. And in many ways, I had my best seven years in Shiloh, with better money, an uptick in prestige, and a sense of contribution to the greater good, however misguided it might have been. Progress, indeed. And along with the addictive boost of adrenaline, Bud's work allowed me to typically accomplish my daily mission by a nice, tidy 4:30 p.m. This allowed the added benefit of time…time spent trying to be a good parent. Family life was good, my kids were healthy and active throughout elementary school, and I still enjoyed coaching various sports for the locals during the evenings and weekends: the benefits of a small-town school district short on budget and staffing. They were always in need of someone to help, especially a rare parent willing to coach teams long before his kids were even old enough to play. True to form, the competition and chess-like strategy never lost its appeal to me, and I continue to fill legal pads sketching out "x's and o's" for football plays, even today during court recesses.

At the same time, I was passionate about making a greater contribution to my little hometown (sounds corny, but true), and working with kids in sports merged enjoyment and my skillsat the same time. Kids responded and flocked to my semi-sermons, maybe because in my mind, I still reasoned like a twelve-year-old. Some parents even transferred their kids to the city school just to have them play for me. Go figure.

This Pied Piper effect on kids, simultaneous with my successful and more noticeable courthouse work, turned into quite a wave of momentum, capped by *Baseball America* magazine, and Hall of Famer Cal Ripken Jr., giving me the award for National Youth Coach of the Year about five years later. That notoriety then led to several local citizenship awards, and when I sought to turn the coaching and mentoring into "more" by founding a local Boys & Girls Club, our struggling little town was able to raise over $1 million for a new facility. In many ways, throughout my tenure with Bud, despite the eternal uncertainty on the inside, life was happy on most days, leaving me both grateful and proud.

Meanwhile, a working relationship and some level of trust and friendship grew with Bud. Daily runs after work discussing the day's craziness usually brought more laughter than sweat. We might rail on Yancey, for example, after watching him smooth-talk a frightened client into paying him an extra thousand bucks, only to come in and agree to the standard plea offer that was already on the table. As a lawyer, Yancey was a master in marketing and maximizing profits. Convince the client of the worst-case scenario, and then go behind closed doors with us…telling enough jokes and drinking enough coffee long enough, of course, to give the impression that we were in an arduous legal battle. Leave the table with a deal much better than predicted to the client, and the client gladly paid for the great result—even recommending Yancey to others around town, mind you—all for a deal he could have gotten for free. We could resent and still admire, get angry and still laugh, all throughout the same set of facts while jogging.

A few years in, Bud began to share his excess real estate work for the two local banks, a market he had come to monopolize by cranking out title opinions between 6 a.m. and 8 a.m. before our office opened. Camaraderie with the other offices in the courthouse—the county sheriff, county clerk, and county tax assessor—allowed him special privileges and access to the Deed Room, so he could get work back to his clients faster than anyone else. He even used office time for private work on some days, as the work was plentiful and profitable, but he knew Chaser and I would never complain—assurances reinforced by his sharing the wealth with us—and he also knew we had the office covered while he was frequently "in a meeting" and unavailable.

Still, the evolution of my relaxation of interaction with Bud did not come quickly. For several months after replacing Donnie Bell, things were often strained and sometimes rocky around the office, much like an arranged marriage with two partners forced into love and trust without having a chance to build a prior relationship. Bud had taken office in January, had appointed me in March, and tensions had already risen sharply by June, when Joe Reznar, our county clerk upstairs, had managed to run his own good thing into a pile of manure—in typical Shiloh style.

Bud walked briskly through the office at 7:00 a.m., not early for him to work but early for him to be done in the Deed Room. Miklos followed him in, and his office door closed behind them. Voices were raised.

"You're killing me!" Bud screamed at one point with a loud thud, possibly a book going across the room. Miklos exited…his solemn face and lack of words for me seeming a bit unusual. Bud summoned me in and proceeded to go cold, as if he had morphed from Sonny Corleone, he of the hot temper, into Michael Corleone, he of the calm, cool, and collected. Typical Bud, as I would learn. He had the capacity for an infamous momentary rage combined with unequaled clarity and depth of thought, and I saw both as he calmly enlightened me with the private scoop about our county clerk, whose arrest was imminent. This would be our first small-town scandal since we had taken office. Reznar was well-known and by all accounts well-liked, and his prosecution was even trickier due to Bud's close relationship with Reznar through political ties and the church. Yes, a second Catholic church member had found himself in legal jeopardy, and unlike the Donnie Bell incident that had happened out of town, this case would stay local. There would likely be a special prosecutor appointed, due to Reznar's connections and friendships, and that prosecutor would require a liaison from our office. Bud was far too shrewd to carry that political hand grenade himself, so our conversation ended with, "It's all yours, Takie. I don't even want updates." I'm not sure we talked again for a month.

Ordinarily, such tension with the boss would have stressed me out, but I have to admit that I was as well balanced and content at that time as I'd ever been as an adult. Amidst all this melee and transition, our second child, Andi (Andromahi, after her great-grandmother Mikey) was born that January. Annie struggled during labor to near death, but ultimately pulled through, and we were on cloud nine. Better work schedule, better cash flow, healthy and happy family, plenty of coaching gigs, and progress on the Boys & Girls Club. *Whatever the Joe Reznar case has in store, bring it!* I thought. I had pined for some more meaningful career action, and I was more than ready. Right now, though, I just couldn't wait for the end of each workday, so I could stop by the house to see Andi and then get to football practice.

As the calendar hit July that year, I was slated as an assistant coach for the local high school and the head coach for middle school team. Practices ran under the lights after dark to beat the heat, so that suited my schedule even better, and Ty, now age five, was old enough to enjoy coming to the field as a water boy. He would spend hours pretending to play on the sidelines, eagerly waiting to run water out onto the field to the gigantic, amazing players (at least they were to him). Neither of us knew he would grow into an all-state quarterback ten years later. For now, he was just my happy son—and that always equals a happy dad.

Full disclosure: Practices lasted two hours, but I'd spend an extra thirty minutes "planning" with the other assistant coaches afterward. Those thirty-minute post-practice gab sessions with me, Walt, Willie, and Andy provided almost more comedic stress relief than we could bear. A lawyer, a banker, a state police trooper, and an entrepreneur, respectively, we all relished the medicine of laughter after such long days. School hadn't started yet, and Ty didn't mind staying late. He would often pull up a watercooler to sit on and listen. We lived only a mile from the field, so Annie didn't mind, either, as she and Andi were usually asleep by that point. No guilt, just fun…endless stories with each storyteller trying to top the last.

On any given night, you might hear Willie talk about our 1986 high school track team, running on that very same field for another of Shiloh's all-time great coaches, Chief Grayson. Chief coached more than fifty years, dating back to Walden High, Shiloh's all-black school before integration. He'd seen and done it all, and he could still wow a PE class with push-ups well past the age of seventy, but Willie had decided Chief could no longer keep count of all the runners coming by the finish line for each lap, so Willie stopped off at the other end of the track near the tennis court to flirt with the pretty girls. Come to find out, Chief could still count just fine, so he had a handle on exactly how many laps Willie still owed, but while Chief's mind was still hanging in, his vision was leaving. He thought the missing runner was me, so I ran extra laps while Willie dated and later married one of the tennis players, Denise.

You might hear how Walt played on some of the best football teams to come out of Rupp County—the mid-1980s Cherokee Mountaineers—not that Walt would brag, but it was just true. Cherokee was all but unstoppable until the school closed a few years later, falling victim to school consolidation from the dwindling coal mines and the surrounding population and tax base. One story Walt couldn't live down, however, despite all their wins, was how he, as an offensive lineman, had managed to luckily scoop up a short, bouncing kickoff one night and appeared headed for his first and likely only touchdown. There was even a picture the next day in our local paper, *The Mountain Enterprise*, of Walt breaking into the clear, eyes literally bulging out of his helmet, seeing nothing but grass between himself and the scoreboard at the end of the field. But if you watched the film, the next thing Walt saw was the earhole of his own helmet, as he was unexpectedly derailed by a ferocious hit out of nowhere. Walt gathered his senses just in time to see the outstretched hand of his own teammate trying to help him up after accidentally running him over: "Sorry, man."

You might hear another storyteller, Andy, a decent quarterback on a very average Shiloh High team in the late 1970s, talk about his disbelief when his father finally convinced him that University of Alabama Head Coach Bear Bryant was *not* coming to sign him to a scholarship, no matter how good Andy thought he was and no matter how long he sat at the kitchen table hoping "The Bear" would show. Andy, then eighteen, might also tell you that to get over this senior year disappointment, he had ventured over to Cass O'Malley's back porch for alcoholic consolation, and that was the first time he discovered that Cass provided another, *more female* menu out of her basement down below. I couldn't let Ty hear that part, nor let him know that some on that "female menu" years ago were now mothers of our current players and upstanding members of the community!

Or, as storytellers go, I might finish up with the tale of the middle school team that came along a couple of years later, a team victimized by the population and enrollment cycles faced in small school athletics. Some years you have tremendous linemen and less talented backs to pass, catch, and run the ball, and other years it's the opposite. But some years, like in 2001, you have neither. We had a team with only thirteen players (there were oddly only sixteen boys in the middle school that year), so we only had two substitutes to go around. We tried to adapt accordingly. There was obviously no scrimmaging at practice—not enough people—and we cut back on contact drills to prevent injury. Beyond only having thirteen players, though, eleven of them were bona-fide linemen, a polite way to say that we could time our 40-yard dashes with a sundial.

Still, we put our smartest lineman at quarterback, and we split the two more athletic kids between wide receiver and running back. Our playbook consisted of essentially toss sweep right, toss sweep left, and throw it deep. And when we got tired after those three plays, we'd run our jumbo quarterback on a sneak to give everyone a breather. Believe it or not, our thirteen kids worked hard and actually won their first game, albeit 2-0 in perhaps the worst football game in the history of the sport. We might still be playing to a scoreless tie if the other team had not snapped a punt out of their own end zone, giving us a safety. That would be the highlight of our season, and, of course, our only win, but that motley crew refused to give in, never losing a game by more than eight points.

Where's the comedy? you ask. Yes, this might be a sentimental tale of underdog perseverance, except for what happened in week five that season. One player had been removed from the school system and placed in detention through Juvenile Court (Takie the Prosecutor stabbed Takie the Coach in the back), and another injured his leg and was out for the year. So, we had only eleven players...any academic suspension, illness, injury, or fatigue left us with not enough players. We were a whisker away from closing up shop.

But that week at the courthouse, Wendy called me up to the front to address a man in our lobby. Before my aggravation set in (that was really *her* job), I saw it was Mr. Tritt, a former classmate of mine in high school and father of our current running back—you know, the best player on our miserable team.

"My son *loves* playing for you, Takie," Tritt said through the lobby window. "And I've got another son, too, so I wondered if it's not too late, can he play? Is it too late?"

I tried to hide my glee. We *needed* players. But the brother of our best athlete? Really? Of course it was not too late, no matter which school policies we had to get around. I hadn't known Tritt very well in school, but we could upgrade to friendship right now. I quickly ran to my office to gather the usual forms—medical release, permission slip, team rules—then I returned to the window, happily handing the forms to Mr. Tritt, making sure he knew that "Practice is at six thirty tonight. Just bring him on over."

To which Tritt replied, "Now, Bob's legally blind. That won't be a problem, will it?"

Crickets.

And so we had our twelfth man, standing alone with me on the sidelines at every game. I wasn't even sure he could see the action. He knew very little about the game, but no matter what position needed a rest, off Bob would run onto the field, trying to find his spot while avoiding any oncoming trains.

The guys always laughed at that story, just like they laughed at me every week during the middle school games that year. None of them volunteered to help with that team. Imagine that. As stated, they were friends, not fools. Good news, though: We finished the season with Bob unharmed, and the players never lost their enthusiasm or desire to play, even when it was obvious how bad we were. We played whiffle ball, tag, and even Red Rover at practice to keep it fun, and though we finished 1-9, by far the worst of all my years coaching, it might have actually been my best work.

Coaches can swap stories *all day*. Literally. Forever. Maybe because then, just like now, the laughs about kids like Bob Tritt reminded you of why you enjoyed life in Shiloh, even while much of it seemed so absurd.

8

FALL FROM GRACE

Nowhere does a public figure or hero tumble so unceremoniously as they do in a small town, where everything and everyone seems larger, whether greater or worse, than it really is. Lou Holtz's old football quote that "nothing is ever as good or as bad as it seems" is apropos, but even he would have had a hard time digesting the swings of fame and fortune in Shiloh.

Somewhat secluded from the mainstream by its infrastructure, particularly roads and technology, Shiloh was in many ways a place that time forgot. The Internet and the Kentucky Transportation Cabinet eventually found their way in, but not before leaving a huge gap between what Shiloh and most other locales found routine. Most Rupp County locals gleefully keep their focus on what would seem small potatoes to any interested outsider—the minutia of small-town government decisions, school personnel moves, and local hospital improvements that would otherwise go unnoticed on the back pages of other local newspapers. In Shiloh, a local physician leaving town or a teacher being laid off due to lack of funding is front-page news. It is true that "All politics is local." Cue our long-lost Speaker of the House Tip O'Neill.

So, needless to say, when the Rupp County clerk was indicted for embezzlement of local government funds, the town was aflutter with excitement or outrage, depending on your viewpoint. Of course, having been the clerk for now more than three terms following the five terms his father held the position, Joe Reznar and his family were among the Shiloh "bluebloods," or the upper crust. It was laughable, really, for anyone to consider themselves "high society" in Shiloh, when most people would barely reach middle class in a larger city, but that is what passed for wealthy in a town where about 80 percent lived below the poverty level. Indeed, in 2012, based on levels, unemployment, education, disability, health care, crime, and life expectancy, the *New York Times* had once labeled neighboring Clay County the toughest place to live in America. In Shiloh, most people were government benefit recipients, and barely trying to survive, or still toiling as blue-collar coal miners, mechanics, or some kind of laborer ancillary to mining, such as a machine wholesaler or a scrap metal recycler. Some might say those hard laborers were simply in purgatory awaiting their eventual injury and enrollment into the poverty and government entitlements. "I gotta get to town today and sign up on my disability," is something you would hear routinely around town. Aside from that, if you were a doctor, lawyer, pharmacist, or even teacher, you were part of the 20 percent that the rest of the town would consider "rich." Doing the math, that leaves approximately six hundred citizens with overinflated egos, or self-importance, beyond what their intelligence or talent warranted. But, since we are all partly shaped by our surroundings, the shelter of the small town would grant these self-righteous souls a chance at royalty, though some might doubt in this case whether the castle, or the kingdom, was anything worth controlling.

One consistent truth for Shiloh, regardless of its otherwise unusual state of affairs, is that ignorance and arrogance still remained our greatest threats. Whether you spy the White House in D.C. or a barnyard outhouse in Shiloh, where public water and sewer lines had yet to reach, the occupants are still equally full of excrement. Only self-awareness of that fact keeps your crap from hitting the fan. One slipup, whether you're just too naïve to know or too conceited to care, can cost years of admiration, confidence, and even an entire career.

Enter Joe Reznar, whose seemingly guaranteed, family-crafted public office and image would crash at ten times the pace it was built. Particularly in Shiloh, the townspeople can blindly adore and worship those appearing to have more talent, or essentially more money, than themselves. But that same group gathers like piranha to feed with similar intensity when the mighty show weakness or put blood in the water. Mob rules apply. And when the mob seizes upon your apparent mistake or character flaw, your "blueblood" friends scatter, in no way eager to put themselves in harm's way. Often among the politicians, it becomes "more important to stay alive," as Sean Connery said in *The Untouchables*. Of course, he also said, "The Lord hates a coward," and every time I had to return to Shiloh to be reminded of how those fake friends had similarly deserted me, I remembered that I hated them, too.

In any event, Reznar's demise seemed to fall more upon arrogance, as, according to the indictment, he had routinely been failing to make appropriate settlements of funds to the local coffers after receiving deed and automobile taxes, marriage fees, and a host of items processed in similar clerks' offices throughout the country. I watched during plea discussions as Reznar naturally first claimed ignorance—but as the boss, that fails to fly. You are *required* to know. Still, Reznar and his attorney—Yancey, of course—hoped his apparent unawareness of some vague office process would be enough to stalemate a jury that might contain one of his few remaining friends. If he could just avoid the appearance of any *intentional* act, even if he pleaded guilty to just the negligent misuse of funds, his "blue" friends would return, and he could possibly clear his black eye by the November elections. Yes, he had taken the May primary unopposed. But as the steady drip of evidence confronted them at each of our weekly sessions, even Yancey's typical robust bullying tactics began to fade. He was the master at avoiding trials, remember? No way did Yancey or Reznar want these details plastered in the paper and lingering as fall approached. Already at the more affluent gossip-laden dinner tables around town, where Reznar had often played gin, talked sports, and solicited campaign contributions, a reasonable mind could no longer accept that Reznar was unaware of the discrepancies between the actual money and his paperwork.

Reznar next tried claiming illness or incapacity, the next most predictable defense for public figures. Suddenly the prevailing rumor around town had Reznar on a high dosage of medication for depression, best evidenced by his foggy demeanor and disheveled clothing, even when he was at work or when walking about town. This gave his family—a wife, an ailing mother, and three teenage sons whom I had coached—something upon which to base their defiance and disbelief. Only they and the family's closest friends still remained indignant that the prosecution was a sort of political witch hunt. Hidden supporters of his election opponent, combined with dastardly prosecutors, were maliciously tearing down an ill, innocent soul for fame and career advancement (yes, ol' Bud had masterfully avoided this hatred by passing the case to me, while all I could do was try to stay silent and look sympathetic at the settlement conferences). Even if he had made an occasional mistake, the family insisted, clearly his years of devout public service should merit sympathy and forgiveness, especially in light of his newly reported medical condition. To the rest of the town, however, it was readily apparent that a clerk's salary did not match his driveway full of five cars in front of a five-bedroom, two-story house, complete with backyard pool while seated conveniently across from the best elementary school in town. The mouths of the piranha mob were watering.

A special prosecutor was routine in high-profile, small-town corruption cases. They would loudly and laughably arrive from the state capital, signaling to all that the law could not tolerate any type of cover-up or protection by the local county or commonwealth's attorney in prosecuting the case. No way a mighty state government employee would ever succumb to bias or corruption, right? Please. Likewise, the local circuit judge would always recuse himself and step aside for a special judge to avoid even the appearance of impropriety, all under the shield of righteousness. In reality, like Bud, the locals eagerly and selfishly ducked such a case, wanting to avoid offending any remaining bluebloods loyal to Reznar's cause or, perhaps worse, avoid splatter from any part of Reznar's corpse that would attract the public feeding frenzy back to them. Even short of criminal prosecution, the wrong alliance at the wrong time could add to the voters' appetite at the polls.

Blame it on bad timing and pressure from the election cycle, or Reznar's reportedly worsening mental state and fatigue, or (most likely) Yancey running out of his retainer as Reznar ran out of money, but they accepted a plea in late August, three months before the general election. Essentially $10,000 extra a month for the twelve years Reznar had been in office—over $1.4 million—was simply too much theft to overcome, not even for Yancey. Strangely, Reznar had grabbed $100,000 in January, which popped up on someone's audit radar somewhere. Holding steady at $10,000 per month might have lasted forever. Perhaps this was Reznar's arrogance, though his ultimate explanation was that he faced a combination of medical bills for his mother and tuition for his first son going to college. Yancey still managed to hammer out a respectable deal. Five years, but he would only serve one before parole if there was restitution. Reznar still had a friend or two to help with that, and better yet, the plea tolled his sentence for six months as he remained on the ballot. Under the delusion that often comes with privilege, he still thought his name and smile could calm the mob and actually win his reelection. Not a chance in Shiloh, home of "trickle-down hypocrisy." Much like the corrupt officials who now ostracized Reznar, a town full of entitlement recipients hated nothing worse than someone trying to get something for nothing.

It always seemed odd that Reznar took the deal on a Friday, and on that next Monday, Donnie Bell's trial came to a screeching halt, as well. After nearly a month of hearing state's evidence in a double murder case, Skinny Don offered only one witness in his defense that morning—himself. His testimony lasted only an hour, as he essentially repeated the story that he had gone to report a bad result to his client. Her spouse came home, grew angry at the news, and pulled a gun. Don allegedly had wrestled the gun away before killing the spouse in self-defense. According to Don, the actual client was still alive and unharmed as he drove away in a panic. His story was no match for the forensics. The jury came back before lunch with a guilty verdict and thirty years.

Earlier testimony said Don had perhaps taken their retainer and done no work at all, and he had already faced reprimand and temporary suspension by the bar for missing deadlines. Another witness pointed out Don's financial woes from gambling and alcohol, intimating that he had shot the clients to prevent yet another formal complaint that would have led to permanent disbarment and a loss of livelihood he could not accept. Yet another alluded to an affair between Don and the client, which the spouse had discovered that night—and that theory goes both ways. Either the spouse pulled a gun on Don out of anger, or Don meant to kill the spouse in order to free up his lover—or even both of them to cover his tracks. Still, no chosen motive clarified the confusion of that Monday. Don had problems, but he had never been violent, and after weeks of his legal team thundering away at the state's witnesses and theories, he offered only his lethargic, almost catatonic testimony as a defense, essentially throwing his hands up. Some even thought he had given up out of depression over the loss of his lover or his life, or both.

LAST NIGHT, 3:00 A.M.

Back then, I was too clueless to even contemplate that such a fight might have been thrown, and too busy with my own life to care. But now, crossing the Kentucky state line into Pike County, just three hours and two mountains away from Shiloh, I was still trying to wrap my mind around a new perspective on the past, knowledge that provided a 50/50 mix of both clarity and confusion.

9

REACHING THE TOP

The scenery brought to mind local attorney Ben Browning, who had earned his stripes across the mountain in Pike County, handling several high-profile cases before the U.S. Department of Labor in the 1970s. Back then, disputes between the coal barons and the union were no longer as bad as they were in the 1950s, but they were still frequent, heated, and sometimes violent. The miners wanted protection from black lung and unstable mine shafts, and the mine operators wanted to keep paying them a pittance in exchange for a twelve-hour day.

The son and nephew, respectively, of the locally acclaimed Browning brothers, Ben had inherited the oldest and most respected firm and legal name in town. Still, Ben had admirably added his family's fortune and notoriety. He won plenty of cases in court, made plenty of money, built the proverbial big house on the hill, and even had a son that grew up to play basketball at Boston University and later professionally in Europe, which in Kentucky, actually garnered Ben more favor than any of his legal victories.

Ben's charmed life changed suddenly, though, when he came home one afternoon to find his youngest son, then sixteen, floating lifeless in the family pool. This happened in the early '80s, and five years later, Ben had followed up that level of grief with disbarment and incarceration after embezzling from his clients' escrow account. Ben had earned reinstatement of his law license in 1994, just as I had returned from law school, and the sympathetic sequence of events repeated throughout town was as follows:

(1) Son's death;
(2) Resulting depression and alcoholism;

(3) Lack of productivity and excessive debt;

(4) Gambling addiction, fueled by both the depression and the debt; and finally,

(5) Theft from his clients in an attempt to pay off unsavory gambling creditors.

Some would even say such hoodlums were involved in his son's death—that the gambling issues began much earlier, or that enemies from his earlier union battles had returned for revenge. Still, the official cause of death remained "accidental drowning."

You would not be aware of any of that from a casual meeting with Ben in the Deed Room, where I would see him at least twice a week. Since his return to law, Ben had settled into a second career mostly comprised of title searches, real estate closings, and trust management for Mountain Miners Bank (MMB), the only bank left in town that did not funnel their work to Bud and the oldest bank in Shiloh. MMB's board of directors still held loyalties to the Browning family that were worthy enough of granting him a second chance. Now in his upper sixties, but looking more like he was in his upper seventies, Ben at least appeared somewhat comfortable, or at least resigned, to his current lot, always with an early morning nod and a "good morning" for an eager newbie like me.

Truth be told, however, Ben had very few clients outside of referrals through the bank. Most locals remained suspicious or at least leery of the whispers and wayward glances that were now attached to his representation. Ben's life proved the difficulty in both destroying and rebuilding a reputation—the latter a near-impossibility in a small town—and one small-town bank lacked the clientele or transactions necessary to keep even his restrained lifestyle afloat. I knew enough of his story to avoid any touchy topics of conversation, and enough to know that I did not want to end up like *him*.

Viewing Ben up close, it was easy to see the sunken, watery, bloodshot eyes that gave a glimpse of a lost soul, one crushed by the successive losses of his son, career, and reputation. Of course, his eyes were also linked in part to his consistent drinking, obvious from the aroma even at 6 a.m. As Aristotle said, once reputation is lost, "…you are like a canceled writing, of no value, and at best you do but survive your own funeral." This appeared to be true for Ben, and while perhaps it was presumptuous coming from a relative rookie like me, I held some sympathy for Ben as a man appearing to go through the motions while playing out the string. At least his professional basketball playing son provided some financial support as well as some sweet ball game tickets to help distract him from his misery.

Sadly, for Ben, his last string was about to be cut.

2002

Miklos was already in the lobby that morning when Bud and I met at the office backdoor at 6:30 a.m. Thirty years in the courthouse through multiple administrations and renovations had afforded Miklos some "access"—i.e., several sets of "lost" keys. We had title work to crank out before the doors opened to the public at 8 a.m., and Bud let out half a sigh and half an eye roll, realizing now that the work would have to wait. Bud quietly buzzed the lobby door open for Miklos, and the two again vanished into Bud's office—nothing new.

It had been months since there'd been a Miklos sighting in the office. You could count on him at any community event that sparked a crowd—a ribbon cutting for a new store, a high school ball game between rivals, or any significant wedding or funeral, for example. But Miklos kept appearances while on "official business" to a minimum. Tricks of the trade for a lifetime politician: a mixture of hiding in the shadows and dodging raindrops while still managing to push his agenda in the desired direction. Miklos could curry favor from or deliver favor to virtually anyone, all while the public saw only a former assistant county judge executive now reduced to the role of humble recycling coordinator in the new administration of Lee Shipp. Or, as the rednecks would ask when looking for him, "Have you seen that little Greek garbage man?"

Miklos's intentionally low profile also built suspense. It was nearing four years since the news about Donnie Bell and his maneuverings for my job. It had been almost three years or so since the Joe Reznar revelation, so I was thirsty for something new. In a morbid sense, I was hovering at my desk like a kid waiting to open Christmas presents… I just needed my parents to wake up and come downstairs to the tree. The title work quashed for the day, I tried to focus on reviewing the day's court docket. It would start at 9 a.m. across the street, but every criminal defendant, child support dodger, and delinquent taxpayer would be lined up at our office an hour earlier, looking to get their cases continued or perhaps resolved with a variety of sob stories. The title work was much more peaceful—and a lucrative income supplement to our "public service"—so you can understand our preference to be in the Deed Room.

Miklos appeared from behind Bud's door and walked toward the lobby. He paused at my doorway and raised his hand as if to speak, but then he diverted his thought to a wink and a grin. If it hadn't been for his typical work boots, suspenders, and newsboy cap, he might really have resembled Santa—or at least one of the elves.

Bud poked his head around the corner and waved me in.

"You have an opportunity here," Bud said as we sat. "Ben Browning's in some serious trouble, and I need to know if you want to handle it."

As Bud unraveled the news, I realized Miklos had left my stocking completely full.

"Apparently"—Bud crossed his feet on his desktop—"Ben has helped himself to a client's trust fund at MMB, and an indictment is expected Friday." Bud shook his head and grinned. "This town's gone crazy, don't ya think?!"

Yes, was the unspoken, obvious thought in my head, followed immediately by *How much did he take?* and, *You want me on this case?!*

"Seems like ol' Ben," Bud continued, "has spent the last two years drinking, going to ball games, and slowly siphoning off nearly two million dollars of Old Doc Jameson's family fortune."

Everyone knew of the late Bryan Jameson, M.D. He was one of the last true family practitioners, operating out of a small office on Central Street for over fifty years, maybe more. Seriously, the diploma on his wall said 1938, and even my poor math skills put him near ninety when he finally retired. Hailing from the age of medicine before insurance companies took over, Doc Jameson would treat almost any ailment with an old-fashioned remedy, and regular patients could negotiate the cost, paying either in cash or in kind services on his many properties. Indeed, Doc had made a fortune as everyone's favorite medicine man, and on top of that, he had married his office manager, Whitney, whose family had literally owned up to a fifth of the county in the 1950s. (Side note: Whitney's niece was Tracy Griffin, the wife of my first boss, yes, "Six Degrees of Kevin Bacon"—or Rupp County—is an easy game to play.)

Anyway, Doc passed away shortly after his retirement, about the time I returned from law school, and Whitney had shrewdly sold the practice and managed the family properties, ultimately selling off much of them to wannabe coal operators, real estate developers, and even the local school system for the newly consolidated high school a few years back. But Whitney had been in the local nursing home the last few years, and thus the trust at MMB had been managed by…you guessed it…Ben. When she finally had passed away last year, her children returned to town to divide the estate. They were furious. Apparently, Ben had avoided arrest for a year only due to back-channel negotiations between the children of the two families, all of whom had shared high school friendships and retained some sentiment for each other, especially as the Browning Law Office was situated right across the street from Doc Jameson's. It was surely only that connection that had allowed such an alcoholic access to such a rich liquor cabinet—pun intended.

"This one's a game changer, Takie. You won't get any higher profile a case in this town, and you've earned it."

We hashed out the details and theories for nearly an hour, as the deed work and 9 a.m. docket across the street seemed meaningless by comparison. Bud and I had evolved. Rivals. Colleagues. Now mentor/mentee. By the end of that first year in the courthouse, about three months after Joe Reznar's plea deal had closed, the mostly unspoken tension had thawed. Bud had gained a little trust and respect from my competence, and I had grown less naïve and less annoyed while learning my penultimate role as Bud's political buffer. The work proved mutually beneficial. I built my skills as a prosecutor along with much-needed contacts and future prospects among the so-called power brokers in town. In turn, Bud built his fortress of loyalty and insulation along with much-needed assistants who were both competent and connected to substantial blocks of voters.

We made even more progress actually from things outside of work. Hell…Bud was as close to a friend as I had made in legal circles. We shared title work in the mornings, and we jogged in the afternoons, sharing thoughts and jokes on the daily nonsense we'd seen. Most evenings or weekends, we'd coach our kids together in T-ball or basketball or peewee football, all on teams well-sponsored by Rodney Morgan, yet another St. Francis Church member who was conveniently both a friend of Bud and one of the five magistrates on the fiscal court. He had made his living as a frequent trucking contractor for Miklos at the recycling plant. Speaking of Miklos…

"You won't even believe the best part," Bud spit out while cackling. The conversation, as usual, had devolved into jokes and amazement at things so absurd yet so normal at the same time. "Ben got busted by confessing at an AA meeting. Told his sponsor in the basement of the church. Fucking janitor overheard, and that janitor's day job is loading trucks for Morgan. Ol' Hot Rod got the story and blabbed to the Jameson children, else they'd have never looked for the two mil...you're talking two hundred million dollars plus in that estate. They would have considered it a loss on investments. I shit you not." Bud loved a good story almost as much as cursing. Any good memory of Bud involved spicy language.

"That's how that your son-of-a-bitch uncle Miklos found out!" Seems Rowdy Rod, as would be his nickname in a Western or a WWE match, enjoyed sharing his hard-earned wealth with youth sports teams but he equally enjoyed sharing any gossip he heard around town. Rodney brought guaranteed laughter on his monthly office visits sharing the news of District Five up in Pups Branch. Just had to be careful not to give him any news in return.

I did not have to be careful around Bud anymore. We were downright gleeful. Bud would now have a monopoly on all the title work in town, as he would surely gobble up MMB—the only bank he did not have—in Ben's absence. More money usually had a way of making a lawyer happy, and my involvement on the case would again shield Bud from an appearance of conflict in prosecuting his main legal competitor. I, on the other hand, finally felt some needed significance, perhaps optimism that this whole legal grind actually had a grander purpose, that I could parlay this case into bigger and better things. Yes, the headlines would flatter my ego, which always remembered Judge Newberry's daily threats of retirement at the end of his next term.

10

GOOD KINDA CRAZY

As was true in any small town, Shiloh's bad news garnered more buzz than the good, even though most folks on most days were quietly busy being kind, being considerate, and just trying to find their way. It is always easy for anyone, me included, to knock Shiloh for its poverty, old-fashioned attitudes, or political corruption—see the Bell, Reznar, and Browning examples in less than four years. Hell, the original settlers and ultimately Daniel Boone had tracked their way to Shiloh across what became nearby Clay County on what was called the Warrior's Path, fighting the British-aided Native Americans along the way, and whether it was over cattle, salt mines, or coal, the town had been at war with itself ever since. The famous Baker-Howard Family Feud before the Civil War had actually required state and federal troops to step in, so it's easy to see the stereotype.

But those who live there still share a sincere sense of togetherness that is *so* hard to find anymore, a simple fun that much of the world has left behind. Our decision to return to Shiloh after law school, to raise a family in that atmosphere, was on purpose and without regrets. Yes, outsiders can point to plenty of crazy—events you just cannot make up—but the people of Shiloh make the world a better place. That same crazy offers much more good than bad on most days, and it was definitely a whole lot more fun.

1981–1987

For those who may never get to visit, I will try to set the scene. You've heard of *The Five People You Meet in Heaven* by Mitch Albom? Well, here's Takie's

51

Five Memories of Childhood in Shiloh, in no particular order, and just the first five that come to mind:

My first friend. I had many sleepovers and teammates while growing up, and I got along with all of them, but the first one to make a lasting impression was Piggy Bee. That name is *not* a misprint, just FYI. Through the sixth grade, I had grown up out in the country, going to the old Cardinal School by the river, the lower-middle-class son of a secretary and a mechanic, and just as poor and white as everyone else. I pleased parents and teachers with my report cards…that's what I had to do…while I played every sport possible…that's what I wanted to do. At the age of eleven, I took much more pride in my wall of trophies than any Honor Roll certificates, and I would gladly play the dumb jock to avoid being dubbed the nerd.

The summer before I went into the seventh grade, Dad got a new job at the Ford dealership in town, so we were suddenly moving to the *city*. Yes, I was clueless, but all I knew was what my classmates and parents believed. I was about to go to Shiloh City Middle, the rich kids' school, a whole school of nothing but uppity doctors' and lawyers' families, kids who raised their pinkies while drinking the carton of milk and wore shirts and ties even to the playground. Oh, by the way, Takie, said everyone, you can expect to be the dumbest one there.

Of course, on the first day of seventh grade, twelve-year-old me was smacked with the obvious truth. In this school just five miles away from my old one, all the ratios of poverty and intelligence were magically the same. In my homeroom that first morning, I was surrounded by housing project kids, each curious to see the new guy. That's how I met Piggy. He was the first black kid I'd ever talked to…and by far the coolest.

I got to school early every morning to hang out with Piggy at the end of the hall. He had biceps the other kids didn't have, he had a tendency to be a little loud, and he always smiled as if he was up to no good. This scared the other white kids away, so I felt special, as the only one he allowed in his "office" by the window at the end of the hall. I anxiously found him every morning, wearing the same plain white T-shirt and sweatpants. Only years later did I find out this wasn't his choice to be cool, but simply all he had.

I was "all-in" from the start. I wanted to absorb how he talked, how he lived, what he thought, and what he knew about all the others. He was amazingly interesting to me, even teaching me how to create comical rhymes about our day, and my talent and liking for limericks and couplets to this day still dates back to Piggy. This one I'll never forget:

> Your daddy in jail,
> Your brother in hell,
> Your momma on the corner,
> Selling fruit cocktail.

Again, what I thought funny or clever turned out to be all too real for Piggy, because one day he simply vanished from school. In the days before social media and cell phones, you could still do that. Not one word from friends or teachers. Not seen at ball games or out in town. He was just gone. It took twenty-five years and my job in juvenile court to realize what happens to kids removed and "placed" by the system, whether it was due to school discipline, crime, or neglect and abuse at home. To the extent that we are hostage to our surroundings, I learned we are all the same. There was a rumor about ten years back that Piggy had surfaced a couple counties over as an exotic dancer, à la *Chippendales*, but the honkytonk bar version. If so, I picture him smiling.

My First Nickname. Piggy's parting gift to me, though it failed to last, was my first and really only nickname (not counting the mean ones from defendants I prosecuted in court)—"PJ." I was in and out of the hospital as a kid for allergies and asthma, and I required shots twice a week for food allergies until I turned twelve. Name about *any* food a kid would pick for lunch, and I was allergic to it. And that includes the *first* food most kids would pick—peanut butter. Nothing serious: My lips, eyes, or ears would swell, just enough to scare my overprotective mom, but those were badges of honor to a twelve-year-old, and well worth the risk. Piggy and his new friend PJ made a habit of sneaking away from school at lunch—across the tracks to his apartment in the housing projects—to enjoy peanut butter sandwiches. Well, *I* enjoyed them while he enjoyed the freakshow of the side effects on my face.

PJ ultimately faded away, along with my allergies, a year later, but my time across the tracks opened my eyes to other nicknames that will forever stick in my mind. There was "Little Man," who clearly was the biggest kid on the block, and there was "Snuffy," who was comically skinny while having droopy eyes that resembled Mr. Snuffleupagus from *Sesame Street*. There was "Milk Shake," who obviously had a little jiggle in his belly and later became a master at post-touchdown celebration dances. Then there was the all-time winner, "Choo Choo," who got the nickname for his addiction to bubble gum but was coincidentally last seen on the train tracks, where he was arrested for assault shortly after high school, then shipped to the state pen. I ran into Choo Choo a few years later, when I was part of a college outreach group playing basketball against inmates. He was in the prison crowd. Then again, just five years ago, long after his release, he showed up as a proud dad to watch his son play on one of my teams.

In hindsight, you can learn a lot from schoolyard nicknames, as kids— especially poor ones—are the most creative and honest among us.

My First Job. Dad was a worker, period. There was *never* a day when he failed to get up and out early, or was exhausted by the end. All for us. He even had three part-time jobs at one point—on top of his regular gig at Ford—while trying to save money as my older brother neared college age. So, the summer after eighth grade, when I was thirteen, he and Mom helped me get a job at the local radio station, and I was excited…honored, even, that I could work like Dad. The paycheck went to Mom and Dad; because I was oblivious to the stress that they actually *needed* the money help make ends meet, for me, it was just a fun way to spend weekend mornings and weekday afternoons between school and football practice.

These types of stations are mostly gone now. No preprogrammed music or prerecorded commentary, just real DJs spinning records with live hourly news, sports, and weather updates. Listen to music and talk sports or current events in air-conditioning. Play a long record, like "Hotel California," and you had plenty of time for a snack or even some homework. Play a segment of *America's Top* 40 with Casey Kasem, and you could even get up on the roof of the building for some sun. I had friends who were bagging groceries and mowing grass. Believe me, there was no better small-town gig for a kid.

Beyond the actual work, the real fun came behind the scenes with the rest of the staff. Just FYI—stations like *WKRP in Cincinnati* really did exist. We had our own "Big Guy," the affectionate nickname of the station general manager who had the voice and persona of James Earl Jones. He could command love, respect, and fear with his voice, all in the same sentence. He had earned a Peabody Award, the radio version of the Pulitzer, for his coverage of the great 1977 flood in nearby Harlan County, and he never missed a minute of the broadcasts. Whether he was at home, in the car, in the office, or on a portable, the radio—his baby—was always on and by his side. We also had "Little Guy," the boss's son and daily office manager, known for his constant cigarettes and goofy laugh, like Ernie from *Sesame Street*. There was also Shirley, a nice-looking secretary whom "Little Guy" eventually married. She was no Loni Anderson from the old show, but you get the idea. There were even a couple of full-time DJs, both appearing to battle issues with substance abuse, depression, or burnout. The contrast between their bubbly on-air personalities and their obvious realities was always impressive.

The rest of the staff, though, was comprised of teenagers like me—kids who would ultimately be kids. For example, during one 5:00 p.m. newscast (5:00 p.m. being our peak "drive time" audience), I had to read the story concerning the death and funeral arrangements of a local matriarch. A fellow DJ, a bit older than me, came into the control room and proceeded to surprise me, resting his exposed penis upon the stereo counter. I giggled on the air right in the middle of explaining the lady's death, too inexperienced to cut off the microphone. I finished the newscast and cut to a song, but not before the phone was already ringing. I answered the phone to a booming, "DON'T LAUGH DURING THE OBITUARIES, DAMMIT!" It honestly could have been the voice of God himself. Lesson learned.

That day notwithstanding, I worked hard and parlayed it into another job as a sports reporter for the local paper. To this day, I remain the only Rupp County alumnus to ever score a touchdown in a high school football game and then interview my coach and write the story for the paper the next day. This ended up being the best experience for writing legal arguments later…taking quotes, stats, and information from multiple sources, and then weaving them together into a tale the average reader finds compelling. Looking back, aside from not laughing during the obituaries, I learned two other things from that early work in Shiloh…it takes multiple voices and perspectives to really get to the true story, and it's pretty easy to sound heroic when you are writing the history.

My First Drink. Most of my youth in Shiloh was spent working to please people—parents, teachers, coaches, or bosses—in hopes of working my way to some vague, magical reward. The rest of the time spent not working to please was spent being afraid of failing to please. Kids like me had no clear picture of college or a career to come. We just knew that Nirvana was somewhere far away from Shiloh, and we lived in fear of being left behind. But some days, I did manage to sample the typical, small-town teenage life around me, mainly thanks to a crew of older college kids who took me under their wing.

Rick, Jackie, and Bo all graduated a couple of years ahead of me, and they would come home from college on most weekends to see Shiloh's version of rural America's favorite Friday and Saturday ritual in the eighties—kids cruising the mall. For hours on end, you could find sixteen- to nineteen-year-olds in their freshly washed cars, creeping at a parking lot pace in the same circular pattern, just trying to see and be seen. We would never join that circuit, mind you, as we were the guys sitting on the hoods of our parked cars telling jokes or yelling obscenities at the passersby. Our weekends were spent pumping iron, reading philosophy, and then spitting our ideas on the world from the hoods of our cars. Our crew defiantly refused to join the cruising herd, for the same reason Rick said they were all GDIs (goddamn independents) and refused to join a fraternity at college. Such social groups were for the needy, the petty, and the conformists, and we would never be so weak. Of course, from the outside, you might say we had simply made our own fraternity, and I for one was grateful they had chosen me as the fourth member of the coolest wolf pack in town.

It was in my summer between high school and college that Rick, Jackie, and Bo helped me on foolhardy adventures I was too scared to ever try on my own…things I knew went against every authority figure I was supposed to please. I was afraid of the activity and afraid of getting in trouble, but I was more afraid of not being a part of my new group of friends. Was I really going to tell the guys to "stop the car and let me out"? Thanks to Rick, who had a sense of comfort with firearms from his retired military father, I fired my first gun (albeit as we took target practice at road signs out the window of Rick's car on midnight rides to the lake). Thanks to Jackie, who had a comfort level with liquor from his alcoholic father, I had my first whiskey and Coke (albeit after I was mortified by my first trip through Cass O'Malley's bootlegging drive-thru, with then seventy-year-old Cass noticing, "Y'all got Miklos's little Greek nephew with you, eh?"). From my heartbeat, you would have thought I was a Russian spy noticed by a CIA operative. And thanks to Bo, who had a fascination with the human body as a future med student, I performed my first stupid human trick (albeit at 1:00 a.m., when the mall parking lot had emptied, as we took turns driving our cars over our straddled bodies while we lay on the pavement).

I learned that bored kids, plus liquor and minus fear, equals stupid. And if you repeat that formula long enough, stupid turns to tragedy. By summer's end, Rick was dead, the end result of a late-night parking lot mix of alcohol, a gun, and uninhibited horseplay. It was an accident, but the gang died with him. I left for college after the funeral, more fearful than ever to stay on the right path. I never saw Jackie or Bo again.

My First Case. While the first legal job with Mr. Griffin was primarily repetitive claims for workers' compensation—back injuries and black lung from coal miners—my first actual court appearance made a far more lasting impression. All lawyers, especially the rookies, took turns handling pro bono cases for indigent clients, and in my first month on the job, I was appointed to represent a father in a termination-of-parental-rights case, i.e., my client wanted to keep his son, and the state wanted to sever the relationship and free the child for permanent adoption.

The facts were simple yet astonishing. It seems a local woman, one with quite a drug habit, had managed to amass eight children by seven different fathers, all by the age of twenty-four. Now, she had vanished, was last seen in northern Ohio, leaving all eight children, ages eight and under, in the custody of social services. The seven different fathers were notified of the final hearing to terminate all parental rights—with the state intending to move the children on for adoption—and only one father, my client, responded in hopes of raising his child. Yes, Big Ted Lacey, as I would learn, had spent money on many bad habits, including drugs, booze, and prostitutes, but he needed a free lawyer to help him try to hang on to his one-year old-son, Ted Jr.

Though I would see it daily in the juvenile court work later, this was my first experience with the most basic conflict arising in cases of neglect or abuse: the natural argument for the instinctual, biological parent–child relationship against a government trying to ensure and protect the "best interests of the child." How far should government go to impose social values or behaviors in the home, and if so, whose values are we imposing? Clearly, total abandonment or physical and sexual abuse are easy calls, but should Big Ted's bloodshot eyes and alcohol breath disqualify him as a parent? Should he leave the child with a sitter three nights a week to go down to pub to drink, fight, and pick up women? Sure, he's not Father of the Year, but is he not to be a father at all? Or if he has a history of drug rehab and prison after supplementing his income with an occasional street corner transaction, does he then lose the right to be a dad?

I struggled to argue Big Ted's case zealously, wondering if winning was actually losing for the child, who might just be better off with a fresh start somewhere else. Were we minimizing risk of harm to the child by separating him from Ted's possible behavior or by not separating him from his natural father? Ultimately, the presence and support of Ted's older sister, who actually helped raise Ted and several foster children, tipped the court in our favor, and Ted was overjoyed. That six-foot-five, 350-pound bear of a man, an ex-college football player and a bar bouncer with hands sufficient to crush a skull, cried as he squeezed the breath out of me. He was the first person I felt I had helped with my law degree, and though I had doubts long after, "Little Teddy," as we called him, did just fine. Like his father, he grew into a local football star before graduating and moving on to college. He even played for me a couple of years, always making me smile while calling me "Godfather"—the name he and Big Ted gave the attorney who had saved him. Guess I learned that most things aren't perfect, but if you care hard enough and long enough—and you get just a little bit of help—things usually get where they need to be.

11

JUMPING THE SHARK

LAST NIGHT, 4:00 A.M.

It was no coincidence that my mind had resorted to conjuring up the more endearing memories of Shiloh just as I could gaze out atop the majestic crest of the Daniel Boone National Forest nearing the Rupp County line. Of natural beauty, Shiloh has a'plenty. Also not a coincidence, as I topped the peak and could see Shiloh in the foggy distance below, the mental recap of my career also neared its pinnacle over the next twelve months in the courthouse, snowballing in both speed and levels of stress.

2002–2003

Ben Browning's case was actually the easy part. The goal was simple: handle the arraignment and preliminary hearing in the lower district court, all while trying to make use of the media spotlight in opposing such appalling thievery, especially by a lawyer and *especially* by one with Ben's prior record. That would be an easy sell to the public. Then, as the case awaited trial, hammer out a plea agreement to garner more press clippings before Commonwealth Attorney Chet Lawson could seize them. Mountain Miners Bank had an ample paper trail of evidence, Ben was up in years and would likely do anything not to die in jail, and the prominent Browning family had the necessary resources and a clear desire to make this go away quickly. That would be an easy sell to defense counsel, too…who, of course, was none other than Yancey Danforth.

Side note: Back then, just the passing thought or mention of Chet S. Lawson would have derailed the story and brought my blood to a boil. Never existed a more complete hypocrite than Lawson, he was maximum hubris mixed with maximum sloth. A Michigan transplant, Lawson set new records of condescension toward all of us poor, intellectually inferior Shilohans (at least that's how he saw it). He spent *every* Sunday at the church sharing his "family values" from his royal pew, and the other six days sharing his "work values" from his royal office. Short version went as follows. Rule 1: Anyone who needed help lacked sufficient morals, sufficient knowledge of the law, or sufficient influence in the election, and therefore they had no case. Rule 2: If Rule 1 failed to apply, Chet's in the middle of a big case and will get back to you. No one could ever pinpoint such an actual "big case," but if he could stall long enough, the really busy, stressed-out people tended to solve their problems elsewhere or just gave up.

Ordinarily, outplaying Chet Lawson for political points on Browning's case would have required Jason Bourne–like tactics. Taking credit, laying blame, and doing nothing were his specialties. But Chet Lawson had accrued his own baggage by that time and was fighting to stay afloat this next election cycle. His high-and-mighty moral authority was finally being threatened by his regular visits to a prostitute, which the religious crowd had ignored for three terms. Worse for Chet Lawson, though, was that his spot and Judge Newberry's post were the only ones up for grabs in the coming election cycle. With Newberry hinting at retirement and Chet's Catholic Church following now in tatters, he was vulnerable. You see, lost in this recount of my career climb was the toll of repeated black eyes and body blows suffered at St. Francis. First, Donnie Bell, then Joe Reznar, and now Ben Browning had drawn a line between the respective Browning and Jameson family pews. There was still a solid political base there, with Bud, Magistrate Morgan, County Judge-Executive Lee Shipp, Circuit Judge Paul Runyan, County Engineer Mo Lillard, and of course, Miklos, but the crew was thinner and getting long in the tooth. Meanwhile, the Mount Pleasant Baptist Church across town had a growing congregation and some viable challengers for seats at the courthouse table.

In any event, a distracted Chet Lawson meant an easy road for me. The Joe Reznar case provided the blueprint; all I had to do was withstand the usual antics by Yancey Danforth. Yancey never wanted a trial in any case, and he had never danced in with a bigger loser on the evidence than Browning. After grinding through several pretrial motions, reams of documents, and Yancey's theatrics at the negotiating table, the case came down to the usual— money. The Jamesons wanted restitution more than they wanted to put an old man in jail, and the Browning clan including Ben's pro athlete son had plenty of it to buy leniency. How much would you pay to keep your loving father or uncle from dying in jail? He had never been a violent man; he just got caught up in the racket of gambling and booze. Heck, *The Godfather* would have actually called those honorable pursuits. He had already lost his son and career to his vices, and to create an even more sympathetic figure, he was now diagnosed with prostate cancer. There was ample room for a win-win compromise. Victims could get made whole, and the headlines and quotes would parade my assault against corrupt, greedy lawyers, telling how no one escaped justice, especially not the rich. I actually fancied that I believed those remarks myself and beat the drums loudly.

In reality, it was less a drum and more a trumpet lightly playing *Taps* while Yancey negotiated the terms of Browning's surrender. Of course, Yancey delayed as much as reasonably possible and pushed the inevitable well into the summer of 2003, knowing that Ben's death looming on the horizon would render the prosecution moot. The extension of good media coverage was fine by me. Ultimately, the Jameson family attorney signed off on their price, while my added demand was for the full jail term but probated so long as Browning surrendered his law license and left Shiloh. Browning's son paid the tab and took his ill father north to convalesce. Ben was dead by Christmas.

Meanwhile, by that same holiday season, my shooting star in Shiloh would never be brighter. There were pats on the back galore for the relentless crusader for justice by day, the caring youth coach and mentor by night. All I needed was a cape. Seriously, it grew almost to a comic extent: If you believed the gossip around town, you would have expected Doc Holliday from *Tombstone* to find me "down by the creek, walking on water." Fame also helped boost local donations and it got our Boys & Girls Club idea started, complete with a paid staff and after-school drug-prevention program. This momentum led to my receiving the award for National Youth Coach of the Year, presented by none other than Hall of Famer Cal Ripken Jr. A month later, the local chamber of commerce would name me Rupp County Citizen of the Year and ask me to ride a sleigh with Santa as the grand marshal of the Christmas parade. Small-town nonsense, truly, and my coaching friends happily ridiculed me with the nickname "Midas." As Bud and I liked to say about most of our work, "You can't make this shit up."

Four years in the courthouse, though, and already some of the bloom was falling off of the rose. In those four years, I had gone from anonymous legal grinding with Mr. Griffin to a bit of small-town royalty with Bud. Still, it was obvious that the Catholic mothership had sprung a few leaks over the past few years, and the rival crowd from Mount Pleasant Baptist always had their sharks in the water to take bites when they could, particularly at the apparent rising Catholic star.

It started in small, only semi-painful nibbles. There was fellow attorney Lonnie Conn, with whom I had played Little League as a child and with whom I later enjoyed weekend softball and basketball games as an adult. He had spread a rumor among other members of the bar that I had solicited Boys & Girls Club donations to line my own pockets. Forget being unfounded, I couldn't even imagine an explanation for his claims. While we were not "close" friends, I saw him at least weekly, and in all respects, our interactions were pleasant. There was another local attorney, Kendrick Morton, whose house had neighbored my family's growing up, who lobbied others not to give to our Boys & Girls Club after his cousin, a convicted drug trafficker, was turned down as a volunteer based on his background check. And then there was Sammy Wexler, a local county school administrator who launched a fairly vicious campaign of propaganda to block the Boys & Girls Club from the use of any school system property or resources. The reason? The club was allegedly a ruse for Coach Takie to lure good ball players to his teams in the opposing school system, where he still coached part-time. Really? REALLY? We were talking middle and high schoolers…in the hills of eastern Kentucky. Breaking news… No one there resembled LeBron James. Only in a place like Shiloh could you find such petty, territorial backlash against such an obvious good cause. Say it with me again: "You can't make this shit up."

None of these issues were overwhelming, though, and Annie and I successfully navigated such roadblocks, ultimately landing a nice piece of land on which to erect and open the club. Still, the pattern of any whiff of progress attracting small-minded haters became apparent. In hindsight, Lonnie Conn truly just couldn't stand not having such notoriety for himself. Kendrick Morton proved to be angling as a competitor for Judge Newberry's judicial seat. And Sammy Wexler? Well, he actually cared more about sports than education or anything else, so he honestly believed his cause in tearing down the club to protect "his" athletes was just. I guess points go to him over the other two for at least caring about other people beyond himself.

Another common thread, however, was the obvious "resistance" building from the Baptist church crowd—including the Conn, Morton, Wexler trio—against the Catholic church group currently controlling most of the courthouse. Despite my pure motives with coaching and the club, and despite my not being a major part of the Catholic crowd, four years was far too long to avoid most folks linking me—and the district judge maneuvering—to Miklos, Bud, and the Catholic company. Add to this the customary wear and tear that accrues as a small-town prosecutor makes daily enemies through his work, and the cumulative friction slowed my momentum, both publicly and internally. You just cannot avoid alienating most families at some point. Between politicians angling for power, defendants angry from prosecution, and the usual piranha public mob always looking for gossip or blood…well, let's just say Santa wasn't holding that Christmas parade seat for me next year. To the townspeople I might have been "gettin' above my raisin'." Comical for sure, as I was so far from being a blueblood, but mountain folk hate an outsider only slightly more than one of their own trying to rise above the pack.

12

CALLING AUNT ELLEN

LAST NIGHT, 4:15 A.M.

The dashboard clock angrily glared at me, like my dad waking up late on the couch to me coming in past curfew from the Rick, Jackie, and Bo adventures in days gone by. It sobered me instantly, just like Dad had, drawing nervous attention to my looming uncertainty, with no plan of attack and no funds to flee. I had dodged such thoughts for nearly five hours in part from shock, but more from already knowing my limited options even before I had hit Fort Pitt Tunnel at the edge of the city. My mind had wandered with a sliver of false hope for a nonexistent solution, some kind of Plan B, but I'd hit Shiloh in less than two hours with only two empty pockets and a story I couldn't tell…and worse, a story that no one would believe. Who could possibly help? The position description called for 1) resources, 2) loyalty, and most importantly, 3) the willingness to give both without understanding why. The potential applicant pool was never more than one…Aunt Ellen.

Miklos had always had cash and property investments, built up from a cloudy mix of sources. There were several small business ventures over the years, some decent and some not, and of course, his hilarious two lottery wins in back-to-back months in the spring of 2000. But mostly there was some family inheritance compounded with his extension of the family business breaking down and reselling scrap metal from the area coal mines. Even after Mama Mikey's death, the estate received a large settlement as part of a class action suit against American Power Company, which had dumped toxic cleaning chemicals into the nearby water supply leading to multiple cancer deaths, including Mikey's. Yes, outside of Appalachia such environmental violations and tragedy might have made national news, but Shiloh folks were used to being spit on, and carpetbagger companies like American Power were good at spitting at us on the way out after they had taken the labor or natural resources they wanted. Miklos and my dad had also received their own personal portions of the settlement, both as survivors of Mikey's death and from their own related health problems. Sadly, they had spent their teens and most of their twenties working the scrapyard for Deo, routinely washing their hands and even eating their lunch while covered in that "cleaner."

But beyond the inheritance and the settlement and lottery, Miklos had a more discreet side. A true blue-collar millionaire, Miklos the chameleon could manage the solid waste dump by day and spend evenings connecting with other "off the books" fat cats in backwoods trailers and cabins—places even the cops wouldn't go for fear of a stray black bear or property owner's shotgun. There was a whole network of guys throughout towns like Shiloh who still kept their money under mattresses and in barrels buried in their backyard, mostly to avoid taxes but also to hide the fruits of, shall we say, "suspicious" pursuits when needed. Drugs, particularly marijuana and oxycontin, alcohol (bootlegged into the dry town), prostitution, or loan sharking—the usual vices or trappings of the poor—provided secret lucrative lives, political influence, and police protection for many of Shiloh's upstanding businessmen. The most enjoyable way to launder such cash, or even car titles and property deeds, as it turned out, was through high-stakes poker games run in these hidden, smoky parlors. And not to paint everyone with a broad brush, but there were also those guys who avoided the crime while blending in just enough to entertain the room, trade favors, and gather any info that might work as political capital later, all while satisfy their gambling fix. One of *those* guys was named Miklos.

As the eldest child and caretaker of the family business and properties, Miklos had managed Mikey's money in her later years, and based on his time spent running her errands and dropping off food or money to her house, he had honorably cared for her until her death. In fact, throughout Mikey's later years, Miklos would notoriously repeat at any family function—almost as a propaganda slogan—that "all the money went to Mikey." So obviously, when Mikey passed without leaving any significant fortune, Terez and Dimi, the other siblings, doubted Miklos's explanation of his expenditures on Mikey's behalf. Far from the first family to fuss over money after death of a matriarch, Terez and Dimi felt their inheritance had been invaded by their older brother using Mikey's money for his personal needs, and Miklos felt pretty unappreciated by his younger siblings after pulling the lion's share of Mikey's caretaking. As always, the truth lay somewhere in the middle. Mikey had outlived much of her lawsuit settlement, and she had a penchant for fancy clothes and jewelry—and for purchasing expensive Christmas gifts for her grandkids—until the very end. Terez and Dimi had mistakenly presumed that Miklos had used some of his own good fortune on Mikey, thereby preserving the family estate, and perhaps he could have been more generous, considering his success that stemmed from family business. But Miklos had declined that path and built up his own position over the years, while Terez and Dimi had both toiled in the lower middle class. Nothing wrong with that, but the reminder of all of this at Mikey's death stirred up the resentment from years past when Deo had favored Miklos over the other kids with the gift of the scrap metal enterprise.

Unlike Miklos, an apparent money magnet, Terez spent much of his life chasing it, a trait he had passed on to me. Dad was always an amazingly hard worker, a selfless jack of all trades with no hours too long to work for his family, but he just never hit the big one. He gave us a nice, comfortable life—nothing flashy—and whether one viewed it as morality or weakness, I had done only slightly more than that for my kids. Comparing my law degree and his inability to speak English until the age of thirteen, some might see failure. With both Mom and Dad gone, their thoughts of me as a loser or a winner, a saint or a sinner were uncertain. Regardless of their view from the grave, and no matter how wistful my thoughts, all they had left me with was the small family homestead, which barely auctioned for enough to cover the mortgage.

So that put me back to Aunt Ellen. Though I hadn't seen her in years, she had been most welcoming after the funeral, with a smile, a hug, and some cookies…as if I was fourteen again and looking for a soft spot to land while dealing with the usual teen angst about my parents. It was hard to fathom the service was only three days ago; it seemed at least a year. Ellen had expressed sincere gratitude for the kind words of my eulogy. She knew all too well my discomfort with—even hatred of—being back in Shiloh, and she knew I had taken one for the team as the designated family mouthpiece, particularly at funerals after I'd been the one to give the eulogies for Mikey, both my parents, and now Miklos. The ceremony had included many of the old guard from the past. Bud and Chaser, Mr. Griffin, all the Catholic church politicians, and even Nan Diaz, the church's choir director and Shiloh Chamber of Commerce president who had nominated me for the Christmas parade gig. Every glance found a familiar face sprinkled throughout the other church members, all connections from the past that were at best unhelpful, and at worst nauseating.

Graciously, Ellen had invited me up to their house after the dust settled from what seemed like an entire town of well-wishers at the funeral. We sat for tea, played with Buddy, her ever playful terrier, and reminisced a lot about life, especially the last few years after I had left town. She had always been so kind, with a kindness you cannot fake, and her infectious laugh rang throughout the basement as we descended the old, rickety metal spiral staircase into Miklos's makeshift garage office. There was Miklos's old desk, literally pulled from the recycling dump, and covered in Post-It Notes just like the dashboard and front seat of his work truck. There was his usual dusty dartboard, pool table, and card table, all the customary "man toys" that men collected before the days of iPhones and Roku. And of course, stacked up beside his old-school filing cabinet were dozens of legal pads, every page drenched with lottery numbers he had tracked for over twenty years.

"Numbers go hot and cold," Miklos had always chuckled. "A man best know the temperature if he's gonna put a handful of dollars in."

Typical nonsense from the wannabe wise philosopher. We all rolled our eyes at Miklos sometimes, even Ellen, and we would have laughed harder at the memory except that he had won twice. Joke was on us.

For the first time in all that laughter growing up, though, I needed Ellen's kindness now. She had given me Miklos's ledger that evening, so that I could count up anything needed to wrap up the estate after the will went through probate. It would not exactly be pain free, as even a casual glance at the book now in my passenger seat could attest. We were talking a book likely older than me, held together more by tape than leather at this point, two hundred pages of handwritten, partially legible scribbles showing credits and debits to any number of accounts ranging from thousands in monthly fuel for his company trucks down to the farmers' market, where he grabbed the occasional apple across from the courthouse. There was handwriting on tape across the front reading only "Miklos/050898." I had opened it just long enough to see the upcoming workload, though I would never complain about helping Ellen, and I had heard enough from her to know she really had no idea of the business. All she knew was that Miklos had left all of his personal assets to her and the business interests to their son Paris, who had long been second-in-command at the scrapyard and was more than ready to take the reins.

My hope was that Ellen's mix of affection and innocence would be my escape hatch. I just needed enough to lasso enough money to at least take a leave of absence from work, lie low, and figure things out. I needed to either find a way to disengage or disappear until it blew over. Surely things would have to move on without me. I had managed to dodge every fight since the fifth grade, so why not one more time? I would concoct some legal mumbo-jumbo to get Ellen to point me to some of the cash on hand...perhaps an account password, a safety deposit box key, or the combination to Miklos's office safe. Ellen should have no suspicion toward me and no financial worry with all that Miklos left behind, so my only fight would be with my own guilt at deceiving her. Yeah, I promise I felt the guilt already creeping up the back of my neck, but I had no choice, and the truth would only put her in the lifeboat with me. Don't look now, but I would have to become the shyster like those I despised. I would have to become my family's version of Ben Browning.

13

FOUR MORE YEARS

Any stress and scheming over money in the past five years had always circled me back to the same story of how my time in Shiloh had imploded. In fact, despite time and distance, any return to town still brought a twinge of rage. I had tried to learn to ignore what could not be changed, to subdue that past personality in my head like Professor Nash in *A Beautiful Mind,* but descending the back side of Elk Mountain toward the past was like sinking in quicksand. You could feel the weight and the inevitable sinking, and the instinctual thrashing about in anger only sank you deeper. Granted, I had healed stronger since getting out, and I had plenty of distraction at the moment, but a man always clenches the steering wheel a little tighter when he sees the woman who broke his heart. Imagine if that was a whole town.

2004–2008

The confusion about me, to anyone looking from the outside in, and to Annie as the marriage crumbled, was that my anguish (or mental illness) came at what appeared the peak of my success. Knocking out high-profile cases, establishing a thriving Boys & Girls Club from nothing, and enjoying a happy and healthy family. Was this not the American dream? My dream? Career significance, family comfort, and community outreach all achieved in my small town? And now the National Youth Coach of the Year Award. Just more hard work and faith rewarded. The year 2004 was essentially my fifteen minutes of fame. Major League Baseball flew me and my family out to Anaheim, California, to be recognized at its Winter Meetings…right alongside Cal Ripken Jr. himself and an assembly hall full of superstars, even Vin Scully and "freakin' Tommy Lasorda," as I referred to him in my acceptance speech. It was a bit surreal for me to take the stage after ESPN commentators had just handed out Major League Baseball's Player and Manager of the Year Awards. It was all a blur of excitement, but whatever I said, the Atlanta Braves General Manager John Schuerholz and coaching staff, Bobby Cox and Leo Mazzone, liked my words so much they offered the whole family a free week that coming March at their Spring Training in Disney World. Ty spent the entire evening playing tic-tac-toe and the "dot game" on napkins with Ripken. That experience, along with watching me throw out the first pitch at a Major League game that spring, was enough for my ten-year-old son to be even more proud of his dad—and that was the best part.

But if the flights to Anaheim and Orlando were the ascent to my fifteen minutes of fame, the descent proved to be more of a sudden freefall. Lost in the whirlwind and hilarity of our Disney vacation was Judge Newberry's decision to hang on for one more term. He had known and endorsed my plans for succession that winter, but as we sat in the Orlando airport awaiting our return flight, he called to break the news that he would be filing for that year's primary election. He had seven kids, one still in college, and over twenty grandkids, some of which still relied upon him for support, so he needed one more term. Of course, I was instantly conciliatory, as, whether judge or local politician, Judge Newberry was "the best there is…in Cooperstown," just as Rusty deferred to Saul's criminal greatness at the dog track in *Oceans 11*. There would be no honor or success in challenging him, and he assured me I'd have no trouble with four more years in my current glow. It was only a matter of time.

But his phone call triggered an avalanche of uncontrolled thoughts in my head. Can a person have a midlife crisis at thirty-five? Or was this burnout from a frenetic decade spent juggling work, the Club, coaching, and family? Either way, my brain began to lose cabin pressure. Annie and the kids were grabbing something to eat a few gates down. I sat there at the airport gate, watching strangers and trying to process my life, trying to ignore the actual sounds of the airport clock faintly in my head…*tick, tock.*

The path so far had clearly gone well, but district judge was the next logical step for me…the end that would justify the means. That was the buoy in the distance, the life raft surprisingly materializing after a decade of monotonous swimming, not in some clear blue ocean but in a muddy, swampy, polluted Shiloh stream. And now the port had just been moved four years further away? I felt a warm wave of resentment crash in. A man dumped his leftover dinner into the trash, and somehow that symbolized my career to that point for me. *Tick, tock.*

It didn't symbolize my family, mind you. I saw them nearing the cashier at the food stand, and for a moment I caught my wind again. They were perfect. A source of complete joy. But I despised the world in which I worked almost as much as I loved them. My public face, the fake mask that withstood the pressure of work…that found significance and importance in what we did—day in, day out—was crumbling. I knew it, and the kid who had gone to law school on a drunken soccer team dare definitely knew it. I wanted no part of law or politics anymore, and I was wasting precious seconds of my life. Hell, even the clock knew it. *TICK, TOCK.*

But what other option was there in Shiloh? One that would provide what I already had, what everyone said I had already achieved, and much more importantly, a good life for Ty and Andi. Was I supposed to come home from this version of the Shiloh mountaintop and just say I was quitting? Go teach or write for the newspaper for one-fourth the pay? Take the loss, downsize the lifestyle, and start over? I could see their smiling faces and ice cream cones approaching. No way could I do that. I had made promises. I would pull the weight. It's what any man does.

But there, at our family's happiest moment, with the airline calling us to board the flight back home, I was shaking at the thought of another four years wading through meaningless courthouse shit. I ducked into a nearby restroom to hide, but the clock pressed on. *TICK, TOCK!*

That's my only real memory of panic, as, for the most part, I settled in to quiet submission. My work was still successful on all counts, and the growing pile of enemy bodies had in no way diminished my value to Bud. I remained a good and loyal buffer. Still, as the attrition mounted, I realized I lacked the stomach for real politics, and the district judge post that seemed such a layup a year ago was no longer easy or certain. Without it as a clear goal, discontentment reared its ugly head again. The county had continuous financial constraints, so raises could not be expected, and with Bud likely entrenched in his chair until retirement, my glass ceiling was actually now a concrete dungeon in the courthouse basement. Work quickly grew more monotonous, an unsatisfying hassle, and what had once provided passion and purpose now seemed useless…a steady stream of the same families not paying their debts, not raising their kids right, not obeying the law. On many occasions, you could track a kid from juvenile court, whether facing crime, truancy, neglect, or abuse, into dropping out of school, unemployment, early parenthood, and eventual criminal activity as an adult. The same guy might pop up on each of the four different dockets in the same week. What purpose did the work possibly serve?

My growing sense of hopelessness even began to seep into my coaching, ever my holiday from the courthouse fray. But I had now coached long enough to see my first fifth grade teams through to high school graduation, and sadly the percentage of my kids ending up in juvenile court, on drugs, or in jail as adults actually matched the general population. Like our court system, motivational speeches and mentoring during two-hour practices were no match for the surrounding OxyContin epidemic and lack of opportunity the kids faced the other twenty-two hours of the day. It was hard to see how the effort mattered at all.

I hung in long enough for Ty and Andi to later play for me, and our time and experiences together remain priceless. They were both truly heroic on the field, terrific players and team leaders, but they both saw firsthand how sometimes the smarter players—those with more opportunity—often "aged out" of the game mentally before their actual playing days were done. They already had the acquired discipline and a vision for the future, so they just did not need to "run through the wall" to add a trophy to the school's case. Sports are fun, and they can teach great life skills, particularly discipline and a solid work ethic, but if you cannot tie that effort to a meaningful vision, it's impossible to invest your heart and spirit. In the words of my first coach, Walker Troutman, a man needs three bones to succeed in life—a wishbone (vision), a backbone (hard work), and a funny bone (enjoyment). I could work as hard as anyone and make everyone laugh, but as I had lost my vision of purpose in the law or in coaching, and long before I ever thought it would have been possible just a few months earlier, I realized I had "aged out," too.

Of course, a clear rearview now sees those thoughts as somewhat ridiculous. Like a poker player who only remembers the bad beats over the wins, you never see or recall in your mind's eye the ones you helped, particularly in the legal system, because those who move forward never need to reenter the system. The true nature of the game in our legal assembly line, the people who might justify your sweat or reinforce your energy, were one and done. The ones who drained your soul always came back for more. And long before 2008, when I might have had the opportunity offered by

Judge Newberry's retirement, I was on empty. By that point, the pride...the significance...the thrill was gone, leaving only a virus of misery spreading to anything I touched. Word to the wise for all husbands: There's absolutely no way to express dissatisfaction with your life and career without your wife taking that personally. You don't mean it toward her, ever. But she's in it with you. That's just the way it is. Hope she's forgiven me by now.

14

RIPE FOR TEMPTATION

LAST NIGHT, 4:30 A.M.

Discontentment, if it hangs around long enough, eventually turns into the double-edged sword of desperation. On the one hand, it can provide needed motivation, perhaps for a dispirited chicken like me to take a leap and make a change. On the other hand, it may tempt you away from your safety zone, toward things outside your strengths—like a singles hitter who strikes out trying to take one deep. Change for the sake of change can take you from the frying pan into the fire, as leaping without looking can land you right in dog shit.

Yes, you see, impatient and aggravated, I had swung for the fences once, at least at my minor league level. Took the path less traveled toward apparent riches and ended in ruin. Considering my customary sense of risk aversion, you could picture Charlie Brown knowing not to try the kick, but then doing so, only to land on his ass. While discouraged and mired in the monotony at Bud's, my tempter's name wasn't "Lucy," but rather a fat, ornery, hideous pit bull of a woman named Viola Wells. The thought that I would have listened to her overtures—just considering his appearance and reputation—tells you just how miserable I had convinced myself to be.

2007

The majority owner and president/CEO of Mountain Miners Bank (MMB), and front-row regular at the rival Baptist church, Viola, or Vi as everyone knew her, was synonymous with Scrooge in Shiloh. She would say she was rightfully serving her fellow shareholders and protecting the bank's bottom line, but she had ruthlessly squeezed many a local for more than twenty years. Most notably, beyond her usual derogatory, cruel remarks when turning someone down for a loan or foreclosing upon their nonpayment, Vi was known for her vulture-like tactics, wherein she would torpedo a loan needed on a good business deal and then, with the applicant out of the way, swoop in and take the deal herself. She also routinely scooped up properties at auction or deeds from the desperate in lieu of foreclosure for pennies on the dollar, as she had all of the inside information on the real estate and full discretion to call the full balance due and force a sale. She used several shell corporations, of course, and though she lacked Wall Street sophistication, she was clever enough to dodge the unknowing or underfunded commoners. Besides, there was no white collar crime division in the courthouse, and Vi kept any local lawyers from taking a civil case against her with preferred interest rates and shared insider tips on deals she skipped. She had a knack for enjoying her work and life, even as 90 percent of the people she passed on the street hated her...the true definition of a miser. Seriously, of three robbery attempts at the bank over twenty years, two confessed they just wanted to shoot her or steal from her. She conceal-carried at all times out of necessity.

Vi actually asked Bud for permission to offer me a job, and once she got permission, she even asked Bud his opinion on how much he thought it would take to lure me into a new career. In Vi's mind, I was the perfect replacement as corporate counsel for Ben Browning. A necessary background in title and trust work, a good reputation to remove the public relations stain from the mess that Ben had left behind, and most importantly in hindsight, just young and inexperienced enough not to sniff out shady operations.

Vi's vision was of no consequence, though, after Bud and I shared a drink and a laugh in formulating our response. Bud would never willingly give up his loyal first mate or the chance to monopolize the local title work once the MMB work went to him with Ben out of commission. He casually gave Vi a figure at two and half times my salary, knowing that would end the discussion. As stated, no consequence. No chance. That is, until Vi actually came back with the money...actually three times my prosecutor's pay when you counted annual bonuses and stock options. I would do their title opinions, advise their board of directors, manage their regulatory paperwork, and otherwise perform NAS ("nod and smile") duties. In other words, Vi recognized my one skill of serving shit with a smile. She wanted me for much the same role I'd had at Bud's, to serve as a public relations buffer pulling in customers with kindness and putting a smile on any bad news she had to deliver.

Aside from the huge pay bump, the bank job offered something steady with seemingly very little stress compared to the courthouse: no possibility of election defeat every four years, and did I mention an enormous pay increase? Moreover, it was something "different"—a lighted path at a time when all I saw was a dark dead end ahead. I actually lost a few nights' sleep over it. Like with most major decisions, I could never determine if a great opportunity was being divinely offered after years of sweat and preparation, or if such luck was a temptation to derail me from my chosen, functional path. Was this time to "strike while the iron is hot," or to remember that "if it ain't broke, don't fix it"? In my usual brain, if in doubt, the stronger fear would win out. But whether you call it burnout, the inability to stomach a full four years in the dungeon waiting for Judge Newberry to retire, or just my one Charlie Brown moment of weakness, I took the gig. I didn't consult Miklos, or Frank, or any other would-be puppeteer. I just jumped. Thought I would be my own man for once, and this appeared to be the proverbial "offer he can't refuse."

There was minimal celebration. I would still have to tell Bud and set fire to the first of multiple bridges. Bud's meter shot well past the prior tension to open hostility, though he managed to admit that while it was a "professional screwing," it was clearly "personal advancement." Even though he was extremely angry, he knew me well enough to understand my inner struggle.

"We'll figure out how to adjust without you. Don't worry about it," he said without even looking up from his computer screen, obviously trying to restrain his words. "You know we wish you well."

He never looked up, only kept typing more ferociously and almost breaking the keyboard until I thanked him and walked away.

If the ending at Bud's proved bittersweet, the bank job was just pure bitter, from start to end. Like the step into dog shit or accidentally touching a woman's breast in an elevator or subway where you cannot escape, there's an instant awkwardness there that you cannot shake. I spent the first three days wanting to phone Bud to admit my stupidity and plead for my job back. Whether out of sheer pride or fear of shame, I hung on, and soon the morphine of money turned me into nothing more than an upper-middle-class addict. I hated work more than ever, but I would show up just the same. How could I dare complain or renege on providing such a better life for my family? But eventually, the virus of hate had reconstituted within the host. A "different" job was a far cry from a "more fulfilling" job. Instead, it was mind-numbingly boring, and after the hustle of the courthouse, it was the equivalent of an air traffic controller being asked to monitor a kindergarten playground. Never would I have more money in my pocket, and never would I be more useless. No offense to those souls who find happiness in banking, but let's just say, the industry and my skillset were mismatched.

The job was actually a revolving circle of nonsense, thanks to one key ingredient…Viola Wells. Once we were inside the bank, it was surprisingly difficult to pin Vi down on what exactly my job required. Shiloh would never be a hotbed for real estate lending or commercial development, so any title work was done before the doors opened, and any regulatory or financial reports were prepped and discussed at monthly or quarterly meetings. So, other than sitting in a large office and straightening the files, tell me again what I was supposed to do for the 300 percent raise? What Vi did reveal was her plan to retire in a couple of years, and she promised to show me the ropes to usher me into her seat. She would retain her ownership interest and collect her dividends, but the day-to-day oversight—and another sizable pay hike—would fall to me. I was fine with the long-term plan, not so much with just trying to get through the immediate day ahead. With me onboard, Vi traveled extensively and stopped in every three weeks or so to give her ideas, opinions, and general state-of-the-union updates. Smiling for an hour while eating a complete plate of her shit, even unsalted, seemed a small price to pay for the salary, but still, the constantly moving and impossible targets tested my sanity. Here's a sample series of our monthly meetings:

Vi: "You're paid too much for just legal work. Drum us up some business."

(I brought in a month full of the typical Shiloh home-buying loan applicants.)

Vi: "That's not the kind of credit profile we want at this bank."

(Ya think?! In a town with 80 percent of the citizens living below the poverty line? Dumbass.)

Vi: "Go get us some of your high-rolling lawyer friends."

(I swallow all integrity and sweet-talk some lawyers to switch banks to get better interest rates on their deposits and access to management [me] when needed.)

Vi: "We can't pay those interest rates on deposits! And we can't loan them money that cheaply! That's not profitable for this bank."

(I renege on the rates offered, smiling while swallowing further crow and insults from douchebags I would never have talked to— let alone tried to help—otherwise.)

Vi: "You've got too much going on in your life. If you want to run this bank someday, you need to be more focused."

(I cut out coaching activities and resign as the director of the Boys & Girls Club, sacrificing the last shred of utility and self-worth to be found in my career.)

Vi: "You need to be more active in social and civic groups. Get your name out there more and develop good public relations for us."

(I wish I was kidding. And 'round and 'round we would go.)

In short, I had never encountered a more self-inflated yet intellectually dense individual. Someone who thought everything they did or said was the most important or effective ever done or said, and yet who was too "obtuse"— to quote Andy in *The Shawshank Redemption*—to ever hear or accept any opposing view. Sadly, she seemed perfect for her job…if only I could ever figure out what that was. Absolute absurdity. I loathed her. Detested the job. And fully detested myself for getting myself into such a mess. But there I was, nearing forty. Had reached the mountaintop of my hometown trying to work hard and stay humble, only to see that those at the summit appeared to just collect money while doing nothing and convincing themselves of their greatness. The family and our monthly bills had already expanded to accommodate to the extra money, of course, so I had effectively painted myself into a corner with few other equivalent options in Shiloh. I had traded trapped *without* money for trapped *with* money…and for someone who valued significance in their work, the lack of *any* utility at the bank was actually much worse. In my mind, the decision was to acquiesce to some form of semi-retirement at thirty-eight. I would have to swallow the fact that I had given and achieved much in my career's first half, and that the second half would essentially consist of sitting still and collecting checks for me and mine. But what might have elevated another man actually deflated me further, and I had to choose to let a little more air out of my life each and every morning.

15

A TRUE OUTLAW

LAST NIGHT, 5:00 A.M.

Taking a right at the base of the forest near the Big Hickory Golf Course directs your mind's eye toward the "Tri-Cities," otherwise known as the towns of Chapel, Orangeburg, and Prosperity, all about thirty minutes from the county seat in Shiloh. All three were thriving communities during Rupp County's coal-mining and U.S. Steel heyday in the 1970s. But 30 years later and just shy of 5 a.m., there was only one red light on the highway, one Shell gas/convenience store, and apparently only one ghost left in town – the ghost of Gill Blackney.

Blackney had risen to glory as a swashbuckling sheriff of "Die-Loh," the town as it was through the '60s, the '70s and even the early '80s while torn between longstanding liquor bootleggers and marijuana farmers, expanding cocaine or heroin importers, and mining union agitators. Judge Newberry had started as the town's public defender during those days, and he told sordid stories of a murder per week as criminal factions battled for territory, either to sell their product or to extort payment for their "protection" from their unsavory rivals. Blackney would never be confused with Einstein or Socrates, but he saw the exodus of good families from Rupp County as the coal-mining jobs evaporated. He saw less middle-class and more mob, and more important than seeing it was his willingness to take advantage of it.

Over the course of two terms, Blackney and his deputies had reached the pinnacle of public support as the new champions of justice—swift, harsh, and reportedly righteous. Behind the badge, though, he also sat atop Shiloh's criminal underbelly in similar fashion—swift, harsh, and reportedly ruthless. Under the guise of law enforcement, Blackney amassed an empire by out-extorting the extorters, out-dealing the dealers, and out-gunning the gun thugs. In his defense, he actually did broker some sense of peace for the commoners around town. He struck fear in the outlaws, and they avoided his wrath only so long as they stayed in their respective hollers and paid him the appropriate toll whenever they crossed the bridges into town.

Some had described this time as "A Tale of Two (Tri-) Cities," a mix of prosperity and violence going back to the Great Depression. U.S. Steel and International Harvester had long provided a pipeline to high-paying, union jobs in what was the "Cadillac" of coal-mining towns. That same pipeline, however, remained open for drug trafficking and criminal transients long after the jobs were gone. Blackney was the first to get a modern-day lasso around the evolving Rupp County economy, and, for that, he was in many ways a welcome relief. As a result, he remained revered and beloved by many long after his notorious demise, a fact still evident by the tattered billboard still visible as I passed through on Goose Creek Highway.

Proud Home of Gill Blackney, an American Patriot!

Yes, Shiloh had "alternative facts" long before Kellyanne Conway.

"Rome wasn't built in a day, but it burned in one," goes the saying, and true to form, Blackney's kingdom proved no different. You see, aside from those rare chameleons like Miklos, the political pendulum ultimately returns to whack everyone. By the fall of 1983, the Kentucky State Police had compiled plenty of corruption evidence on Blackney, likely holding it to maintain leverage for use at the optimal time. Over the years, Blackney had surely collected dirt on and brokered profitable deals with the KSP—most troopers were far from infallible in my experience—but they still outranked him on paper and in the court of public opinion. Worse for Blackney, the lead detective in charge of his KSP file was about to turn up the heat.

In twenty-five years, Detective Nathan Grant had built up an impeccable reputation in law enforcement. He had no known history of missteps or dishonesty, and he had successfully investigated a high-profile adultery/embezzlement/murder fiasco involving the local school board superintendent in the early seventies—the kind of case people remembered. In addition, having started out on the governor's security detail and being a lifelong member of the Catholic church, he had the ample state and local political connections that allowed a man "options." As the election cycle of

'84 neared, and as the Catholic church crowd was planning their courthouse takeover that would last for the next twenty-five years, Grant made his move. Armed with years of accumulated notes, witnesses, and even recorded statements from Blackney, Grant retired from the state police and sought a second career as the Rupp County sheriff. Whether by intelligent design or cosmic coincidence, Blackney was about to see his skeletons exposed…along with his desperation.

It was hard to gauge which Blackney held to more tightly, his image or his illegal income—and what was his master plan to save both? A loud, emphatic, record-setting raid soon took place on a drug deal between the county's top two crime families, complete with front-page headlines and propaganda Grant could not match. Through his own paid informants, Blackney had actually planted the seeds of the transaction, including the time, location, and his tacit approval, so the fix was in. He would swoop in and break up the deal, double-crossing the thugs he had set up. And what was the cherry of valor on top of this double scoop of concocted courage? Blackney had arranged for one of his own deputies to wound him during the raid—a non-life-threatening gunshot to the leg—leaving him an injured hero in the line of duty and, per his plan, an immovable object in the minds and hearts of the voters.

But stepping-stones that give safe footing at low tide often shift and sink when the water reverses course and crashes back in. As you might expect, Blackney had far too many enemies and known pressure points after having crossed virtually every ethical line during eight years in office. His deputy eventually squealed, and Blackney not only lost the election in May, but he ultimately faced arrest, exposure of his enterprise, and up to twenty years in prison.

The prosecutor at the time, Commonwealth Attorney Paul Runyan (yes, the same Paul Runyan now occupying our circuit judge post), garnered great acclaim from the case by his willingness to take down a fellow public official and not take the easy road and recuse himself in favor of a special prosecutor from out of town. He did this despite multiple death threats from Blackney's supporters, some disgruntled dealers none too happy with the loss of their status quo business arrangement. Runyan, however, had grown up next door to Blackney—literally—and he would prove tough enough to match such tactics. He had cut his teeth as the prosecutor in all those murders that Newberry had defended. He packed heat, talked tough, and was ego without fear twenty-four hours a day. A decorated Vietnam War hero who was never without a story of his adventures, he was exactly Rupp County's brand of legal whiskey. He would springboard from that case to the circuit judge position in 1988, leaving his flimsy, spineless assistant, Chet Lawson—the one with whom I had dealt during my time in the courthouse—as the town's chief prosecutor. Thankfully for local justice, Runyan could oversee Lawson from the bench, often correcting any obvious weaknesses shown in plea agreements.

Grant and Runyan's respective pedigrees and integrity still had them hanging on as sheriff and circuit judge during my courthouse days, notwithstanding a steady epidemic of crime morphing from illegal alcohol and marijuana through cocaine, heroin, OxyContin, and later, methamphetamine. Somewhat worn but still stubborn and pious, their remaining authority over town presented an interesting backdrop of scenery, as Blackney had been released from federal prison in late 2006. Grant had personally appeared at every one of Blackney's parole hearings, and Runyan had essentially become supreme ruler of the Rupp County legal kingdom, complete with shotgun on the wall behind his bench, loaded pistol under it, and a quick, harsh wit for all criminals sprayed out via his newly installed closed-circuit court TV. Runyan fancied himself as interesting and entertaining to all, including himself, but his old adversary, Blackney, was not without his own sense of humor.

Upon his release, Blackney promptly returned to live at his family homestead, conveniently next door to Runyan and his wife. Through a thin set of willow trees and a worn picket fence, Runyan and his wife came home nightly to a staring Blackney, rocking on his porch with a shotgun noticeably spread across his lap. Careful not to provoke the judge beyond a stare and a slight grin, Blackney committed every evening to practice such annoyance of Runyan, and the message was clear. Meanwhile, Blackney became more vocal around town, spreading to all within earshot his intent to retake his rightful place as sheriff in the 2008 election and to rightfully return Rupp County to its oppressed people (whether he meant liberation of the law keepers or the lawbreakers was open to interpretation).

The proverbial match in this increasingly pressurized powder keg was lit when Sheriff Grant arrested Blackney's twenty-five-year-old son, Gill Jr., for drug possession (oxy not in an appropriate prescription container) and for driving under the influence, second offense. Half the town saw this as a Blackney son following in his father's drug-dealing ways and getting his deserved punishment, but the other half screamed sabotage by Grant against a viable political threat. Shiloh didn't need CNN and Fox News to be just as intensely divided as the congressional Democrats and Republicans. By early 2008, the elder Blackney had filed as a candidate against Grant just as Grant was walking Gill Jr. into Runyan's circuit court for sentencing per his plea agreement. After much apprehension, Runyan stuck to the terms of the negotiated deal—two years probated on certain conditions—thereby not making the son pay extra for the sins of the father. But Runyan could not resist rubbing some verbal salt in the wound…actually, sixty minutes of a sanctimonious sermon from his mount, all crafted for the viewing public.

The rest of the thirty-year saga played out relatively quickly.

During the course of the sermon, Gill Jr. mouthed off to Runyan, something to the effect of "Shut up, ya old bastard, and get on with it!" (Granted, he was not alone in that sentiment after an hour of Runyan's preaching.)

Runyan went ballistic with indignation (his customary response to any sense of disrespect). He added a year to the sentence, set his gun out on the bench for all to see, and screamed, "One more word, sir, and I'll solve this problem! And you can tell your father the same thing for me."

The camera caught it all.

And ten days later, just eight weeks before the primary election in May, Kentucky State Police discovered the body of the elder Gill Blackney just across the Rupp County line in Owsley County. The corpse had been burned inside his pickup truck parked at the edge of an abandoned coal mine two miles deep into Beech Creek, across the Salt Works Swinging Bridge. The burning came postmortem, though. The cause of death was a gunshot wound to the back of the head.

16

THE WRONG PATH

The unraveling twists between Grant, Runyan, and Blackney undoubtedly grew into the Rupp County story of the year—if not the decade. As the stories swirled around town, the main facts were these:

One of Sheriff Grant's current deputies, Amy Haller, had met with Blackney and two other men, both known for their drug and prostitution entrepreneurship, at an abandoned shack in Beech Creek. This was the morning before the body was discovered and the last time Blackney was seen alive. Most notably, KSP detectives tracked most of the timeline not from the other men (they each lawyered up and said very little), but instead from Sheriff Grant's wiretap files. Yes, Amy Haller had worn a wire during the meet, and the discussion involved oddly vague statements concerning the ongoing Rupp County drug trade.

The truth proved to be maddeningly elusive in light of several forks in the story and with both sides putting out plausible theories at each turn. On one curve, either Sheriff Grant had authorized Haller, his primary undercover narcotics officer, to infiltrate Blackney's connections in an effort to obtain evidence of his renewed criminal activity (good for Grant in fighting crime) or as part of election reconnaissance (bad for Grant intentionally using public resources for his private benefit). On another level, it was possible Haller had acted alone as a rogue deputy with unauthorized wiretaps (bad for Grant showing ignorance and lack of control of his own staff), and she would have also done so for her own protection while scheming with Blackney to remain on as deputy and manage the drug trade should he win (obviously a bad look for Blackney).

Beyond the motives behind the meet, yet more angles concerned how things ultimately ended in murder. Possibly Blackney discovered the wire, forcing Haller to defend herself (unlikely, considering the mob-style execution)? Maybe Blackney was a victim of the scoundrels he had so often crossed, lured to a negotiation as a ruse for a hit (though this would still not explain Haller's presence unless the two events were wholly unrelated)? Or, per the ultimate conspiracy theory, thanks to the closed-circuit court TV video just two weeks earlier, perhaps Grant and/or Runyan had taken Blackney out the old-fashioned way, as Runyan had warned he would do on camera, either in person or by a hired gun.

The eventual prosecution of Haller and the others, as well as the accompanying lawsuit of the Blackney family against the county, went on for the better part of a year but still left things murky. Haller and the others were tagged with sealed federal indictments reportedly linked to their racketeering schemes, but strangely, while awaiting trial, both of the other two criminals met their demise, one by alleged suicide and the other during a prison lunchroom altercation. Haller, as the story goes at that point, entered the federal witness protection and was never heard from again. The Blackney family made lots of noise in the papers and on local television at every court appearance, but once the criminal loose ends were tied up, the county subsequently settled the lawsuit. Whether a just result, convenient consequence, or conniving coverup, no witness or charge ever implicated Runyan or Grant. And the remaining Blackney clan apparently had a price to finally let it go.

Still, the extreme scrutiny and public bruising did appear to take its toll on the sitting sheriff and circuit judge. Both now running unopposed in the May primaries, Runyan and Grant were heavily favored to win new terms that November. Nevertheless, per the street gossip, both cowboys independently decided to hang up their spurs that summer. Long in the tooth, short on energy, and with egos covered in Blackney slime—whether justified or not—Grant decided to devote more time to his grandbabies in June. Runyan would hang on past the election, perhaps trying to block off any undesirable challengers for his throne, but then he issued a similar public statement early in the spring of 2009. Again, in a vacuum, facts such as these could be totally innocuous. Add in some context, though, and you might think the retirements were either a getaway car (if you think Grant or Runyan put Blackney down), or that Blackney got some modicum of revenge from the grave in forcing them out (if you ignore the bullets and burns on his corpse). More likely, this was just a political war without a winner. As usual.

2009–2010

Never could the town have been more abuzz or divided, and never could I have been more oblivious. I had left the circus of the courthouse and politics behind for the enthralling bank gig as Scrooge's glorified personal assistant, remember? By the end of the Blackney scandal and lawsuit in the spring of 2009, I was nearing a year and half in with Viola Wells...in other words, still trying to pin her down on exactly what my job required. Admittedly, I had followed the political news, although in my defense, the size and fury of the story was hardly ignored by anyone.

In the midst of my more affluent misery, a buzz on the office intercom alerted me to a visitor, and a quick glance up found none other than Miklos in one of the waiting chairs outside. I honestly could not remember seeing him on any serious business since he had brought in news of the Ben Browning case down at the courthouse. For such a long time, no see was partly Miklos's usual MO, but it had been more my own doing since jumping to the bank. He disapproved of my decision, and he thought I had dodged him at holiday dinners; he was likely right. He knew it. I knew it. And now I would finally get to hear him say it.

"Well, hello, sir! Look at you in this fancy office!"

He reached out to shake my hand while spreading a bubbly smile and accent usually reserved for family functions. I was caught off guard a bit, but I was perhaps distracted while trying to cover my desk with files and open some computer programs to appear busy or important somehow.

"Hi, Miklos. It's good to see you. Please...take a seat. How's life treating you?"

"When it rains, it pours," he said as he shook his head and chuckled. "And I think it is raining politicians this week."

I mustered my usual small-talk smile. "Been reading the news... I was wondering how all this will impact Bud and everyone. Always figured you would land on your feet, as usual."

After a slightly awkward silence, Miklos's face grew more serious.

"Did *you* land on your feet, Takie?"

We paused in silence, both knowing the real answer even before I spoke otherwise.

"I'm doing okay. Just trying to keep my head down and work hard." Again, when in doubt, revert to stock small-talk phrases.

"Well, I'm not trying to pry or make you feel uncomfortable," said Miklos, confirming that my bluff was ineffective. "It's just that I was a little surprised by your move. I understand the money, and it's a position of respect. That's not my point."

I'm sure I looked perplexed, a face Miklos was used to seeing.

"If I can talk freely here, Takie, I was and still am more concerned about Ms. Wells. I didn't see her here today."

"She's rarely here," I replied. "On most days, I guess I run the place." I didn't feel agitated, but it might have sounded like it.

"Well, it may not be a big deal then," Miklos backpedaled just a bit. "You are more than capable, Takie. You have a lot of experience in many areas, and I'm sure you investigated your decision. It's just that I've known Ms. Wells for almost forty years. In all that time, I've never seen anyone work with her and leave happy."

I sat for a second. I had known he was right about that six hours into the first day on the job.

"Miklos, I fully hear what you're saying," I started, "but I'm not sure it would really matter. This could be the worst job in town and Viola the worst lady in the world [again my 'tells' were showing], but I was going nowhere at the courthouse." Yes, now I was feeling agitated and wanting him to know.

"I worked hard for fifteen years, and I would gladly have done another four or seven or even fifteen if it meant getting somewhere, but I wasn't seeing or hearing any options…including from you, Miklos. I can do without much return financially, and I honestly don't need gratitude or fame, but the work needs to matter. If it was just a dead end and small potatoes, I might as well do that here and at least get paid."

That was probably the most self-interested speech I had ever put forth, aside from talking to myself while showering or driving.

Miklos re-crossed his legs and paused, his face a mixture of compassion and resolve.

"Then, how's this for an option?" He was still trying to be Santa to his nephew while ignoring that the kid had just punched him in the gut.

"Judge Runyan has just retired, leaving an open seat as circuit judge. There will be a special election this November. Yes, you would have some opponents, but your name and experience still carry some weight. We could even spin it that you left Bud's to separate yourself independently in preparation of running...so that Bud would be insulated from making enemies."

And this was where I bit off my nose to spite my face. One minute after being completely honest with him, I recoiled. Inside I was flattered, excited, hopeful, even vindicated. But sadly, I was also hurt, angry, and most of all: chicken.

This is what came out:

"I just really burned out on the whole scene, Miklos. And my heart is really not in running for office. I thought about that before I made the jump. Even if my skin was thick enough, I'm just not sure I care enough to go through with it. Those things require great enthusiasm from more interested men like you, Miklos, and I'm just not sure I see the point anymore."

You cannot con a con man. Even if I really had had no interest, I should have had the balls to express my anger honestly...tell Miklos that I resented him not helping more. That I had taken a backseat to Bud from the start. That I had to wait so long. That I hadn't made more money. That I had to feign respect for ignorant wannabe political puppeteers. Even if I felt guilty later for dumping that undeservedly on him, at least it would've been real. Not the wimpy and insincere "*It's not you; it's me*" speech.

We talked a few more minutes, but my lasting memory was Miklos's expression thereafter. It was the same face my dad had made after forbidding me from seeing my first real girlfriend at fifteen because he *knew* she was in the process of breaking my heart. He was part sad at my pending hurt—and that he had to step back and let me learn about heartbreak for myself—and part disappointed that his protégé had failed to avoid such a pitfall, that his life lessons had not fully succeeded. The feeling in my gut had always been that Miklos gave up on me in that moment. And aside from small talk at holidays, that actually was the last meaningful conversation we ever had while he was alive. Every. Damn. Time, I return to Shiloh and still get hit with the same memories and emotions—always bittersweet.

17

BAD TO WORSE

THIS MORNING, 5:30 A.M.

About midway through the half-hour drive from the Tri-Cities to Shiloh was another unavoidable signpost reading MADSEN-GRIGGS LAND COMPANY. I had let the courthouse and politics go. The law? Good riddance. The Boys & Girls Club and coaching? Trying to help the town? Gone. Color it burnout, selfishness, or stupidity. Whatever. So, what does the man with little left need? A friend to help him lose the rest. Enter my old coaching buddy, Andy Madsen.

Part entrepreneur, part sports fanatic, part philanthropist, part politician, part coach, part drinking buddy and all-around party guy, Andy was the life of any room or conversation. You might call him Miklos 2.0, and full disclosure: The behind-the-scenes political chameleon would have been the best match for his interests and skills. Of course, Shiloh already had its Miklos, and openings for political power broker in a small town weren't exactly advertised on LinkedIn or open to the public. Plus, even as a would-be successor, Andy had some weaknesses. He was more modern and more American, which is a nice way to say he was louder, more impulsive, and a little less discreet. Andy and I had grown close coaching together and watching our sons' progress through various sporting events. Andy had helped me as an intermittent assistant coach and Boys & Girls Club volunteer, and I had helped him with intermittent financial and legal advice concerning his various businesses. Socially, he displayed genuine kindness and altruism. From this, he had a long list of friends and was a master at having his good deeds on display for all to see. But financially, he had tried and erred in many business ventures over the years. And from this, he had alienated a long list of unsatisfied investors, creditors, and customers, and these events were set on equal volume. His accrued enemy list had surpassed mine from all the courthouse work...perhaps another source of our longstanding camaraderie.

2009–2010

My talks and friendship with Andy accelerated after the move to the bank. We each missed our coaching chats, and neither of us had much to occupy our appointment calendars. Now going on fifty years old, Andy had long refused to join the nine-to-five crowd and spent most of his days covering Southeastern Kentucky in his pickup truck while on a cell phone, trying to broker deals on mining machinery. Find one mine looking to downsize and a new strip mine looking for a good deal on startup equipment. Connect the two and set up delivery of the auger, roof bolter, loader, or truck for a modest broker's fee. Several guys around town had made good money in that line of work over the years, yet another economic offshoot from coal mining, and Andy's energy and personality were perfect for such a gig. He had done well for his family for several years, and some locals envied his luxuries, which included nice sports cars for his kids, season tickets to Kentucky basketball, and even a Florida vacation home. But Andy was not one to save for a rainy day—that's part of his charm—and coal's ultimate downturn was contagious to all those attached, including him. The resulting scarcity of equipment deals had led to Andy's steadily sinking financial ship, notwithstanding his admirable attempts at several other business startups. There was nothing he wouldn't try—telecom services, industrial cleaning services, even microwave handheld foods—but the same community that cannot afford one cannot afford the others. Although not wholly his fault, this path had run him through many a partner, investor, and friend, but my door remained open. He was fun, and he had visions of grandeur, and I was desperate for both at the bank.

Beyond my empty schedule and spacious office, Andy was also welcome at Mountain Miners Bank based on his connection as Viola's nephew. Though they were not extremely close, Vi seemed to like Andy despite his lack of money, and I never had to look over my shoulder when Andy was hanging around without any real banking purpose. Our chats were always entertaining, covering the state of Rupp County politics, area high school sports, and Andy's latest business ideas. Slowly, our lunch talks moved to the back booth at the local Pioneer Village Café, not necessarily for the food but for the privacy. And as you might expect, our talks eventually reached a business proposition that Andy had for me.

Andy had identified a row of neighboring duplexes as a good source of positive rental cash flow and, after paying down any necessary mortgage over the next ten years, it would turn into just the retirement income Andy would need as he hit sixty. We would be 50/50 partners on the property ownership and net income, though the initial down payment would be 65 percent me and 35 percent Andy. That was the best he could do, and I could pay myself back first as cash became available until our equity shares were even. He would need my extra cash and better credit score to secure the loan, and that was my price for him letting me in on half of what was otherwise his own apparent diamond in the rough.

To Andy's credit, he had done extensive legwork on some attractive properties. These duplexes were well situated in the center of town, and they had a reputable owner with profitable earnings records and a documented customer base going back twenty years. Even with any overhead, needed repairs, and a new mortgage, we would net an extra $500 each per month, all for about an extra two days' work, split between us. He would handle any complaints, applications, and service calls, a good fit for him, and I would handle the accounting and legal needs, also fitting. After the mortgage, that would go to $2,000 each monthly, plus we'd have the debt-free property to sell when we desired later in life. Even as the king of risk aversion, I was having a hard time seeing the downside.

Optimism and greed notwithstanding, I still had doubts by nature, and my only available counsel is this area was, unfortunately, Viola. On top of wanting her experience in business evaluation, I likely needed clearance with her on having a side business income while on salary at the bank. She had literally dozens of rental properties, of course, so it wasn't a major concern, but not knowing her well, I wanted to earn her trust with all of my cards on the table.

Vi sat across my desk that morning, casting her usual Humpty-Dumpty silhouette and sipping her coffee. Her face said, *You're out of your depth*, in the same tone of Philip Seymour Hoffman as a condescending Art Howe in *Moneyball*. But I ignored it. I liked our plan and, somewhat surprisingly after I laid it out, so did she. Even after open discussion about Andy's cash flow issues and prior business failings, Vi acknowledged the good prospects.

"Sounds like something I would do," she said as we lightly toasted each other with our coffee cups. "Cheers. Welcome to the club, sir. You're on your way." I had rarely seen her hideous grin or her apparent pleasure with me.

Seriously, she was just a patch of green fur away from the Grinch after he got home with the town's Christmas gifts.

And with that, our business plan was fully hatched. As autumn approached, we had the incorporation, the financing, the property, the tenants, and some extra cash. I had needed an adventure and I wanted financial freedom, maybe even enough to ditch my current ridiculous job sooner than expected. Excited, Andy and I were already discussing other properties and expansion, and according to Shiloh's supreme money miser, Viola, this was the secret handshake world's guide to wealth. Hell, I might ultimately vindicate myself to Miklos and the courthouse crew. What was there not to like?

Sadly, my brief bubble of economic growth sprung a leak after a visit from Kendrick Morton in late September that year. He sauntered into the office in his uniquely arrogant Ichabod Crane way, leaving the viewer to wonder if he wanted to be sure everyone noticed him or if he honestly was afraid of falling on his old, frail frame. We were nowhere near friends. In fact, I couldn't remember seeing or speaking to him in several years, especially after his cousin's volunteer application had been rejected at the Boys & Girls Club due to the man's drug-related criminal history. Some in the courthouse scene had even wondered if he had retired. In my current line of work, odds were, he had a deceased client with an estate to carve up and he needed to know what assets were in play, that is, available for use in calculating his fee. As usual, I restrained my sigh and pressed play on the usual cassette tape in my head. *Let's just get this over with.*

But Morton proceeded to meticulously unveil the allegations of an unnamed bank customer, who, according to Morton, had applied for a loan at MMB in hopes of purchasing our same duplexes earlier that summer.

"Takie, I'm not here to threaten you. I'm not going to take the case, and I come here only out of professional courtesy," he said. It was hard to imagine words that fit a face less than these words and his face. Courtesy? Please. I was the king of passing out bad news with kindness, remember? And he could use a few lessons. His smug grin said clearly that he came to gather intel if possible and, if convenient, cast a stone or two. Either he had a resting smile face like the Joker, or as I would find later, he clearly enjoyed delivered this message.

"In all honesty, though," he continued, "this has all the appearance of pretty-clear wrongdoing, something that typically ends up in litigation. I have to admit, I'm pretty surprised you would do such a thing."

1. He said no threats. 2. I had *no idea* what he was talking about.

"I've got my hat in the ring to replace Judge Runyan in the special election this November, so splitting the town in two with a case like this isn't worth the money right now." He talked as if I actually had *any* concern for his plans. "So, I referred the prospective client to an attorney out of town. He wasn't comfortable with any attorney in town whom he feared might take it easy on you. He only trusted me enough out of our relationship through the church."

"What in the hell are you talking about?" I'd have said it with more anger but for being completely dumbfounded.

"I'm not here to get you to confess, and I really don't want to know anything more than I already know," he said with supreme arrogance. "But I dug enough to know that this fellow has sufficient proof that the bank unfairly turned him down for his loan, and then you ended up with the property a few months later. The math is simple."

Alright, now I was mad. I had hated him with fire long before he poured this gasoline on the flames. He couldn't pull off the Kevin Bacon routine from *A Few Good Men*—that he had no "passion or prejudice" but that his "client has a case" crap. His glee oozed from his pores. Clearly, he still harbored the grudge over his cousin's rejection by the club, and going by his move for Judge Runyan's seat, I suspected he wanted to poke down at me thinking I might want the gig. From that angle, and his reference to a fellow church member, I even wondered if his Baptist church connections were loading and aiming another political shotgun at the Catholics. What he failed to understand was that I cared for none of his possible motivations, and no way would that old, arrogant bastard condescend to me from across my own desk.

"Fine, sir, message received," I said as I rose to walk him out. "Appreciate the notice, and I'll look into it. Now, please do whatever else it is you think you need to do, but do it from somewhere else."

The prosecutor side of my brain instinctively took over once the door shut behind him. I had a narrow focus from the clues, but searches for loan applications by members of his Baptist church on the duplexes' property earlier that year had all proved a dead end. I tried a few days to discreetly trace any possible scenario, any possible documentation throughout the bank…nothing. Nothing, that is, until the next Saturday morning. I was in the office only briefly, mopping up some paperwork in an otherwise empty bank, as Viola strolled in for an unexpected checkup. As usual, she was just passing through from one week of travel to the next, ever the semi-retired boss slowly choking the life from me. But I figured now was as good a time as any to tell her that the bank—and I—might get sued.

"Ah, hell, Takie, he's probably talking about that little Bennett kid… Jody Bennett," scoffed Vi. "He nosed around here a couple of times back in the summer, asking me about possible rates and the process, but I think he might be a little 'slow' or something. Clearly, he had absolutely no business sense, and he was doubtful on his needed down payment. Kid's just a part-time kindergarten aide and youth pastor, so I would've diverted him to you—no offense—except that I have to see him at church."

No offense taken, unless you count a little offense and longtime confusion as to how Vi reconciled all those church sermons with her actions at the bank for all these years, but I guess you could say that about a lot of churchgoers, not just in Shiloh. Still, she sipped her coffee and kept right on.

"Plus, Harry Westwood had recommended he come to me." Westwood was the prior owner of the duplexes, our eventual seller, who happened to be a longtime customer of the bank and by all accounts, an honorable local businessman worthy of Vi's attention up until he retired after selling his duplexes to me and Andy.

"Anyway, Bennett never even returned the application packet, even after he came back in two more times for the same conversation. Harry then came by around the first of August to ask about the delay on Bennett's pending loan, and he and I both then realized that Bennett was not just two steps slow, but perhaps also two marbles short upstairs. The kid was talking a sales price a mile apart from Harry's final offer, and then was throwing around loan numbers as a done deal even though he had never even completed the application for us to process." The lack of a completed application explained the lack of documentation on the computers.

"You see, even if he had given us all we needed," Vi cranked on, "he said the purchase price was $300K, and Harry had never offered to sell for less than $400K. So there was no deal to be had. And even if they *had* struck a deal, the kid wanted to borrow four $450K, well over 100% of the purchase price, with nothing down. No way *any* bank considers that, and I told him as much the last time—the fourth time—he came by. I told him thanks, but maybe he should consider the other, less conservative banks in town."

Maybe my chuckle at his explanation had made my earlier nerves obvious by comparison. "I've been sued a dozen times over the years, Takie," she attempted to comfort me, while almost bragging. "If you want a piece of the pie in this business, that's part of it."

To the unaware, Viola the Grinch actually appeared to have a heart.

18

HITTING ROCK BOTTOM

Viola's reassurance put lawsuit worries to the back of my brain and put me back on my mindless grind. Managing the business with Andy had thankfully occupied some of my empty time and thoughts, but even the combined peak of monies couldn't offset the valley of mediocrity. Blah, blah, blah… I did keep a side-eye on the news to see that the Mount Pleasant Baptist Church crew had captured the two vacated political seats, Morton as circuit judge and a former Blackney deputy hellhound named Lundy Travis as sheriff, so I knew enough to be reminded that I would still hate being back in the courthouse, too.

You should picture these uneventful thoughts early in 2010 as the three-month quiet before a six-month thunderstorm. Here were the initial raindrops:

- Lawsuit was filed against the bank and against me personally, claiming I essentially interfered with Bennett's loan application and stole his deal with Harry Westwood.

  (No worries. There was never an actual completed loan application, and there was never a "deal" or agreed-upon purchase price between him and Westwood.)

- Bank insurance was handling our joint defense, so no legal fees for me, but during first strategy conference, I'm floored to hear the complaint sought $5 million.

  (Ludicrous. As in, I actually had to read it myself. Still, no worries. You could buy the entire county for $5 million. What an idiot.)

- "Local attorney sued for $5 million" makes for a great headline in the local paper.

  (Okay…now some worries. But surely forty years of good living outweighs one baseless lie.)

- Kendrick Morton, now circuit judge over the case, refuses to recuse himself, and he astonishingly denies a Motion for Summary Judgment; referring the case for mediation.

  (More sickening headlines; more wayward glances and whispers; another month of misery…but hopefully the insurance company will settle the case for its nuisance value, and we can all move along.)

- Mediation proves pointless. Youth pastor AND HIS ATTORNEY—with a straight face—will take nothing less than $3 million. Laughable, if not so utterly ridiculous. The policy limits were $1 million, and the settlement value of the claim was $10 K tops, just to avoid litigation expenses.

  (Shaking my head. $3 mil? Let me get my checkbook. He clearly picked the wrong deep pocket for his expected lottery jackpot. There would be no easy way out. Can't battle wits with an unarmed man.)

The trickle of rain had evolved to a downpour. We were going to trial. Six more weeks of headlines, gossip, stress, and shame. Testimony on closed circuit television. I cannot overstate the growing rage on this page. AN ABSOLUTELY BASELESS ACCUSATION. And we get to listen to a parade of enemies from my past tell their version of all my misdeeds. Imagine how many—the criminals, the deadbeats, the jealous, the offended, even those who would just love to take their shot at a small-town do-gooder—all lined up and eager. It was an old-school public hanging, back when folks used to pack a picnic and enjoy the show. By the end of the plaintiff's case, his side of the gallery was standing room only, and my opposing pews were empty. Even my own family couldn't bear to watch, and I preferred to suffer alone anyway. The protections our legal system provided, such as summary judgment or exclusion of irrelevant and biased testimony, required a willing and impartial judge, but I didn't see one of those, just Old Man Morton up there with his occasional grin.

The charade of testimony finally complete, there was one more chance to end it. The parties would argue a Motion for Directed Verdict, essentially a request for the judge to step in and throw the case out, to make a finding that no reasonable person or jury could award in Bennett's favor based on the complete lack of evidence. Maybe now that Morton had taken my pound of flesh publicly, now that he had to know I was no future political threat in this town, just maybe now he would call off the abuse.

Seriously, even Morton should rule in my favor. The kid's case was a farce anyway, essentially "I wanted the deal, and Takie ended up with it." The rest was all just an emotional play for money. Never mind that he never had a deal, never completed a loan application, and never had a loan request that even could have been approved. This was a poor, church-going little guy outmaneuvered by the sleazy lawyer, Takie; the greedy businessman, Westwood; and the deep-pocket bank. Please, jury! Here's your chance to strike a blow for the little guy against all that's corrupt. How often do you get that chance!? In any other courtroom, the judge would have quashed the case long before, but most definitely now. That's EXACTLY why the system allows a Directed Verdict—for undisputed facts that have NO CHANCE to win under the law, rather than give an always unpredictable jury the chance to take justice off the rails.

The court recessed the Friday before what was to be Judge Morton's fateful ruling, and Viola had bristled through to her office at the bank without her typical nod to me as she passed by. Yes, when not in court, I was still trying to nod and smile at the bank, pretending not to be preoccupied or shamed by the headlines and gossip. Bank policy memos had directed no talk about the pending lawsuit around work, and Vi's semi-monthly visits had left little time to get any feedback from her during the trial. Color me completely paranoid and anxious at this point, and her sudden odd e-mail invitation back to her office didn't help. She tossed the newspaper at me as I walked in.

The headline read, "*Oxy Docs Done In: Morton Orders $500,000 for the County.*" Apparently, after adjourning our trial session the previous afternoon, Morton had accepted a plea agreement in an infamous drug trafficking case—an investigation orchestrated by new Sheriff Travis—wherein two Memphis doctors, the husband-and-wife team of Reza and Rinkoo Hanji, had accepted responsibility for illegally prescribing boatloads of oxycontin to Shiloh-area residents. Despite their personal greasing of the largest pipeline of pills into Eastern Kentucky to date, the cooperative deal allowed them only five years' probation and even covered their adjacent federal charges, as well. By any legal estimation, they had sold Morton the Brooklyn Bridge, and even gotten a handsome tip for their service. Nevertheless, the article focused on the doctors' surrender of their medical licenses, giving Travis great press as our new "Walking Tall" sheriff, and their $500,000 "fine" that would go directly to the county for a community youth center to fight teenage drug use, thereby painting Morton as the new wise and compassionate "Solomon" from on high.

Those were the angles that came to mind as I quickly scanned the article, and I might have thrown up in my mouth a little reading about Morton and Travis's unearned acclaim, but I needed to figure out Viola's intent by showing it to me.

"I just opened an account here for that five hundred K," Viola started while drumming her fingers on the desk as I looked up, "only because of the goodwill I've built up with the local magistrates over the years. This is the kind of account we hired *you* to bring in. Fat chance of that now."

Point taken. I slithered back to my office, as the downpour of the storm was now torrential. MMB's Board of Directors would next summons me via e-mail to their next meeting, which was the first Wednesday of every month and just four days away. This was obviously ominous, and my later attempt at small talk with Viola that Friday afternoon—to maybe feel her out on the meeting agenda...and maybe to get reassurance that she was at least still in my corner on the lawsuit—was met with a light shrug and "I've not heard anything about it."

If the storm was raging in my mind that Friday evening, what would happen that next Monday morning in court would open the floodgates. Morton not only didn't stop the bleeding, but he handed the jury salt and opened the wound for them to pour. He proceeded to dismiss every one of the twelve counts of the complaint—all six against the bank and all of the similar six against me—except one, telling the jury at the very end of his sermon that there seemed to be enough evidence "to consider" the last count of tortious interference against yours truly.

As succinctly clarified in *A Few Good Men*, a trial is "not about truth so much as placing blame." A sympathetic guy, even if ignorant and without cause, felt harmed, and a jury of small town piranha would like to blame someone. With the bank and its team of lawyers literally packing up and walking out just before the jury was released to deliberate, Morton had effectively served my head up on a platter as the only available human sacrifice. I didn't stay for the verdict. Anyone with trial experience knew what was coming. My attorney stayed and called me later. After three hours, judgment was for the plaintiff for $614 K. Repeat that, please? I had already expected the worst, but even when *any* amount over $1 was ridiculous, the jury had managed to top a whole trial of absurdity with a number completely out of left field. The jury's choices on damages were $0 (what he proved) or $5 million (Bennett's calculations literally made on a church napkin using his mind as a high school graduate with no business expertise). Somehow, the jury opted for its own inexplicable figure…just more spice for such complete bullshit.

I honestly didn't care about the figure. There was no way to collect that from a guy like me. Morton had ended any hope of Bennett getting paid when he cut the bank and its insurance carrier loose (if Bennett only knew). If I cut Morton any slack, it is *possible* he might have thought there was no way the jury would go for $5 million, so they would have to come back with $0. In this way, perhaps Morton would have allowed the kid his day in court while being able to blame the jury for his loss and not take a hit with any of his church- or family-connected voters.

I can only base the possibility of this motive on Morton's surprising, but rightful action a week later, when he granted a judgment notwithstanding the verdict (JNOV), throwing out the jury's decision as inconsistent with supporting evidence. That's right, sports fans. The judge ruled that the jury had no legal or evidentiary basis for awarding the judgment against me. He was overruling their verdict and entering his own judgment in my favor. Case dismissed. Ya think?! No idea where his common sense, legal acumen, or compassion had been the last three months. Maybe he simply knew what I did: that he had taken his pound of flesh, and that the monetary judgment was irrelevant. It was the loss of my dignity, of my pride, of my self-esteem that the flood had completely washed away. He could now close the floodgates, having accomplished his mission while still ultimately carrying out justice in the end. From his standpoint, it was win-win.

In between the jury's absurdity on a Monday afternoon, and Morton finally cutting me loose the Monday after, I got the bonus prize of the high noon Wednesday meeting with MMB's Board of Directors. Such a title grants them far too much prestige. Just five fat cats, all of whom were exactly the small-town, uppity sons of bitches I would've hated long before my current mess. Most importantly, among them sat Viola. Yes, the ass who had cleared my deal with Andy beforehand. Yes, the ass who had actually dealt with Bennett and not told me anything about it beforehand. Yes, the one who had told me she had "no idea" about this meeting beforehand. She sat there silently throughout the whole meeting, saying nothing other than to actually add that, in her opinion, I hadn't done due diligence on the deal and had apparently not learned anything from her tutoring over the past two years. She had mastered the art of lying, though all I could hear in my head was Miklos saying, "I told you so." Meanwhile, the other four explained their positions in words their legal team had prepared, all afraid their "in-house" angry attorney might try to retaliate and burn their house down.

They overestimated my "give a damn" at that point. It was incredulous and yet so obvious. Sad yet so laughable. Ironic yet so sincere. After all, they were assholes just being true to themselves. I'm sure they were eventually going to get to "resign or be fired," but I had long since slammed the door and walked out on the meeting. On all of it. Picture that as a last lightning strike obliterating anything still standing after the flood.

19

KICKING THE CAN

Call me petty or immature. But hanging in Shiloh over the next two years had brought on some emotional regression. Ordinarily, I fell back on any number of coaching or philosophical quotes to conquer such adversity, Wooden's "be more concerned with your character than your reputation," for example. But my ultimate victory in the lawsuit came without any public vindication. Neither the judge's ruling in my favor, nor the two wins later against Bennett's appeals (yes, the poor kid's likely still incapable of comprehending his lack of a case—both the sad part of the story and also the point) met the same fanfare as the trial had before. Just like every newspaper correction hidden in a back-page paragraph, hardly offsetting the damage of the front-page headline, there really is very little social justice for the wrongfully accused. Cameras only find the arrested going into jail, rarely the cuffs coming off upon release, because the mob only turns out to watch an execution, not exoneration.

2011–2012

I kicked around in Shiloh for those next two years after the trial, trying hard to ignore, to rebuild and restore, but that was impossible. I promise, I tried. But full disclosure: I let the mob get the best of me for a while. Whether true or false or right or wrong, a small town NEVER forgets. You are forever defined by your mistakes in such a place, and the fact that I HAD NOT MADE A MISTAKE constantly stoked my anger and resentment—at every face I saw, including the one looking back at me in the mirror. I wanted to scream the truth from the mountaintop by day…and I wanted to slide a rope around my throat by night. Both thoughts were equal parts useless and exhausting.

Your doctor, your friends, or your wife may call it depression. But I felt no irrational sadness or apathy toward life…instead it was just a clear, obvious lack of hope. Most men are wired to work hard, and they can generally grind away at any assigned task—any one issue—for as long as it takes, especially if it helps or protects those they love. They will dig any hole, break through any wall, meet any need, make any sacrifice, so long as they 1) see an eventual path to progress, however long it may be, and 2) retain some control over that path. As I used to tell Annie while I was making her miserable, I can swim or tread water forever if I can see the island or lighthouse or at least a buoy in the distance to mark my progress.

If progress and control provide a man with his power, the trial's aftermath left me only with kryptonite. I had marked advancement in Shiloh through chasing a cause or cold hard cash, but now I had a career sinking in quicksand. We stayed afloat with a mix of shifting income from a disinterested private practice combined with part-time odd jobs teaching at the local college, coaching, and as a contracted fill-in for other attorneys taking depositions and attending disability hearings. There was no denying the downward trend, and having spoiled my best political and financial routes—and still hating the notion of becoming the next Yancey Danforth—my Shiloh alternatives had gone from slim to none.

I had digested that at this point, though. Setbacks come. Being a sin-eater is part of manhood. You swallow the struggles and the hopelessness so that the rest of your loved ones can thrive. You just keep digging. Sure, your career is stagnant, but you can measure progress in other ways, through the milestones of your children and the life you provide for them, for example. Maybe you spearhead another charitable project or set out on any number of personal adventures, like writing a book or running a marathon. These were uptown problems. The bills were paid. The kids were healthy.

But the usual mechanisms only work with a singular focus, and this reversal of career progress was also accompanied by a complete loss of control in multiple other areas. The issue was no longer just an unsatisfying career. The following problems arrived at nearly the same time:

a) The stress of slow erosion of the business with Andy. My legal bills had hit us hard. And Andy had borrowed from the business to offset an enormous loss in one of his other ventures. We tried in vain to float the business cash flow, but combining Andy's pattern of robbing Peter to pay Paul and my pattern of financial mediocrity, any capital investment, along with our personal savings, soon salted away. Mark Twain might have been referring to friends like me and Andy when he said, "History doesn't repeat itself, but it sure does rhyme."

b) The emotional wreckage led to estrangement at home and ultimately divorce. There were the usual feelings of failure, regret, hurt, and guilt customarily associated with any breakup, and the added time I spent away from Ty and Andi added pain beyond agony, as being a decent dad was my most sacred and last remaining identity to lose.

c) The loss of self-esteem hit me hard. In hindsight, such an admission is exactly as weak and self-centered as it appears, but to get at the complete truth, you should know that the piranha mob had worn me down. I managed to wear the mask and go through the motions on most days, but occasionally, their persistent whispers and glances had me on retreat. Not caring what others thought was a lesson I'd learned in childhood, but my ego had been seduced by the crowd during my earlier fifteen minutes of fame, and now I was jilted. I even skipped a couple of Ty and Andi's ball games out of shame and self-pity, and I can see now that there was actually much more shame related to forsaking them just to avoid the meaningless judgment of strangers.

Again, most men can tackle any one of these particular issues—whether work or family or internal pressures—with endless enthusiasm, but it's the convergence of major issues that usually leads to a man's demise. I grew to hate every inch of the town and every minute I had given to it, and that hate eventually metastasized internally before finally infecting our family. I would live and learn. I would even survive. But that recovery would be done alone, and on many nights, intoxicated. Yes, a person often clings to basic routines for comfort during periods of high distress, and I rightfully downsized life to just the basics during that time frame, whether due to budget constraints or my desire for social isolation or both. Still, I managed to add one new ritual—a nightly visit to the back porch of Cass O'Malley.

In my defense, Andy had dragged me along the first couple of nights, trying to give me a friendly tug out of my self-imposed evening exile. But I left my cave for Cass's brew the next six months after that all on my own accord. It took a couple of weeks for Cass to recognize my face as a regular. After all, it had been a dozen years since I had cautiously knocked on her door—at Miklos's behest—to ask for political support in a possible run for office back in 1998. At the same time, though she had sparked rumors as a witch for her ability to get around so well even into her early nineties, it was possible that she was losing a step mentally…possible that is, until she proved me wrong.

"Why don't you ever come downstairs, Takie?" Cass asked dryly as she passed me a brown-bagged bottle of vodka through my car window.

"Say that again?" I had heard her question, but I was startled by her first words to me outside of stating the price of my order each night for the past two weeks.

"Oh, don't be silly." She waved off my question. "I've known you your *whole* life, child. Don't you think it's time you saw the rest of my store?" I'll admit I was curious, and I only had my lonely apartment waiting. She had long since read my face. "Pull your car 'round the bottom of the hill. I'll open the door for you."

Walking across her creaky wooden floors was like taking a step back in time. There was a log cabin feel to the place, like I'd stepped into an old Western, complete with a shotgun over the bar, rocking chairs by the fire, and nostalgic black-and-white headshots of dignitaries on the walls. I saw both famous passersby and local kingpins…even Miklos. I recognized faces from both the Catholic and Baptist church crowds. It appears all religions bowed to liquor.

"You like those, huh?" Cass was proudly pouring a drink, and now, in the light, her smock and physical frame actually reminded me of Mikey in later life. I'd put Mikey's toughness up against anyone, but Cass might have had more sass. She was still wearing a tiara, as she had every night at the drive-thru, and rumor was she'd never taken it off since an NPR special had labeled her the queen of mountain bootleggers back in the 1990s.

"*Bar* stands for bartending but also bartering, young man. A good bartender hears and trades information, and believe you me, I've been entertaining and trading on people up here for years…and that goes for just about everyone."

"Well, I guess you do have kind of a monopoly, Cass." I smiled while accepting a first round of vodka and raising my glass to thank her. "So, I reckon that does guarantee high traffic."

"Don't kid yourself, Sonny, my business ain't about me. It's about this town keeping order. The cops love the control. It's crime, but it's contained at one location and keeps out an element they fear could be worse. They know I can feed them a ton of information on people they're tracking, the good and the bad, 'cause like you said, *everyone* comes here.

"The politicians just want their contributions. It's a vice they can't publicly endorse, but they don't mind when I give to their campaign requests…damn extortion, if you ask me. The preachers allow me here because they know that without *me*, without any way to get a drink, this little town would vote wet, and they can't bear the thought of losing their little church flock to Mr. Al K. Hall." She paused to savor her position of power. "The hilarious part is that they ALL want a drink and a woman on occasion, discreet like, so as not to disrupt their other lives. Hypocrites."

With that, she might have summed up more Rupp County politics in one paragraph than I had mastered in ten years. "I get it." I giggled, in part from Queen Cass's tirade and in part from the drink.

"Look, young man, at my age, I have to work fast. Ain't got time for you to play coy. I know you as Miklos's little nephew from back in your high school days. I know you as Miklos's little nephew who came huntin' 'round here wantin' to be a politician a few years back. I know you did a great thing with that Boys and Girls Club, and I know you've had a rough go of it past few months. I read the papers. I've got Cammy and Patty in the back, and I know you went to high school with them. You want some time?"

I was still adjusting to Cass's wide world of bootlegging, but I already knew I was not that desperate yet. Guess I had failed to reach complete rock bottom. No offense to Cammy and Patty. They were just good ol' middle-class kids from Cardinal, just like me, and rest assured, I knew I was no one special. But I also knew their lives had veered into drugs and prostitution after high school, a life they had never left. I had seen them periodically passing through court, either chasing unpaid child support or dodging solicitation charges. Cammy and Patty had actually garnered some minimal fame as two of the original "guardrail girls" during the oxycontin and methamphetamine epidemics starting in the late 1990s. Shiloh had very few city streets to walk, so working girls usually hit the rural highways, waving down coal truckers to exchange favors for cash or pills. While I was enamored with Cass's underworld, I had no interest in that part of her high traffic business.

From that point, I was a welcome visitor in Cass's bar. I hung out on occasion, just about an hour or so each time and only late at night when the place was empty, just watching television and escaping the world. She would sometimes offer me a meal, though I was never able to pin down if she operated an actual grill for customers or if she was just being nice to me. "Beans and franks are what I make best, if you want any," she'd say, her way of offering a late-night hot dog and side of beans, but I never ate much those days, just wasn't in the mood. True to her word, she let me sit, she never pestered me about the girls, and she understood my desire for privacy, so if she had company, she'd let me know by just ushering me on through her drive-thru outside.

Late that summer, though, and well into a bottle of vodka, I was staring into space in one of Cass's rockers when I noticed someone over in the corner sitting near the fire. I looked behind the bar for Cass, just in time to see her disappear into the supply room. I peered closer at the figure. It was hard not to be attracted to her form, even seeing it only through the blanket she had draped around herself, but it was hard to lay eyes on her face with her baseball cap pulled down low, ponytail hanging out the back. I got up to move closer—I couldn't resist—and as she looked up to accept my offer of a swig of vodka, I could see it was Amy Haller.

You may remember Amy as the deputy sheriff who was part of the last meeting with Gill Blackney, the outlaw who was shot in the head and burned in his truck. You should also know that Amy was my first crush when I was ten years old, all the way back in elementary school at Cardinal. A complete tomboy, she had won me over by getting my brand-new baseball hat back from our school bully, a ferocious, six-foot, twelve-year-old girl named Twila. I promise I am not making that up. I honestly feared Twila might cut me into pieces for dinner, so I had decided to forego the hat—until Amy intervened.

I lost track of Amy after I transferred to the city school later, other than to learn she had turned into the county's best basketball player, as well as its best-looking girl. But still the tomboy at heart, she reappeared in time to ask *me* to the junior prom when we were sixteen. She proceeded to swear me to secrecy before telling me she was trying to get distance from an abusive, older boyfriend. She just wanted a fun night out, to let things settle with him, and she felt she could trust me. I was shocked, both at her selection of me and at the fact that she'd lost her way. That was just not her style, just like the prom was far from mine, but I relented and went, for her. I guess I still had a crush, even though her college-guy ex had circulated the word to everyone that they were still together. I got a few dances and a thankful kiss on the cheek that night, but it was obvious where her heart was. She was just hoping to make him jealous…it was her way of punching him back, and she cut out early to his waiting car outside.

Of course, I had come across her years later during my time in the courthouse. The boyfriend had died of a drug overdose, and a later marriage of hers had died due to her neglect. The law enforcement career and uniform suited her, but the job's late hours and emotional strain rarely suits any spouse, at least for the cops I've known. She had vanished during the Blackney investigation a couple of years back, by all accounts whisked off into federal protection, though it remained a mystery whether the danger was due to possible retaliation for her role in his death or possible retaliation for her role in fingering someone else.

But there, in those two rockers by the fire in Cass's twenty-first-century "secret saloon," we played the game of "What the hell are *you* doing *here*?" My stories were boring by comparison, fumbling attempts to explain life while still maintaining some manhood. I guess I still had a crush. In exchange, she gave me two hours of complete distraction, flooring me with three revelations in particular:

1) She *had* killed Blackney, but not as a part of any conspiracy. Yes, she had worn the wire and infiltrated his drug ring to gather dirt, just as Sheriff Grant had directed her to do, but later denied. He could not be seen using public resources to protect his own campaign. But after the infamous Beech Creek meet, Blackney had apparently decided to use her body as well as her undercover drug money, and she drew a hard line at that, a lesson she had learned all too well from her first boyfriend.

2) She had not gone into federal protective custody, but instead she'd bounced around several local safe houses before "settling" in the loft above Cass's bar about six months before. Sheriff Grant had initially overseen her placements, but she no longer knew the monthly visitors who still brought her installments of groceries, clothing, and cash. She didn't know how long she would be expected or allowed to stay, and she often considered running away, but Cass would always persuade her against it. Seems cranky ol' Cass had a soft spot for more than just me, and Amy spoke highly of her, except for: "Never eat the food. Cass told me she killed her first

husband, Frank, and chopped his body up into the hot dogs. That's why she calls it 'Beans and Franks.' I honestly think she's telling the truth." Color me eternally grateful for my lack of appetite.

3) Lastly, she had ventured down from her loft that night not by chance. She had seen me come and go, and she had asked Cass's permission to approach me. According to the rest of the night and to my sixteen-year-old memory, she still looked and felt exactly the same.

20

A RECOVERING ATTORNEY

THIS MORNING, 5:45 A.M.

It had been six years since I'd left this graveyard of a town, and almost a decade since the lawsuit. That's a lot of time for healing…a lot of distance and perspective. Yet I *still* could feel the albatross around my neck every time I returned, whether it was to see the kids and my parents for a holiday, or even now, as I pulled into the Dairy Queen parking lot at the edge of town. Though it was trivial, small-town stupidity in my rearview, I had to acknowledge that the trauma at the time had resulted in real pain for me, and though I had despised the town from head to toe, I also had to acknowledge my likeness to the town in one respect: I would never forget. I'd never forget how forty years spent trying to do the "right thing" were so swiftly erased. I'd never forget trying to derive some sense of career significance by "giving back" and contributing to my hometown, only to have that town's response just reinforce my failure. The locals had used me up, tossed me to the curb when they were done, and revealed the town for what it is in many respects: ignorant, ungrateful, and beyond repair. Even among the bluebloods and my so-called friends, like Frank Coxton, the upper crust that rode my wave of celebrity just a few years before, I was treated like a leper. You could just as easily have called me Joe Reznar.

I might still be drowning in the wasted anguish and anger over my legal career in Shiloh but for the coaching. One silver lining of losing the bank gig was my return to the one line of work I would gladly do for free. Hot July practices at the beginning of football season sweated out my true spirit along with the toxins from nightly trips to visit Cass. The enthusiasm of the kids, the hope of a new year, the laughter from the old coaching stories—all were good medicine—and even the field itself seem to provide a sanctuary from all the white noise in town. Staying busy every night past 10 p.m. distracted me while I healed, and with Ty, in his heyday as the team's star quarterback, and Andi, now twelve, happily taking on the role of water girl, I got plenty of quality time with them. At the end of a long losing streak, it was finally win, win, win.

Football season led into basketball season, and I spent my last winter with good ol' Earl Starks. Now retired from teaching, Earl was finishing up his last two years of coaching, helping out cash-strapped Shiloh City High for free. With Earl, the school got coach, bus driver, locker room carpenter, and all-around ambassador. His hilarious quotes and jokes, and his literal twenty-four-hour supply of coffee in his office were welcome mood boosts to me, and in his semi-retired mode, he allowed me all the input and control of huddles and practices I desired. We never spoke much about the lawsuit or my other outside stressors, but I think that was his way of telling me what he wanted to say...that I was still capable of helping others, still worthy of respect, and still able to enjoy at least part of my life. And, of course, his motto for life still applied: We worked hard daily, did our very best, and tried to help the kids we were influencing find their way.

Speaking of kids, we were blessed with a mix of hilarity, talent, and hard work that year, and as a result, I will never forget my last team in Shiloh. Accordingly, in old-school fashion, we branded the best of that team with lasting nicknames. There was "T-Y," which was the way I yelled for Ty, our unselfish point guard who continually bailed us out with his pinpoint ball-handling, passing, and sarcasm, and yet he was always harder on himself than anyone else. There was "B-Tay," a shifty, sneaky, skilled, left-handed post man and wannabe gangster rapper, sadly trapped from greatness in his five-foot-eleven, 220-pound accountant's body. There was "Vlade," our gangly, smooth-shooting six-foot-six center named Aaron, who could take over a game and would gladly join B-Tay on the hip-hop circuit, but he struggled with our entire team's fatal flaw—we were just too nice. Teams almost always take on their coach's personality, and as a lifelong "first mate," perhaps I failed to inject enough killer instinct. Despite the great kids and our wondrous fun, that bunch fell just short in the small school regional championship.

2013–2016

If coaching was my life preserver, the rope that pulled me to shore in the midst of the quicksand I fell into six years ago came out of nowhere—from Judge

Mitch Allen Kohn. Judge Kohn had grown fond of me through countless Social Security disability hearings I had practiced before him dating back to the mid-1990s and my time with Mr. Griffin. Like Judge Newberry in Juvenile Court, Judge Kohn had raised me from a pup in the courtroom, politely guiding me and shrewdly protecting me from my own mistakes when needed, all while I learned the ropes. When the work was done, we would always enjoy swapping a post-hearing sports or legal story, trying to top each other's jokes or commentary on current events.

Beyond the fun, I was amazed to learn of our similar career paths through the course of our interactions. Here was a former college football player with a widely varied legal career, including previous time as a rising star in politics, albeit far beyond the Shiloh ghost town level. Try former workers compensation commissioner for the entire state of New York! Kohn had glad-handed with the New York governor and made the front page of the *New York Times* before he opted for a more secure and less stressed world as a judge of disability claims.

Of course, on the downside to him, Social Security sends new judges to areas with the most applications, usually remote towns like Middlesboro, Kentucky, where greater unemployment and poverty generally coincides with greater desperation and disability applications. So, picture this feisty Brooklyn native, with later suburban roots as a kid in both Queens and Long Island, laying down the law in small-town coal country. His story hadn't tracked all the way from Athens, Greece, like Uncle Miklos's, but in the reaction of the Appalachian locals, you could see the resemblance. His personality took over any room, as he was part the reserved, wise sage of experience and part unbridled, boisterous optimism and joy. Think Buddha mixed with the Ghost of Christmas Present from *A Christmas Carol*, and I was always grateful to see his name on my cases, until he earned the right to transfer back up north just about the time I had left the courthouse for the bank.

Heading into the fall of 2013, Ty had graduated from high school and was prepping for college, and I was set for another round of football coaching, still trying to blend into a new sense of normal. It was at that point—after not seeing him in almost five years—that Judge Kohn reached out to me to gauge my interest in a federal gig as an in-house attorney for Social Security. By all accounts, it was a fairly boring, anonymous job, reviewing cases and writing draft decisions for judges like him, but it came with good benefits and low stress. The government had just lifted a longstanding hiring freeze, so this was the first opportunity to be had in a while, and though I wasn't sure he knew all the details of my current scene, he knew enough about me to know I was looking for a change, even back in 2008. He thought it would be a great fit and he offered himself as a reference. After weighing his knack for wisdom and my lack of alternatives, I drank his Kool-Aid immediately and had my application e-mail sent before he hung up the phone.

The new job gave me just enough footing to slowly extricate myself from the ongoing career misery; it also gave me a chance to refocus and, most importantly, to relocate. Like it did with Kohn's initial placement from New York to Middlesboro, Social Security shipped me from Shiloh to Pittsburgh to start down a whole new career path. There was no better painkiller than distance and a fresh start, and I was an instant addict. Once there, despite all the previous turmoil, my two basic superpowers remained: I could softly deliver bad news with kindness, and when given hope for a future and a singular focus, I could outwork just about anyone. For delivering friendly, quality public service, better skills there would never be. Among the misfit toys—like me—who typically washed up on the shore of a typical government office, I was Midas once again.

From there on, once I took the leap, Judge Kohn kept me under his wing as my de facto guardian angel. I even got to spend eighteen months in the same office with him in Greensboro, North Carolina, as he had transferred again, seeking a warmer climate to please his wife. Once he got there, he jumped a mound of bureaucratic red tape—well beyond the call of duty—to pull me in from Pittsburgh, because 1) he knew I wanted to be closer to the kids in Kentucky if possible, and 2) he considered that his personal mission: to help people progress along their chosen paths.

It was that time in Greensboro that accelerated my recovery, as Judge Kohn, or "Big Brisket" as his friends and former teammates affectionately called him, made two demands of those around him. You a) stay in the moment, perfect for dousing my depression from the past and anxiety about the future, and b) enjoy your life as an energy or common thread that connects us all. He was constantly working on his spiritual evolution and receptive to new lines of thought, and his beliefs were what had us down at the local homeless shelter on a Saturday morning serving up his famous pancake breakfasts with a side dish of wisdom to anyone who would listen. (Side note: If you want good eats, find your nearest ex-offensive lineman.) It was Brisket's beliefs that allowed us to take risks at work, to create and implement programs other offices wouldn't try. Yeah, we risked failure, but he understood that the first guy through any wall always gets bloody. Those risks were invigorating, and that vibe of enthusiasm and joy—no matter what the task—was contagious. It was leadership you couldn't help but follow.

Big Brisket was a guy who left a rocky home life as a teen, taking a job tending bar even before graduating from high school. And at seventeen, already out on his own on Long Island, he brokered a deal with his high school principal to earn a diploma if he finished his first semester of college while simultaneously getting the local college to admit him as a student if he brought them a high school diploma by the end of the first semester. He worked both schools against each other to create an opening for himself, and he had used his hard-earned, self-made skills to reach down and help a floundering soul like me. I admired him instantly.

On any given day, Big Brisket might hit you with any one of his many commandments, such as:

- The secret to being likeable is not caring whether or not people like you *(have a thick skin)*.
- Sometimes you just need to start now and worry later *(don't overanalyze)*.
- Be accountable for the output, not the input *(keep your eyes on the prize)*.
- Understanding brings peace; confusion brings emotion *(learn first, react second)*.
- Smart is just dumb after mistakes *(be grateful for your experiences)*.
- No one will ever value you more than you *(don't let others define your worth)*.
- Let others seek status; we seek to create *(seek to help everyone, not yourself)*.
- No one can beat you at being you *(life's quest is for who and what needs you most)*.

I think Brisket liked my simple translations of his more intellectual and spiritual designs. Maybe he liked my country drawl or the motivational coaching speeches I gave the other employees. Maybe he just liked a guy in need of a good sermon every now and then. But mostly, I know he liked our instant, easy, unspoken partnership, and I know he considered me part of his mitzvah in bringing me closer to home from Pittsburgh. What I don't know for sure is whether he understood the emotional healing he brought me, too.

Fast-forwarding two more years, after a total of four promotions and working in five cities, all happily endorsed by Big Brisket, I had charged upward to a position right alongside my mentor—one finally combining significance, security, and accompanying self-esteem—as the chief administrative law judge. After nearly forty years in Shiloh, my four-year tour had taken me through Pittsburgh, Greensboro, Omaha, and Savannah, all scenery and achievement beyond anything attainable in my little hometown. Most in Shiloh would never know, nor would they care if they ever did, that in the corners of my mind I considered it redemption against the whole damn town. Hell, I wasn't even a first mate for once, and I did it even without Miklos's help…go figure.

21

DEAD ON ARRIVAL

Thanks to my Big Brisket spiritual sensei, you might consider this my own personal *Shawshank* escape, with Judge Kohn's boisterous voice taking the place of Morgan Freeman's narration as I had "crawled through a river of shit"…and "come out the other side. But that was a just a movie. The *Shawshank* hero escaped to waiting wealth and a new, unencumbered life in full view of the Pacific Ocean. In real life, you may escape a tornado with your life, but you still have to rebuild your home that is left in shambles. Yes, Brisket had restored my hope, which the movie would philosophically describe as "a good thing, and maybe the best of things. But to paraphrase the legendary pugilist philosopher Mike Tyson, "Everyone has a plan (and hope) until you get punched in the face."

The analogy is perhaps that of a football team racing out of the tunnel, stoked by a terrific pregame speech and the confidence that comes from a week's preparation. Your belief comes easy under the protection of the locker room, the strength in numbers from your teammates, the fountain of inspiration from your coach. Then you're spit on by the opposing fans, they run back the opening kickoff for a touchdown, and your best player tears up his knee. It's just adversity—the same for everyone. You play on and live through it, but life is always easier said than done.

So, despite my heavy dose of Big Brisket optimism, the mopping up of my prior mess moved at glacier speed, and rest assured, I had to face the fact that some things—like my financial straits—were possibly on a decade-long plan, if not downright irreversible. It took another year and a half, for example, long after I had left town, for Andy to come up with another partner to buy out my interest in the business, so we were continually bobbing for air against the monthly waves of debts and stress. With my parents already buried and both kids now off to college, there was no reason to keep any property or business interests in Shiloh, and I all but gave it away to Andy's new guy. Granted, the ultimate peace of mind from severing the dead weight of any remaining Shiloh tie was priceless. Good riddance. But even without that baggage, it took three more years to find any financial peace, as the deep hole from Andy, the divorce, and multiple moves to follow the work would require years of climbing to reach the surface.

And then sadly, apart from the money woes, not even the accrued success and recovery garnered from six years on the road could prevent my internal struggle on just a two-day stopover in Shiloh. It was the same cycle—mostly exasperation, then nausea, then an instant urge to "get the hell out of here"—and it had risen three days ago at Miklos's funeral and then quickly returned this morning while I was driving into town. My resistance and balance had improved some over the years, but I still had to work to stay level about who and what I am. None of that babble mattered at this point, at least not until I could solve my Pittsburgh problem. I *had* to be here now. As the hired hands at Miklos's scrapyard liked to say in the face of undesirable junk, "All that garbage and fifty cents might get you a cup of coffee."

THIS MORNING, 6:00 A.M.

Just past 6 a.m., and after driving all night, I still felt not an ounce of fatigue. I had escaped to a corner of the Dairy Queen with a cup of coffee, trying to give Ellen the courtesy of waiting until seven before knocking her door. This was as good a place as any to hide and avoid anyone who might recognize an old face like mine with a tall tale attached. The usual codgers were rolling into the regular breakfast scene at the DQ, where weathered retirees came looking to swap stories over coffee and solve the same world problems they had solved the day before...the same problems my dad had tackled, and old Deo Sideris before him. Though far from productive, the typical old man quorum in Shiloh was generally harmless...just men still trying to feel significant—sounds familiar—all while avoiding their wives' dreaded "honey do" lists. Most of them would tell you they loved their "honeys," but they'd just as soon "do" the coal mines. I was all for them—just as long as they left me alone.

2016–2017

I grabbed a stray newspaper to help pass the time just as a sliver of daylight began to peek over the mountains and kill the darkness. Clearly, anyone ever expecting "news" in the Shiloh paper had usually just set fire to 50 cents, especially so in the last few years. Whether by attrition after the fall of most every public figure in town, or whether by chronic fatigue of the townspeople at having to live through such a circus, Shiloh had returned to some semblance of calm during my time away. Indeed, in six years of my weekly checks on the paper's Internet postings since leaving town, the only decent ripple was the arrest of Lee Shipp, the county judge executive, for conspiracy to distribute narcotics (OxyContin) by Sheriff Lundy Travis only to be later cut loose with charges dropped by Chet Lawson, who was still clinging to his commonwealth attorney's post while prosecuting as few people as possible. Either Travis had nabbed his first big fish in his personal war on drugs, and Lawson lacked the spine to follow it up, or Lawson had honorably blocked Travis's shady, politically motivated investigation of Shipp. Nothing new in Shiloh, of course, as a person's view of events depended on his or her party and/or church affiliation, and the possible changing of that view remained an impossibility—also nothing new. Regardless, if that was the only crazy news in over five years, Shiloh felt like Lake Placid.

Nevertheless, occasionally even the most uneventful icebergs actually bring down the *Titanic*, and despite my burning eyes and a slightly dazed mind after the all-night drive, the lower headline "MORTON AND TRAVIS FACE INVESTIGATION" compelled further study. As I read on below the fold, it appeared that over the past year, the State of Kentucky had opened investigations into Judge Morton for possible abuse of power and into Sheriff Travis for the potential misuse of funds. Morton's issue arose from the $500,000 deal in the now-infamous Hanji fraudulent oxy prescription case. Per the story, the husband-and-wife team of Dr. and Dr. Hanji had made a sweet purchase of their freedom—as encouraged and accepted by Morton— that did not sit well with Frankfort politicians, particularly after it surfaced that the money, initially earmarked for a youth community center, was later diverted by a subsequent Morton Order to a new playground and basketball court for the private school attended by his grandchildren.

Meanwhile, Travis might have set a new record for ethical violations, using local tax dollars to 1) wine and dine a *20/20* video crew he had invited to do a "ride-along" television profile documenting his courage in the line of duty, 2) maintain and repair his personal vehicles, and 3)…drumroll please…purchase his annual memberships to multiple Internet dating sites. He basically was telling the ghost of his mentor, former sheriff and complete outlaw Gill Blackney, to "Hold my beer."

On any other day…and I mean ANY…OTHER…DAY…this story would have sparked me to amazement, some out-loud laughter, and upon some reflection, perhaps a feeling of satisfaction. I promise it would not just be out of petty, vengeful spite, but more from the immature avoidance of my looming problem. Guess a job coach might shade my varied character flaws by at least saying I'm a proven multitasker. But the voice in my head knew I was just stalling now and I really couldn't any longer. It was the same voice that had kept me afloat in the post-lawsuit quicksand, the same voice that had pushed me to take the new job and leave Shiloh, the same voice I had heard in all those cities alone, and the same voice spurring me on during the long drive this morning despite all the fear and uncertainty. I could put the voice in Earl Stark's country twang, and say, "Takie, it's time to shit or get off the pot." I could make the voice loud and proud like Big Brisket, and simply hear, "Go *now*. We can make it cool later." Or I could resort to classical *Shawshank* and hear Morgan Freeman say, "Get busy living, or get busy dying." But with due respect to all of those gentlemen, I knew it was nearing a quarter of seven now, I knew Ellen's house was just two minutes away, and I already knew she was my best option. What I didn't know was whether any of the voices in my head knew how this movie of my life was going to end.

22

THREE DAYS GRACE

The DQ sat only about a mile from Miklos's (now Ellen's) house, which sat in the middle of the town's best neighborhood near the top of Bluegrass Hill. Their house was far from the fanciest, nice enough, not so much that it would stand out, but it was the most connected—sitting at the crest of Shiloh's steepest Moo Cow Curve—and it had the best view overlooking downtown and the courthouse scene. The house, the style, and the view...all were quintessential Miklos.

The winding back road runs you past the Catholic church, and it felt strangely hollow passing it in the wake of Miklos's overwhelming memorial service held there just three days before. Public speaking was not a concern, mind you. Taking on a public persona and cueing the prerecorded tape in my head remained my "special sauce," if I had one. I had eulogized Mikey in 1998 and had spoken on behalf of the family while burying both my parents more recently, even while under the added pressure of my purgatory status with this hellhole of a town. Still, of all the speeches amidst all the uncomfortable circumstances, the most difficult words to find were those I had buried alongside Miklos.

THREE DAYS BEFORE

First, the enormous congregation turned up the heat a bit. Everyone... EVERYONE knew Miklos. The leader of the only Greek family in a small town, bearing a strong resemblance to Nintendo's Luigi, and with a name like Laskaris and over forty years in public service, Miklos had made his mark on almost everyone. And that didn't even touch his magnanimity that drew everyone in. Safe to say, the service was standing room only—great for showing Miklos and the family the town's reverence for him, but not so great for a reluctant keynote speaker taking yet another one for the family team.

But it wasn't the people. That was the point, damn it! I had long since relearned the hard way not to care what "they" thought...especially "these" small-minded birds. And I was now long gone, moved on, rebuilt and redeemed, beyond over it, so why the boiling anger at the sight of all of them in the church that day? Why, if I had hardened myself to stone on my travels, did I have such fragile bones that day?

Because it WAS the people. Both points of a double-edged sword. The same people unworthy of a second thought, not an ounce of my precious energy, were the same ones looking down at me, as if *I* was the one who was second rate. And you would never convince them otherwise. Walking up to the podium, I could see the pity in their faces in every pew of the church, accentuated by their fake smiles and halfhearted nods. How dare they condescend to me? After a lifetime spent outthinking them at every turn, yet playing down to their level in an effort to fit in and help them despite themselves, how could it be that they were painting *me* as the dumb one? I was the one thinking chess to their checkers. I just never understood that Viola wanted to play.

I know... I know... All that is just self-righteous bullshit. I just got outplayed...got caught unaware. It was my fault, not theirs, and so the anger always circled back to my own self...for wasting my time...for not seeing all the angles...and for wrongfully thinking of myself better than any of them. Forget *all* of my whining. I had taken a wrong turn in life and paid a steep price to get back on the highway. That was on *me*. I just hate the seemingly eternal humble pie I had to eat on every visit. It will always seem that the punishment didn't fit my crime, especially when THERE WASN'T ONE. Don't get the circle spinning again, please.

Dodging the demons in the crowd that day was only half the noise in my head, though. While resolving my own personal self-esteem argument with a resounding "*It's not about me!*" the competing voices in my mind never noticed the rising tide of emotion as Miklos lay behind me. Right or wrong, in some ways Miklos's death represented a deeper loss than even the death my father. Not necessarily because of Miklos's attempted investment in me or his mentoring of me in the courthouse, but more from his role as patriarch in our little Greek clan. Catching the eye of my children, Ty and

Andi, in the gallery, words of family pride were fighting to get out, while thoughts of sadness were choking them back down. It had been downright cool being a part of the Greek lineage and history in that otherwise bland Appalachian town. We had tried to cultivate our differences, what set us apart and above the crowd, in Ty and Andi. At least at the time when they both left town for college, we had successfully instilled that rightful respect, love, and admiration for their family traditions and values, and Miklos had been integral to that. Beyond his stature around town, it was the little things. He was happily the family glue to the end, even as it frayed badly. He was the guy who made the thoughtful toasts on special occasions, the guy donning the silly hat and noisemaker at parties, the guy instigating the board games—and cracking the best jokes—after a holiday dinner. He told the best family stories, all that we had left of Mikey and Terez after they passed. And I hadn't said more than hello to him since that last day at the bank. Pardon me while I wipe a tear.

The family anchor, and our chain of connection with it, was now gone. Ty had earned an economics degree, like his father, and was actually thriving in Las Vegas as a professional poker player. Andi was halfway through her training in electrocardiography, with a 4.0 GPA, and she was likely halfway to marriage while still in love with her high school sweetheart. Still, their potentially changing view of the family was worrisome to an old dad who had invested much sweat and pain to maintain that image. I hadn't held on to much of my personal pride since the bank ordeal, and the kids undoubtedly felt my self-loathing while lurking in the town shadows during brief, uncomfortable visits. There was no way to count the cost of that in their hearts, the cost of seeing their father—the one who'd been appointed the pillar of family honor—crumpled in the corner with a broken spirit. Shame on me for showing such weakness while I wipe another tear.

The timing of the cracks in the family armor added more angst. Things were spread across distance now, so it was tough to sustain ties even in the best of times. Lots of commuting to see the kids had kept us as close as possible, and I always gathered a hug or a kiss when I could, but especially with Miklos's family glue fading away, would there ever be enough opportunity, enough time together, to heal all of the wounds? To fully restore any lost faith in their family, their heritage, and—most of all—in me?

With that thought, any anger turned to adrenaline and spurred me to battle at the podium. Yeah, my eyes traced the flash cards of my past—a reunion of faces and associated thoughts, including puppeteer Frank Coxton, magistrate Rodney Morgan, former sheriff Grant and former judge Runyan, County Judge-Executive Shipp, former bosses Bud and Mr. Griffin—we literally could have held the memorial service in the courthouse. But my mind tiptoed over and around their faces. I kept my eyes on the prize. This was far more important than *any* of them or *any* of the baggage I might still want to carry on their behalf. This was for *Miklos* and all that he'd meant to us, for his sobbing wife, Ellen, in the front row, for my dad and Mikey, for all the family members who came before, and for Ty and Andi and all the family members who would come after. I needed words they'd remember and keep in their heart.

So, over the course of about ten minutes, I shared stories of Miklos to his friends and loved ones, but mostly, while I had the chance, I sent subliminal thoughts to Ty and Andi. And true to form, I managed to hide my mind's inner division behind my words' outer clarity. I quickly reverted to my old habits, using the rule of threes, just like the old coaching sermons did…or did it go as far back as *Sesame Street* with "a loaf of bread, a container of milk, and a stick of butter"? No matter, lessons in three parts are catchy, and the kids always seemed to remember things better that way.

"It's not easy saying good-bye to any loved one," I started, "let alone an entire family's guiding hand. Every family has one. But this family thankfully gets good medicine today along with any pain. We get to remember how proud we all were of Miklos's accomplishments in life, how much impact he had despite the fear he must have felt coming to America at the age of thirteen…with barely a penny in hand or an English word to speak. Early on and throughout his life, he portrayed a feeling of peace that only comes from knowing that you are more than the lot of your daily life. That takes a clear vision, and the family left behind was always a part of that picture. And now that family gets the joy of adding to it."

Even while saying it, I realized Miklos had left me the old man among what was left of the Shiloh Greeks. Picture that old man's arms wide open, trying to embrace Ty and Andi with words from across the room. Cue another tear.

"Aside from his vision, we get the obvious truth of his joyful life." Yes, besides the rule of three, I was always fond of communicating in movie quotes, and this was my favorite afterlife reference via Morgan Freeman in *The Bucket List*: "Ancient Egyptians believed there were only two questions to answer at the heavenly gates. 'Did you find joy in your life? And did you bring joy to others?'" Without a doubt, in the Hall of Fame of joy, Miklos was a first ballot lock on all counts, whether it concerned family, work, or play.

This was a shot at the one thing ANY parent wants most—for their kids to find their version of happy—somehow, someway. And now I was wiping my face of the tears streaming down.

"Speaking of work, our family also gets a great example set by Miklos. No one becomes a jack of all trades like Miklos—and succeeds at all of them like Miklos did—without relentless energy. As quick as Miklos was with a kind word or smile, he was equally quick to roll up his sleeves and get as dirty as the work required. And knowing that, it's time for us to say good-bye, because knowing Miklos, he's in a hurry to be on his way."

Translation to the kids: Keep working hard for what you want and know that I'll always be around if you need me.

"Everything really comes down to a saying of an old football coach of mine, the late Walker Troutman [yeah, I know, more coaches...now you're starting to see why a kid of mine might start to roll their eyes at times]. In perhaps the best seventh-grade Social Studies lesson ever, Coach Troutman hit me with the 'Three Bones' needed for a good life: the wishbone, the backbone, and the funny bone. In other words, have a clear vision, work hard at it, and enjoy the ride. I've never forgotten it, and I've never seen it lived out better by anyone other than Miklos."

Please tuck that in your hearts, Ty and Andi. I'm out of tears, and that's the best I can do.

23

THE FAMILY BUSINESS

I wasn't much for small talk—ever—even without the Shiloh piranha circling, and especially not at weddings or funerals. It always seemed redundant and useless for the bridal party or grieving family to have the same uncomfortable thirty-second conversation with literally everyone who had attended. You can leave a gift or sign the guestbook—if you just *have* to know they know you were there; and leave a card with a message—if you just *have* to share your "caring" thoughts. Having experience in hosting both events, though, I'd bet money that very few brides, grooms, or grieving family members remember anything you actually say. Newly married couples are too excited; families left behind by the deceased are too sad. So, I'm not putting that on the guests of honor; it's on the wannabe socialites wasting life standing in the reception line.

Accordingly, I had bellied up to the bar for the eulogy, for which my reward was a loving hug from Andi and a handshake and kiss on the cheek for Ty. That was plenty of give-and-take in my book, so when Ellen offered a safe haven with coffee and cookies at her house, I was fumbling for my car keys and heading for the back door of the church before I'd even accepted.

"Sure thing, Ms. Ellen," I called to her. "I'll meet you there in a couple of hours when things settle. Take your time. Hope the service went as you hoped."

"You always speak from the heart, Takie," she said as she hugged me. "And it's always been a good one." I broke the hug off early to avoid more tears.

Later that evening, I'd reminisce with Ellen, discuss the estate filing requirements a bit, and ultimately leave with the *Miklos/050898* ledger, which was still in my passenger-seat floor. And while waiting in my car at the top of Bluegrass Hill, fresh from the cathartic eulogy, I almost drifted into a peaceful nap. Consider me foiled again.

I rolled down my window to see Paris's friendly face sitting high in his pickup truck, which had woken me up with its headlights before finding its place opposite my car in Miklos's horseshoe-shaped driveway. Everyone liked Paris. And he was the same kind soul now—even after his dad's funeral service—as he was on every other day. Just as always, Paris was in "Dickie's" attire, or some semblance of rough khakis and button-down shirt, the kind of clothes that can satisfy for a business casual meeting, a rural church service, or the dust and grime of the scrapyard. He was younger and more handsome, he wore a baseball cap to Miklos's newsboy, and he was a tall, thin drink of water to Miklos's Luigi frame, but otherwise Paris appeared to be not only Miklos's firstborn son, but also the perfect successor to the family business.

"Hey, man." He kicked his hat back off his face. "Thanks for the kind words about Dad. Mom and I...*and Dad*...really appreciate it."

"No worries, sir. My pleasure." The words came out before my lips could halt that partial lie—there *was* pleasure in honoring Miklos, just not necessarily in addressing the crowd. "Nothing I said wasn't exactly true and completely deserved. We all loved Miklos. I'm sure he knew."

"Just know I'm sure that wasn't easy to do," he said with a nod that could have meant respect for public speaking at all, but more likely for speaking in front of the old courthouse gang and the locals. Paris and I had never talked since my self-imposed exile, but as was true in any family, you can find an unspoken, hardly camouflaged elephant in every room.

"What's the old saying: If you can't get rid of the family skeleton, you might as well make it dance?" I used humor as my usual deflection of pain, but George Bernard Shaw had a point with that thought. You might as well laugh at the misery, especially once it was over. I wasn't sure I had ever quoted such a thinker in regular conversation, though. Color me half-proud and half-drunk on endorphins from the emotional release that completing the eulogy had brought.

Paris chuckled at the joke, then turned a little pensive.

"I know you're up here waiting on Mom to go over Dad's stuff. And I'm sorry you're stuck dealing with that. I can pay someone local if you're not up—"

"Shush, Paris," I cut him off. "You know I'll help. Don't give that another thought."

"Well"—he pulled his hat down low to gird his nerves—"I know this will come at you out of left field, but I'm not sure there's a right time for this other favor I'm about to ask."

And from there, he hemmed and hawed his way through ten to fifteen minutes of the recent history of the scrap metal and recycling business, general contracts and cash flow stuff, most of which I could see coming. It wasn't rocket science, but I had yet to see the whole picture.

"I say all that to tell you that the business is fine"—he swallowed—"but I need some advice on a big decision about a partner."

My first reaction was literally to try to crawl into the passenger seat away from him. No way he was asking *me* to partner with him on the business in *Shiloh*?

"I'm just not sure whether to keep Miklos's partner on as my own," he continued, oblivious to my horror. "But heck, Takie, I'm not even sure I have a choice. Or even what my options are."

"Hold up, Paris. Miklos had a partner? I thought he owned the business outright after inheriting it from Deo?"

"Nah"—Paris stepped out of his truck—"why don't you come inside with me? Let me show you some things in Miklos's office." I followed him in, half-stunned, half-curious.

Paris rifled through various files and papers on Miklos's desk. Basically, Miklos was the kind of old-school record-keeper who overwhelmed his accountant with a box crammed full of receipts and invoices every tax season, and if anyone needed a particular document, only he would know its location. It was a mess, but it was *his* mess.

Paris finally laid hands on a folder in Miklos's bottom desk drawer, and the folder contained what appeared to be a vague, boilerplate partnership agreement between Miklos Metal and Recycling, Inc., and VPL Enterprises, LLC, Pittsburgh, Pennsylvania.

Long story short, as I skimmed the agreement and Paris explained the history as he knew it, it dawned on me that Miklos indeed had a business partner. I vaguely remembered Mom and Dad sharing various gossip in the front seat of the car—the kind of stuff that rarely sticks to a ten-year-old kid—about Miklos once running into some financial trouble… That would have been in the late '70s. I always had the impression that was when Miklos got into politics, and that the cash infusion, both from his public office and the contacts that came with it, had righted the family scrap metal ship. Apparently, Miklos had also secured needed capital through a 50 percent fairly silent partner in Pittsburgh. And by "fairly silent," I mean nonexistent to anyone except Miklos until about a month ago.

"Dad was old school." Paris circled the desk, a bit too antsy to sit still. "He wouldn't even take Tylenol, like Mikey. You know they wouldn't do doctors. Just didn't trust them *or* their drugs. So, I've got no idea how long he knew about the prostate cancer. Figured it ties back in to the American Power mess, and I'm guessing it was already really bad before he ever had it diagnosed…"

"…just like Mikey," I finished his thought.

"Anyway, Miklos hit me with this partner news along with his prognosis…only when he had no choice but to get his affairs in order." Paris shook his head, as if still struggling to believe it was true. "Takie, I've run almost every part of this business for over ten years now, but the books were his thing. Dad always played things close to the vest, whether it was cards, politics, or work, so I have to admit I was floored.

"It's been weighing hard on me for three weeks now. He set up a meet with this guy…this Mr. Vangelis. I have his number, and he's expecting my call now that Dad's gone…but you know me, Takie. I'm a worker bee; I'm not a dealmaker like Dad was! Would they consider it if I want to buy them out? Can I even *afford* that? Can I survive without their help? Hell, maybe I should sell the whole thing to *them*!!"

Paris was clearly getting agitated. It was true that he was as hard of a worker as you'd ever meet, but he was a hands-on, scrap-yard, loading-and-delivery type of guy, and he lacked the particular skillset to match Miklos's talent for tact and negotiation. Hell, basically Paris was way too honest for such dealings. So, when he finally got around to asking the favor, I had to laugh—but I also had to say yes.

"Look, man, I just need you to meet them for me. I figure you can tell them you're coming on as Miklos's replacement on the legal and financial side of things. You're a lawyer, you have skills I lack, and you're family. It makes sense. Just feel out our options. Find out what and who I'm dealing with. And, of course, if you actually *do* want to be a partner—do the books and give business or legal advice—you can do it from out of town. That offer is on the table whenever you get back. What do you say?"

I really didn't want to say what I knew I needed to. I spent a few moments thumbing through Miklos's old legal pads full of the lottery numbers…head down, *pretending* to think. I did notice that one pad seemed to hold nothing more than doodles, a whole page full of "050898," the same number as on the ledger. I still wasn't sure if that was just his lucky lotto numbers, an account number of some sort, or maybe a safe combination. But the silence had gone on long enough.

"That's not exactly a soup question, is it?" I giggled at my instinctive deflection, even when I knew what the end result would be. "You know you can count on me, Paris." I had very little interest in dropping another anchor in Shiloh, since I finally had life moving the direction I wanted it to move, but the words kept coming out. "Just set it up and let me know."

Typical me, I had three emotions at once. First, there was comedy in the thought that I could play the shrewd businessman in light of just getting outplayed by the likes of Viola. Then there was a brief flash of anger—at everyone, the whole town I was still a part of, at Miklos for dying, and at Paris for making this request to draw me back in. But mostly there was loyalty and love. I had already taken two weeks off work for the funeral and to tie up any loose ends, and I'd likely be able to even see Andi at college on the way back through from Pittsburgh, so there was really no excuse. My family needed me—especially Paris. Like I said, everyone liked Paris.

24

FRIENDS AND ENEMIES

THIS MORNING, 7:05 A.M.

Passing by the church and thinking back to that evening with Ellen and then Paris, I couldn't help but wonder how that was just three days ago. A lot of life had transpired since then. I'd always pictured memories as cards added on a daily basis to an ever-expanding card catalog or index in my brain…and the fewer the cards, the larger and more vivid the memories were, and the easier the recall. That's how time slowly erases or camouflages visions of the past. They're still memories, but they grow ever smaller against the larger picture, so much so that you often cannot lay eyes on them amidst the endless rows of cards. Strangely, that's how I already felt about Miklos's funeral, rapidly fading into the background, now covered by the events of the last three days and in part by unexpected news from my best friend, Walt Isaacs.

You really only have the heart and mind to properly sustain one or two real friendships in life. Anyone who says they have more than three likely has none. Despite my intentional lack of job postings for friends, Walt had filled the friendship post for me for thirty years. We shared a love for our kids, a passion for football, a distaste of arrogance and lawyers in general, but mostly an unspoken bond that only came from growing up together in a town like Shiloh. Walt was the kind of friend whom I could not speak to for months but then immediately find my rhythm with again, like Clyde Frazier and Pearl Monroe. That was a good thing—and necessary—because if friendship was a crime, we likely lacked probable cause for an arrest. There was an occasional wave or nod between windshields going to work, a tip of the cap or an understanding shrug from the crowd after a local football game (a longtime coach himself, he understood the game and my coaching frustrations), and one decent birthday gift, when I bought him tickets and a hotel room to go to a Steelers football game in Pittsburgh, our shared favorite team since childhood. Otherwise, even as his neighbor two doors down for over fifteen years, we had worked out in our garages and basements, but I had been in his actual home—or he in mine—exactly once, when I had prepared and dropped off a will for his wife. The lack of real contact was likely proof of my weakness as his friend, or a testament to his strength as mine. The choice is yours.

Instead, throughout our mirrored lives in Shiloh, right down to similarly successful careers, similarly aged kids, and similarly square-footed homes, Walt and I did our friendship by text. I guess we had similar texting thumbs, too. Once a week on average, and definitely no less frequently than every two weeks, we'd swap lengthy posts usually involving business, politics, football, our latest workout ideas, or just the comedy of the day. During many 6 a.m. exchanges, the topic would go no further than the hilarious grammar, or lack thereof, offered by Shiloh's local radio celebrities. We were far from academic snobs—I promise—but as Robert DeNiro said as Capone in *The Untouchables*, "Like many things in life, you laugh because it's funny, and you laugh because it's true."

A lot of times, though, and thankfully so, you could just file our texts under the general heading of "life." It seemed we could never meet an issue that was foreign to the other. Walt had the same concerns about health, fitness, and longevity as we headed toward fifty, the same jaded notions of the local small-town bullshit, whether from wannabe puppeteers or backbiting piranha, and the same struggles with guilt and worry over our kids that comes with divorce. Thus, we frequently rejoiced in the success of each other's kids as if they were our own, because we both knew that was a key to any potential happiness of our own. Particularly through the tornado of turmoil that had hit me in the last five years, Walt's texts and thoughts were a needed buoy helping to keep me afloat, mentally and physically. He innately understood it all, and he truly rejoiced at my escape and recovery. Not trying to overdo an analogy, but he really was Red to my Andy in *Shawshank*, and we often joked that I should save him a spot at my new location on Savannah's Tybee Beach.

So, of course, even though we had already shared any needed thoughts through eye contact at Miklos's funeral, Walt had texted the appropriate condolences. In fact, such an occasion actually prompted an invite to stop by Walt's office while in town. In dozens of weekend stopovers since leaving Shiloh, this would be a first. The immediate joke back from me was that the eulogy had "moved" him and found a hole in his manly guard. He would have seen it coming, and he could just as easily deliver a quick-witted comeback or the unspoken agreement that I was right. Like I said, a real friend.

TWO DAYS BEFORE

There were ample reasons for us to meet, though. Paris had set up the meeting with Mr. Vangelis for the second day after the funeral, so I had twenty-four hours to kill, and on top of rehashing funny stories, I could take the opportunity to get an idea of Miklos's accounts for the estate's inventory. Yes, you see, Walt had built his career in banking, famously restarting his career after walking out as a young head teller at Mountain Miners Bank several years back, his personal protest made in disgust at what he saw Ben Browning doing to clients' accounts even before Browning's first law license suspension. After knocking around some in retail sales, he returned to banking, rising up through the ranks, and he was now vice president in charge of the local branch of Black Diamond Bank (BDB), a regional Appalachian chain headquartered in Pennsylvania, and notably Miklos's favorite. It was good to see Walt's loyalty and hard work—and integrity—be rewarded, both financially and geographically, as BDB's numerous locations gave Walt options to transfer or move even further upward once his kids were grown and fully on their feet.

Walking into the local branch, especially in Shiloh, still activated my Spidey sense from the prior bank trauma, even if just from the familiar sounds or smells. Basic dog psychology: After the first smack of a rolled-up newspaper, the pup is on edge every time he hears it crinkle. At least Walt's spacious, private office, and his warm smile and handshake, quickly offered us needed sanctuary from the main lobby scene.

"Sorry about your uncle, T," he began, "but it's really great to see you."

"Understand on both counts, sir, promise, and you've not changed a lick," was my genuinely happy reply. Though he was slightly more worn in the face and just a bit softer along his lean frame, Walt was still well ahead of the curve among forty-eight-year-old bankers. He presented a full head of hair, trendy glasses, a light scruff, and his typical button-down shirt and khakis. We could have been brothers.

"Tell me something new," I engaged and deflected simultaneously.

"Well, I'd better start from the top." He grinned. "I'm leaving the bank next week."

"Say what—?!"

Walt had texted a few times in the past year, expressing some dissatisfaction at work. He resented excessive micromanagement from BDB's corporate headquarters, particularly after his twenty-plus years of success, and he deservedly wanted to spread his wings. But Shiloh lacked many jobs like this one. Regarding that dilemma, I'd already been there, done that.

"Don't laugh, T." He was still grinning, and he had successfully hidden the ball, because I had no idea what was coming. "I'm moving over to Mountain Miners Bank. I'm actually taking Viola's job." Now he was laughing.

My chuckle was not immediate. Just the thought of Viola still boiled my blood, but I managed to cool quickly. "This feels like being told you're pregnant, sir," I said with a smile. "I'm happy for you, but should I be worried?" His laughter grew.

"Say no more, T," he said as he caught his breath. "I promise I've been batting this around in my head a long time, and it's the right move. Huge raise and full autonomy over there. I'll finally be in charge. No one looking over my shoulder, so long as the board and the shareholders get their desired bottom line. And James is settling here with his wife, so if I'm going to be a good granddad someday, it's best I find a way to stick around."

James was Walt's eldest son. He was a couple years ahead of Ty in school, so he had already been out of college for a while and was now a teacher and a coach in the local school system. All of this sounded great, and it would be wholly expected and celebrated for a good guy like Walt aside from 1) his surprising comfort with riding out the rest of his life in Shiloh, considering all of our pining talks about getting out, and 2) the glaring elephant in the room...

"And what about Viola?" I had to ask.

"You really have to let that go, T." He knew my complete hatred of the woman after repeatedly talking me off the ledge during the lawsuit.

"She's really gone this time," Walt went on, "not hanging on there like she did with you. She actually retired. Aged out, along with a few others. No office. No nameplate on the door. Even liquidated her bank stock. I've dealt only with Frank Coxton and some of the other newer board members and shareholders over there, and I made Viola's presence a deal breaker before talks went any further. They're looking to turn things over now, be a bit more customer-friendly now that she is gone. And you know how I know this for sure?"

Well, I'd already withstood news equivalent to a surprise pregnancy. What was next, twins? "How's that?" I asked.

"Viola's leaving to run your duplexes!" His laughter became full-blown howling. "That old bitty bought them at auction a few months back, T. Andy struggled after you left with no one to keep a firm count on his expenses. He finally drowned in a constant string of family and other business catastrophes…typical Andy. The old hag scooped up a good deal without remorse, even after she helped facilitate the original deal—knowing how much you guys had invested—and after refusing to help Andy—her own nephew—refinance and save the sinking ship. Typical Viola."

I had to laugh along with him. I was actually numb from irony, and no other reaction but laughter seemed to fit.

"Guess I should take the compliment that it was definitely a good deal, eh?" That was my attempt at a joke. But I had truly struggled with taking a leap with that property, and even though Viola had truthfully endorsed the deal beforehand, her eventual purchase did at least confirm I had some business sense.

I went on. "Well, forgive the lack of unbridled joy on her cash-filled retirement, but I'm happy her move made a spot for you. You deserve it." He knew those thoughts before he ever heard them expressed out loud.

"It's time for both of us to make progress, T, and that means you really have to let that old stuff go. She's not worth it for sure. Hell, this whole town's not worth it. You *know* that." He was coaching me now, speaking my love language. "Any angst you still hold is on you. In the ridiculous newsfeed around here, you're not even back-page material anymore. Promise. Even those over at Mountain Miners know what Viola did…and what you *didn't* do. I already knew that when you were going through it. I had worked over there, remember? But they openly concede it now. Lawsuit's long over, the board has turned over some, and Viola's finally gone."

"So, I can expect an official public apology now?" He was right. I did concede that apparently MMB had taken on a more Catholic-friendly vibe, with the addition of Frank Coxton on its board, for example, and now Walt, but I could still be sarcastic about it.

We went on to catch up and laugh for another fifteen minutes before Walt's next appointment arrived in the lobby.

"You know I could talk all day, T, but duty calls." Walt always came off professional somehow, even when texting jokes. "You know the drill."

"Of course, sir." I rose to shake his hand. "You always boost my spirits."

"Find me anytime, for anything, T, same as always." His voice got the most serious just as he was walking me out.

"Same here. You know I'll always come running." I was halfway gone. "Hey...forgot to ask you... I'll be probating Miklos's estate here locally. Rough picture of what I'm dealing with? Pretty sure he had all of his stuff here with you."

Walt gave me a one-eyebrow raise, à la Dwayne Johnson. "I wish." He smirked. "Your uncle had two or three hundred grand a month coming through his business accounts, but none of it ever stayed. The cash flow generally broke even, and he made a large regular monthly transfer to PNC in Pittsburgh. He had a small safety deposit box here, but I always figured any real cash or loans must have been over at MMB...or buried underground somewhere." He smiled at his own slight faux pas, considering Miklos's burial had taken place just the day before.

My immediate thought was *Oh joy!* I couldn't wait to track all those transactions in that ledger and try to decipher any outstanding debts and creditors. Just my luck as the only lawyer in the family. Typical Takie.

After I left Walt, I was out of safe landing spots in Shiloh, so it was time to grab a coffee and get moving north toward Pittsburgh. My plan was to drive today, then stay overnight and be fresh for the meeting with Vangelis tomorrow. Maybe even catch a couple hands of poker at the Three Rivers Casino, a favorite stomping ground during my time there. I was thinking of poker chips sitting there in the McDonald's drive-thru, and debating whether to sleaze my way into a senior citizen coffee for 99 cents—yes, a few years too early—using nothing more than charm and the gray in my beard, when my car was literally jarred by a collision from behind.

I whirled to see what had happened, as anyone would, only to find two glaring middle fingers aimed at me, both framing Bud's gleeful grin. Unbelievable. What a blast from the past.

We proceeded to grab coffees, with Bud always double-barreled on caffeine, and then we pulled over side by side in the parking lot, talking through our car windows. "Hear you're heading up north," he barked in his typical Southern redneck drawl. "Could you spare a few minutes?"

I never questioned how Bud *always* knew the goings-on around town. He just did. That was his superpower, I guess. Regardless, the trip was derailed momentarily for a good cause. This I had to hear.

25

MY LITIGATION HAT

In the haze of uncertainty surrounding my pending Pittsburgh journey, and caught off guard by Bud's sudden jolt, it was easy to miss the fact that the town's four-term prosecutor had just rammed my car and flipped me off, all easily visible to the McDonald's drive-thru staff. Why would an accomplished, reputable professional pull such a stunt? you might ask. Well, my guess is that Bud would laugh back, "Because I can!" That truly was Bud's sneaky, playful inner nature, and he had long ago mastered the ability to pull off a practical joke without ever being linked to the deed. In fact, despite a personality that would bump vehicles and flip people off in traffic, prank-call radio talk shows pretending to be a crazy old lady, and leave anonymous porn-store gifts at office birthday parties, Bud had managed to maintain a pretty stiff image around town. To the commoners, he was a "by the book" lawman with a hot temper, if provoked. He was one who often would take a pound of your flesh with a long cursing tirade, even when he was cutting you slack, and he would readily bring hell down upon you—complete with books thrown across his office or the courtroom, if you pushed back foolishly against his plea offer or other recommended course of action.

"Hey, I didn't know if I'd see you again while you were in town," Bud started. "Really just wanted to tell you I'm sorry about Miklos. In all seriousness, we're gonna miss him around here."

Bud recounted a couple of recent jokes and stories about Miklos, and he was always a colorful storyteller, full of swearing and changing accents and imitations and analogies. Always analogies…he was perhaps my only rival on those. But the usual fun seemed jaded by the sad subject matter of Miklos, as well as my waning connection—and desire for such—with Shiloh. I sat in silence for what seemed like ten minutes as Bud downed his first cup and started on the second. I wasn't sure I'd ever seen him in soliloquy mode that long, so I thought it best to let him roll.

"You know he always tried to help you, right?" Bud's eyes moved from his hot coffee directly to my face. "And that's even after you left the courthouse. You may think the whole town left you for dead, that all your so-called friends were fake, and that even Miklos turned away. Tell me you don't. I'm not saying I would have thought any different. I get it. But it's just not true." His show of empathy turned my head—not because I thought that he felt it necessarily, but that he spoke it out loud. My eyebrows were rising, and my lower lip was dropping as he continued.

"He tried to get you not to go to that damn bank, remember? He told me so. You were better off with me, but you thought he was small-minded, trying to hold you down. You thought I just had self-interest in keeping you." He paused to sip, always with that half squint that hid either his burnt tongue from the coffee or his grin from thinking, *I told you so*. I was somewhere between agreeing with him and punching him in the face, which only confirmed his words as true.

"We never really talked once you left the courthouse, Takie. We all just wanted to help. And we all knew it was only a matter of time with Viola. But once the lawsuit went public"—he swallowed hard—"well…we're all still politicians, I guess."

"Yeah, well, that makes *one* of us," I finally mustered. "What's the old joke say? If you're not the lead dog and you never change your position, you're always looking at the asshole of the dog in front of you." I smiled to avoid a show of anger, but I was truly just stating a fact. "I think that's true all over, Bud."

He chuckled under his breath. "Well, just know that the lead dogs still get hit with shit, too. Your pain was Miklos's agony. That whole time. We had a few long talks about it, and he cared more about family than ANYTHING else. And if you think that miracle federal judge job that got you out of here wasn't him still trying to help you, you need to wake up. Feds hiring a bank guy in the middle of the post–banking crash recession?! That make sense to you?!" His voice raised a bit, and I was starting to feel like the mopes sitting in his office, indignant over their criminal charges going in and just thankful

140

not to have a life sentence coming out. "Miklos cashed in a lot of favors for *you*, far beyond anyone else."

"Look, I get it," I said as I finally had to cut him off. "You may be right, Bud." I was now considering whether Judge Kohn had actually coordinated with Miklos when he was helping me get my job. "But Miklos is gone now, and I'll soon be gone, too, so no need to relive it all."

He stared at the nearby mountain. "It's not the past you should worry about, that's true, but right now it's your future you need to think about," he said ominously, still staring in the distance. "That's the other reason I wanted to catch you here." I had started to put the key in the ignition, but I pulled them back out. This ought to be good.

"Looks like this thing with Judge Morton is heating up, and the Ethics Committee meets in Frankfort this week to decide on his removal. I'm not sure he'll survive it. And if not, you might wanna stick around." He turned and started to grin. "You might finally be the judge here after all by the May election…just like you and Miklos always wanted!" He slapped his thigh. "Just don't expect me to call you 'Your Honor,' you son of a bitch."

A headshake and eye roll from me, and now I was starting the car. "Always the joker, eh? There's really nothing left for me here, Bud. I've got this meeting in Pittsburgh for Paris, and then I'll deal with Miklos's estate, but after that, this is not my town anymore. So, enjoy your time." Color me a little miffed and overdramatic as I dropped into reverse to pull away.

"Hey"—he was still keeping his cool—"just keep your litigation hat on, okay? Be ready for anything and keep your options open. If you learned anything from me, or from Miklos, or even from Viola, you should have learned that. Everything is part of a negotiation." Was he talking about Pittsburgh? Was he trying to help me? Was he trying to be Miklos to me now?! Full of wisdom but impossible to understand?

"I've gotta get on the road, Bud. How the hell do you even know about this trip, anyway?"

His smile widened as if he had finally "won" the conversation. "We are who we are. And I wouldn't be me if I didn't know. That's what I'm good at. And you're good at deferring, at playing nice, at pretending to be out of your depth when the stakes get high. All I'm saying is that I knew enough from

Miklos to know that his partner up north is a serious player. Just look out for yourself for once. Play to win."

Thanks for the advice, Bud. And thanks for ruining my drive to Pittsburgh.

Despite my consternation while leaving the parking lot, I'll admit that for the next seven hours on the road, I focused very little on what Vangelis might say or what Bud might have meant. In general, every drive out of Shiloh brought a lightness and freedom to my mind equal to the weight and shackles I always felt going in. And after being stationed in Pittsburgh six months on my first federal assignment with Social Security, I knew my way around. Cool city. Full of bridges, rivers, and personality. My thoughts were mainly on the poker room at the Three Rivers Casino or on a Penguins game, and I had called ahead to reserve a room at the Heinz Factory Lofts, where I had stayed during my tour of duty there. Yes, the old Heinz industrial site had been remade into fairly nice apartments, and I would be just a bridge walk away from downtown and any action I wanted.

As for the Vangelis meeting the next day, I maintained a healthy indifference without any real skin in the game. I would play my role as Paris's counsel, gather intel, and get out. The Kentucky Lottery always said, "You can't win if you don't play." Well, you can't lose, either.

THE DAY BEFORE

The day of the big meeting lacked fanfare early on, unless you count seeing former Steelers great Franco Harris among the street vendors and shops in Pittsburgh's Strip District. I braved the cold in exchange for a retro breakfast at DeLuca's and a couple of Steelers and Pirates souvenirs for Ty and Andi...a fair trade. Otherwise, I napped some, found a gym, and was ready in plenty of time to walk toward the Pennsylvanian for the late post-dinner meeting Paris had set up to start at 9 p.m. Originally this had been a lunch deal, but Paris had called to tell me Vangelis had to move it later. Seemed a bit strange, but it might *force* me into another night at the casino. Guess I could manage that sacrifice. Plus, I was still the king of indifference. No harm, no foul.

The Pennsylvanian is a swanky, high-rise hotel on Liberty Avenue in downtown Pittsburgh. Crafted from the old Union Station, its architecture and train town history alone was formidable to any outsider. You can't help but stare at the handcrafted rotunda as you walk in, and as you approached the front desk, you half-expected to see famous gangster Joe Siragusa or any other Pittsburgh equivalent of Lucky Luciano or Al Capone. Speaking of tough guy, I recognized the doorman. It took a second for me to match him to my memory, as I was thrown a bit by his uncustomary fancy suit and shiny shoes, but his hulking figure was unmistakable. I smiled and gave it a shot. "Hey, Maurice, is that you?"

He eyeballed me a second—with enough hesitation to make me worry—but then he nodded. "Old timer...long time, no see." Maurice was a mountain of a man, the kind that, when standing in a doorway, erased the door. He had lived a few doors down from me during my time at the Heinz Lofts there in Pittsburgh. He had been twenty-three then, fresh out of Florida State and chasing his dream as a defensive end on the practice squad for the Steelers. We connected over football and weights. I admired his superhuman strength and dedication to his dreams, and he shared his admiration that an old man like me had any strength or dreams left at all, I guess. I had also helped him with a ride one night, a ride without questions when he had ended up stranded well after team curfew—doing the wrong things, with the wrong people, in the wrong part of town. I always got a smile and friendly "Old Timer" in the elevator after that. He had bounced to the Kansas City Chiefs and at least one other team before I lost track, and I didn't know if he even still played, but it was clear he was still carved from granite. He would scare any stranger, and when he parted his arms from across his suit to open the door—revealing his shoulder holster and hardware—he even scared this friendly acquaintance.

"Boss is expecting you," he said as he walked me into the elevator and pushed the button for the penthouse. "Top floor is his. Just make yourself at home. He'll be right with you." Something was slightly amiss, though I couldn't put my finger on it. Maurice had given me the "Old Timer," but not the smile.

26

A JOB INTERVIEW

The fifteen-second elevator ride was noisy inside my head. Bud's "don't pretend to be out of your depth" argued with my indifferent "let's just get this over with" until the door opened, and a third voice in my head interrupted with "Did anyone notice Maurice packing heat?!"

The elevator opened, and after a couple of minutes spent perusing the nicest office I had ever seen, my mind started to quiet. The arguing voices were distracted by an array of documents and photographs touting Vangelis's apparent family and business history, along with an amazing view of the Allegheny, Monongahela, and Ohio Rivers. A framed Greek flag and map of Greece stood out on the wall behind his desk. There were several political frames, too, collectors' buttons from several presidential campaigns, and even black-and-white photos of handshakes with LBJ and Ronald Reagan. Impressive all around, but nothing that would solidify any level of interest in the Shiloh scrap metal world, even as he entered the room quietly from a side door I had yet to notice.

Vangelis was slight in stature, about five-foot-eight and likely no more than 140 pounds. He wore a terrifically old-school combo of military crew cut and three-piece suit. He glided across to his desk with hardly any sound, and he set his vintage gold-wired, square spectacles up onto his forehead as he pulled a cigar box out from his desk drawer. He had to be in his eighties, but he was far from frail, and he exuded energy and focus that belied his years. I liked him instantly.

"Please...take a seat." He gestured graciously. "I have to say, it is an honor to finally meet the 'brains' of the family. Miklos had made that clear about his nephew on several occasions." He smiled and lit his cigar, still standing behind his desk.

"Well, thank you, sir. I guess I should try not to disappoint." I shook his hand and unbuttoned my coat to sit. "I have to say I might not be as informed about you as you are about me. Paris tells me you were Miklos's partner?"

Vangelis laid out a brief overview of his business arrangements in no less than a dozen small towns across the South, Midwest, and Great Plains. Long story short, it appeared that VPL Enterprises, or Vangelis Power & Land as he called it, held contracts or subsidiary companies in these towns dealing with the reclamation, recycling, and resale of metal in the steel and mining industries. The parent company managed the orders and national marketing campaign while the small-town affiliates provided the manpower and the actual materials. In addition, the small-town partners were counted on for political influence, tax incentives, economic development funding, government contract preferences, and whatever else came along that might be needed or applicable. It was easy to see why Miklos was perfect for such a role.

Vangelis mixed a tone of kindness in with his reserved, succinct demeanor. The skill to say only what was needed—nothing more and nothing less—can only be honed from experience and intelligence. I liked him even more.

"Please forgive me, Takie…may I call you that?"

I nodded.

"You drove a long way, and I neglected to offer you a drink. Care for anything?"

I acquiesced, and as he turned to pour the vodka, I noticed what appeared to be an older picture of Miklos, Ellen, and Paris among the family photos placed across the mantle above his fireplace.

"So, you and Miklos were in business for a long time, eh?" I was just gathering pedigree data now, trying to get my trip's worth of information, but I had already sized up the bulk of my assessment for Paris. I'd say the old man likely had some business enemies and personal skeletons—thus the armed Maurice—because you didn't make it to the Pennsylvanian Penthouse

145

without sidestepping some landmines or even planting some of your own, all to the detriment of your competition. Meanwhile, his business interests in Shiloh seemed legit, and I definitely got no vibe of ill intent toward Paris.

"Over fifty years, actually," he said as he handed me my drink. "Miklos was my longest-running business partner, and I've had many. I couldn't have had a son, let alone a colleague, more reliable. He brought Ellen and Paris up for a game or a special occasion every year or so. I considered them family."

"So then, you're eager to continue the venture with Paris?" My game plan was obvious. I would play polite for a drink or two, encouraging him to extend the business through Paris. Worst case, if Vangelis declined, I would broker a nice buyout package for Paris and even suggest some potential replacement partners if the old man desired. Either way, I would politely excuse myself from the scene, and in less than an hour, I'd have a stack of chips and a seat at a poker table.

"My interest actually lies in partnering with *you*," he said. "That's why you're here, isn't it?" This was his most direct punch landed after almost an hour of dancing around the ring, apparently trying to gauge my intentions or trustworthiness. I was going to spar another thirty minutes and take my fall, but he had rung the bell early for whole other round of discussions.

"Actually no, sir, and I say that with all due respect. There's no doubt from all I know of Miklos, and in this first impression of you, that this is a good—and I mean *GOOD*—deal for the right person, and that you would be a tremendous partner to have. But this line of work"—I backpedaled in my chair—"and working in Shiloh… Let's just say you deserve a more interested, and more committed, associate. Like Paris, for example, and yes, I realize he lacks Miklos's political polish and insider know-how at this point, but he knows the business and he works extremely hard. He would do anything you ask and then some."

He paused a moment for a sigh. "Are you finished?" His voice never wavered, still kind and compassionate, as if he was only concerned with my well-being. "You're sure?" He put out the cigar and moved from behind the desk, sitting to the side and looking right into my eyes.

"Forgive me again, Takie, but there's no doubt in my mind you are Miklos's perfect successor. In fact, I know if he were here, he would handpick you himself. Like I said, Paris is family to me, and I've watched him work and grow since he was just a young boy, but Miklos always assured me that you were the one with the intelligence and political savvy we need. And as far as commitment goes," he continued, "it sounds to me like you got derailed for a bit with some bank nonsense, but that you always had a desire to be a substantial, formidable man in your own hometown."

Just how much *had* Miklos shared with this guy? Color me just a little spooked. "Again, I can't thank you enough for the kind words. But, sir, you underestimate my lack of desire to be in Shiloh. I've pulled up my roots there, and I've got a good job as a judge elsewhere. Surely you will come to understand."

"I find your comments very interesting, Takie. I respect your thoughts, and we would like nothing more for you to do as you please, but what you desire is impossible. Do you really think that Miklos's death makes any difference to what we are doing here?" He looked down at the floor in thought, then he actually smiled as a father would to son after being asked for permission to stay up all night on a school night. "Let me explain something that perhaps you haven't realized, perhaps angles you haven't seen through your own personal stress. Over all these years, there are people who have grown to care deeply about our stake in Shiloh, people who grew to care about Miklos and, through him, cared about the members of his family... like you. Those people protected Miklos in exchange for all of his great work, the great money he made for them, the many favors he did for them. And those same people are protecting you *now*...including *me*."

I was riveted, on the edge of my seat, and I would've enjoyed the show, like watching Pacino admit he's the devil in *The Devil's Advocate*, if not for the creeping fear up my spine of what I might be about to see. All those years in the courthouse face-to-face with criminals, seeing the same deadbeats at the grocery store, the movies, the Little League field, and I had never felt the least bit threatened, never sensed an ounce of danger. The sudden awareness of this level of fear, including the thought of Maurice's guns downstairs, was chilling. My thoughts moved fast, and they repeatedly circled back to *Get the hell out of here!*

"Sir, we just met. Yet you talk as if what you say is easy, like you are asking me to walk the dog." I stood up and put on my own newsboy cap to leave. "I told you. I have a life. I'm a federal judge, and I've worked hard to get where I am. I've got my own promises to keep, my own family to care for and protect...and I have no interest in *this*."

He never moved in reaction, other than to smile again. "Funny…it sounds like there's a judge spot down in Shiloh just about to open up. Don't you see? This partnership just might be in *everyone's* best interests. Go back to Shiloh, Takie. Go home. Plan things out with Paris. Give things a chance and see what happens. If you believed in Miklos, then believe in me."

I had begun to walk toward the elevator, but I stopped. "And if I *don't*?"

"Well, no one's holding a gun to your head." He was still smiling as he gestured with his hand to me, as if to let me be on my way. "But if you open that door, the protection you *and* your family have, all of that trust, will no longer exist. You'll be out there, all on your own. And it's tough to make it that way, especially with all the others you care about being involved." He still spoke kindly, as if he was doing *me* a favor. "You should not see it as an offer you can't refuse, but rather one you *shouldn't*. This is a great opportunity for you, and your loyalty to your family—and your town—in its time of need will not go unrewarded. You should ignore your emotions. They are always petty. They always hold people back. Think objectively, and then take our job offer as Miklos's replacement."

He reached into his center drawer. Yes, I actually feared a gun. "Here! Take these!" He tossed me a bag of poker chips. "Enjoy the casino tonight. I'll expect your answer within twenty-four hours."

The voices in my head were stunned and silent as the elevator door closed, initiating my descent. At the bottom, I walked out past Maurice, who simply handed me a blank business card with a phone number penned on the back. "Boss said twenty-four hours. You and Paris should call him." He still offered no sign of a smile, and I didn't feel like one anyway.

27

DIGGING A HOLE

THIS MORNING, 7:30 A.M.

*D*ig! I reminded myself again, even as I'm distracted by Grandmother's gravestone just a few feet away. The same gravestone I had helped set in place twenty years before. The same grandmother I had helped lay to rest.

DIG! Even as distracted as I was by the rustling of the leaves in the nearby woods behind our old family homestead in Cardinal. *Surely,* I thought, *it's just an alarmed squirrel or a raccoon…a stray dog, perhaps. No way it's a person combing through a fog-covered hillside deep in private property at 7:30 a.m. Not in Shiloh, Kentucky, where you might meet a shotgun before a "hello." No way.*

DIG!!! Even as distracted as I was by an aching back…by burning shoulders, forty-eight years of wear and tear were now haunting me. Determination to stay healthy all those years—religiously so—had garnered respect from the gym rats but no love from my body while trying to finish this *real* manual labor. My frame was now subtly deconditioned, a bit loose in the cage. I would keep digging frantically…until sweat dripped from my forehead and nose, through my customary scruff, and off my chin.

Finally taking a knee a moment—partly from fatigued lungs, part from a scattered mind—and leaning partially on the shovel and a nearby rock, I could hear the squishing of sweat in my sneakers and pants, and my prevailing thought was still, *What the hell am I doing HERE?* Here in the middle of our family cemetery disturbing my sweet grandmother's rest, behind her old house I had grown to love, in the middle of the small town I had grown to hate.

How the hell *did* my life get here? This desperate. This lost about what to do. This afraid of whom I might be dealing with…even wondering whether any of it could possibly be true? Was there anything even buried here? Or was mine just a mind tricked by grief? I couldn't help but cast a glance toward Miklos's neighboring tombstone, the dirt on his grave still fresh from earlier in the week. Maybe it was just sheer shock from a life now turned upside down. Nothing the way it had seemed just yesterday. Nothing as familiar as it had been even fifteen minutes ago.

And suddenly, there among the family ghosts, came laughter… inexplicable, uncontrolled laughter. It could really be a grand, multilayered conspiracy unraveling before me, or this could just as easily be my own absurd act as a devolving madman, but either way, the path of my life up to this point seemed absolutely hysterical.

It was hysterical that *this* was my best proposal after seven hours of driving and thinking, my grand silver-bullet idea to dig up my grandmother hoping to find Miklos's secret stash of money—a gangster's "go" bag of cash I might find to grease my getaway. And to think that Vangelis had said I was the "brains" of the family. But that, indeed, was the sudden, intuitive leap my mind had made while pausing by the Catholic church on the way up to Aunt Ellen's a few minutes ago. The original plan had been to fleece Ellen for a possible password, account number, or safe combination—anything to access some hidden cash. But sitting there in the parking lot, rehashing the circling thoughts of Vangelis, Miklos, and Paris, I was left with: 1) Walt's confirmation that Miklos held very little cash at Black Diamond Bank, and the fact that Miklos hated Mountain Miners Bank with Viola, so any cash was likely kept on his properties somewhere; 2) Miklos notoriously saying at every family function that "all money went to Mikey"; and 3) the cover of the ledger lying in my passenger seat—the only financial records I had found in Miklos's home office—with the duct tape across the front reading "*Miklos/050898.*" I came to realize that wasn't a safe combination or an account number, as I could literally hear an alarm going off in my head. That was the day Mikey died.

Implausible? Likely. Desperate? Definitely. But even granting the thin connection of a weary mind going on no sleep just past 7 a.m., I failed to see any great risk in trying. It would be in an isolated place (on family land), it would not cause harm to anyone (not counting Mikey), and the evidence (dirt) would be easily replaced. Worst case, if I was completely off-base, I'd be back to square one with sixteen hours or so to figure out a Plan B—no worse off than I was right now. So, I grabbed a shovel from Mikey's old washroom shed and checked a few windows in her vacant house, just to be sure that no transient was squatting for the day. I slowly rolled with my lights off up the trail to the family burial site and got to work.

Making the scene even more surreal, about ten minutes into my misty morning adventure, I struck gold. The clank of the shovel on metal below brought a strange mix of fear and sinister joy. I had never stolen anything before. Had never even won a toy in a cereal box. And yet the partial sense of relief I felt at the sight of the metal lockbox made this very first theft seem like winning the lotto. Up to that point, I had been feverishly afraid to ask anyone else for help. Afraid that someone might see me there. Afraid of what I might find. Afraid of finding nothing at all. Still afraid of what I might have to do from here. Afraid of what might be done to me. Just afraid.

I dusted off and dragged the box into my trunk. There was a combination lock on it, but *050898* worked again. It was too good to be true. Cash in bundles, perhaps a million, maybe more. I would count it later, but it clearly looked like Miklos had packed himself a parachute, one that hopefully no one else knew about. That would be the ultimate jackpot…money no one would ever come looking to find. All I had to do was refill the grave and get on the road. I was not sure where I would go yet, but the cash would buy me some time to adjust. But the discovery *was* too good to be true. Sounds of an engine filled my ears, with headlights moving closer. I had a shovel in hand, a car trunk still open, and a fresh dirt pile beside me. It was Paris's truck pulling up.

Perhaps I was too tired to react quickly, or in the famous words of Detective Murtaugh in *Lethal Weapon*, maybe I was just finally tired and "too old for this shit." Either way, I saw no point in scurrying off. I just spiked the shovel into the dirt and propped my forearms across the top of it. Besides, I had already forgotten my anger at Paris for ushering me into Vangelis's snake den unprepared, but seeing his innocent grin reminded me quickly how he had thrown me to the wolves.

"Now, before you start, Takie, you know I'm sorry," he said as he merged his usual Kentucky drawl with Gomer Pyle humility. "I was afraid you would never go if you knew the whole story. Can you honestly say I was wrong?"

I put up my hand to cut him off. My whole life, I could never hold on to anger beyond six hours. Seriously, give me six hours, and I could decompress from anything. The Pittsburgh drive had been seven, and I had dropped most of my aggravation toward him somewhere in West Virginia. His wife and children and mother were all counting on him, and his pinch now that Miklos was gone was obvious. No need to make him say it. Besides, it was impossible to stay mad at Paris. He meant no harm to anyone.

"So, you up here…that's good news, right? You're gonna stay and help?"

A little confused, I pulled the shovel and started refilling the hole. "Not sure what you consider good news, Paris, but I'm about to get the hell out of here, and that's good news to me."

"You mean Vangelis didn't send you here?" He still leaned on the hood of his truck, but his head tilted, like a watchdog that had heard a noise. "I thought he would have pointed you to this money to help keep the business going…and maybe as a bonus for sticking around. You aren't seriously leaving me, are you?"

I started digging a little faster to match my thoughts. "Paris, what choice do I have here? I'm not seeing any other options. I ran through over a million thoughts driving back, and I'm still not sure what we're dealing with. I'll admit that old man spooked me. The only thought that sticks is that I want no part of this. I'm out of here. And to do that, I need money. Maybe I can set up Andi and Ty in a safe place if needed…maybe you and yours, or anyone else who needs it. Maybe I restart life and drop off the grid if needed. Maybe it's just insurance to hold on to."

"Now, hold on a second." I could see the dots connecting on Paris's face. "You're not getting this. Running is not going to work, Takie, especially not with *his* money. How did you even know it was here?"

"I didn't know for sure?!" Exasperated now and slinging dirt as hard and as far as I could, I went on. "Told you there was no plan, but this made as much sense as anything. You knew it was here?!"

"Not for certain, but Dad came up here a lot." His words now were tinted with sadness. "Figured he was just visiting Mikey's gravesite, but when he'd come back dirty, sweaty, and tired, I had suspicions. Dad always told me what I needed to know and nothing I didn't. So, it kept things simple for me, and I knew not to ask."

"Look, I don't know how to say this, Paris. You know I want to help you. You're family…and not just any family, a real friend. I remember all the Chips Ahoy and Super Mario Brothers nights we spent in middle school. But this is real, Paris. This is a YOU problem, and I can't make it mine—"

"But it *IS* yours!" Paris almost screamed his interruption, totally out of character for him. "I need to tell you something, Takie." And he paused a moment to recoil, so much so that I noticed the scraping of the shovel, my heavy breathing, the crickets nearby. "He's a murderer. The old man has killed a dozen, maybe more…and that's just the ones I heard about. It goes back even before our family came over here from Greece."

"And you didn't tell me that before sending me to Pittsburgh?! And you think somehow that knowing that now would make me want to *stay*?!" I had stopped digging at the word *murderer*. "Look, man…he might be pure evil, and I get that you need the business and not the partner, but *you* need to get that. It's not on me."

"But he's our grandfather!"

Paris had just one-upped every one of my remaining thoughts.

"Don't you get it?! Vangelis is the *V* in *VPL*. Vangelis. Parisi. Laskaris."

"Bull*shit!*" I slammed the shovel onto the ground near my car. "Our grandfather died in the Greek Navy, before they came over. Mikey told me that story herself, many times."

He shook his head and crouched in his work boots like a coal miner about to smoke a cigarette and contemplate life on a work break. "I realize this is hard to fathom, Takie. The navy story was smoke-fed to Mikey to cover his entry into the Greek National Intelligence…the NIS. That's like our CIA. He was planted in Pittsburgh as a foreign agent after World War II. The business was initially his cover, but he kept going in it after he exited the military. He's been connected at a higher level of government, business, and wealth than you and I have ever known—and he also plays by a different set of rules.

"He brought Mikey with the kids over when he became just a civilian, and they tried to be normal, but she couldn't stand what he was. He loved her, I guess, much like a man loves a prized watch or a car, but she begged to get away—to get *out*—and I reckon he loved her enough to at least put her *here*. Isolation was the price she paid to protect Miklos and Terez from that kind of life.

"Deo was never even her husband, just 'family muscle' appointed to guard her and the business. And when he put Deo down, Vangelis lured Dad to take over. I know part of that decision was on Dad—he was tempted by the power and the cash—but he didn't really have much choice. The old man had killed Deo, and he had threatened Mikey and the rest of the family if the local favors and money ever stopped flowing. I actually think he may have finished Mikey off just to keep Dad in line, and I wouldn't be shocked if he had taken Dad out somehow over the money you found today—money he learned that Dad had siphoned off from the business for us over the years. Vangelis came from Greek prominence, and Mikey came from nothing, remember? He owned her…he owned all of us… We're just his pawns…his decorations."

"Did you just say *he killed Mikey*?!" I was still between catching up and giving up.

"Yes, damn it! *All* those cancer stories were phony. He killed his own man, Deo…his own wife…likely his own son. You think he would ever blink at killing you or me?! You can't be that naïve!" Paris had always deferred to me intellectually, but I now felt like he was a lead detective scolding his rookie partner. "Bottom line"—Paris dusted his hands and stood up—"we can't run. We have to deal with this straight-up. And I *need* you."

No matter Paris's needs, though, I had had enough education. Gone was the courage of the morning, the chess player who had tried to think it through, who had followed Bud's advice and responded in his own interest, even to the point of digging up a grave and stealing stacks of cash. What remained was a man scattered and scared, who was under the weight of the cold dirt, the weary all-night drive, and the pounding of Paris's words. The guy in my head who struggled with big decisions now had more than he could handle. I was checking out.

"I can't deal with this, Paris. Not *him*, not Shiloh, not anymore." I picked up the shovel and headed to close the trunk of my car. The hole was not fully filled in, but at this point that was irrelevant. I was picking up steam. "*You* need the business! *YOU* need this life! I get it! But that's not me! I'll *NOT* live like that!" I slammed the trunk so hard I could hear the lockbox of cash tip over inside of it.

"Then I can't let you leave with our money!" I had missed Paris's complete desperation, his presence right behind me as I reached the back of the car. He grabbed my arm and spun me around. He shoved me backward and advanced. "Do you not understand that he will *kill* me?!! My family?!!"

Caught off guard, I raised the shovel as a cross block. And for several seconds, we had all four of our hands locked on the shovel and two pairs of eyes locked on each other, two men as unsure of the fight as we were about life. I finally launched him backward, and as if in slow motion, I saw him stumble over the still-unfilled-in grave hole, reach out instinctively—arms flailing for a stop that never came—and then came the *crack* of his head and neck against Mikey's tombstone. The sound was simultaneously indescribable yet forever unforgettable. A spattering of blood came from his mouth and nose, but otherwise, the world stood completely still. And in that moment, Paris—and life as I knew it—was gone.

28

A TERRORIST PLOT

I'm not sure they make self-help books for those who have accidentally killed someone, say even a stray pedestrian on a lonely highway, let alone a loved one at close range. But I was struck by the level of mental clarity that was retained even without such guidance. Granted, it took a few minutes. In the immediate aftermath, there was first dry-heaving at the vivid realization of death at my hands, followed by pointless pacing between Paris's lifeless body and the car, gathering a thought of what to do but then experiencing an opposing thought and reversing course before I could ever reach a target. In reality, my struggle was bouncing from the sight of Paris, with the paralyzing shock, guilt, and anguish that brought, and the thought of Ty and Andi, with the immediate spur to survive, to shift this story, to save them somehow.

The calamity inside my head was quelled by sirens…many sirens…all growing louder and closer. Were those for *me*? Already?! How could anyone know about this so quickly? All the thoughts you might expect. I heard the sirens pass through on the highway fronting Mikey's house. It was a steady stream of cars and sirens, maybe even ten, all eventually growing fainter. Though it never hit me to question what could possibly be such an emergency at that moment, requiring almost every sheriff and state police car in Shiloh, it did crystallize for me that I had to think and move. Fast.

First question: What do I do with Paris?

Proposals:

a) Take him to the scrapyard and pretend he was a victim of an early morning robbery? The sun was already up and the workers already there.

156

b) Leave him as is and run? Too much guilt in that. Paris's death had taken place because of his desperation, not because it was deserved. He could be lost and undiscovered up here for a couple of days. He was family, and I owed him more than that.

c) Dump him up behind Viola's duplexes? If I must move him, maybe I should jam up an enemy at the same time? I admit I had not yet reached that level of strategic planning in my journey into criminal activity.

d) Maybe just bury him here? Winner! In a world of bad options, this seemed the least evil. The hole was already there, and he'd be next to Mikey and Miklos, as he should be.

Strangely, I methodically rolled Paris into the remaining hole and remember the exact hour and fifty-six minutes it took to refill it. It wasn't pretty...and it was far from discreet, but I couldn't say I didn't want him found soon and buried properly if I could avoid connection to me.

Second question: What do I do with his truck?

Proposals:

a) Move it to the edge of the scrapyard? The street beneath his home? An abandoned roadside somewhere? None of that matched the location of his burial, and after I dumped the truck, how would I be able to get back to my car?

b) Leave it there? This was an easier call. I had not touched the truck to create any fingerprints, and I looked through it to ensure he had nothing in it about me. There was nothing to tie me to it, and the presence of the truck made it more likely they'd find eventually Paris. The sooner the better for my guilt, so long as I'd be gone.

Third question: What tracks needed covering, , and what path should I take from here?

Proposals:

a) The shovel? The only thing I had brought. Put it in the floor of the backseat and dispose of it once on the road. A faraway dumpster would do.

b) The money? I opened the trunk to straighten the money and get it back in the box and close it up, lest any random police stop might call for an officer to take a peek.

c) My clothes? I grabbed some sweats from my duffel bag in the backseat. It was those or the hanging suit and tie I'd worn to Pittsburgh. I'd toss the dirty clothes from the gravesite in a dumpster, one separate from the shovel, just to be safe.

Again, with a strangely clearer mind after the tragedy, I noticed a handwritten page folded among the money. Some kind of chart or index... perhaps a table of contents. I could sort that out later. For now, it went neatly inside the ledger in the front seat. I locked the cash box and was ready to roll.

That only left the question: where to go? I had quickly ruled out leaving town abruptly. That would only create suspicion. I still had Miklos's estate to deal with and believe it or not—if I played this out—yet another funeral, this time for Paris. I paused to dry-heave one more time. Exhausted and smelly, like any gravedigger, I wondered where in this tiny town I might lie low and be safe? I didn't need post-homicidal clarity for that question, as my newly refreshed Shiloh "friend list" was still just one name deep. I needed Walt.

It was around 10 a.m. now and fully daylight, and so I routed around the south side of town on Highway 80, avoiding the Dairy Queen, the Catholic church, and the Bluegrass Hill direction toward Ellen's, from which I'd come that morning. I passed through the old community of Cardinal where I grew up. There were plenty of unseen dumpsters to ditch my clothes there. My old elementary school building was still standing, but long since abandoned, a decent metaphor for my heart at that moment—maybe not abandoned but definitely empty. Cardinal was asleep 24/7, and I figured that was good. Even better, Shiloh seemed just as sleepy as I passed the three red lights on the "bypass" highway around town. It was strange not to see patrol cars aligned around the courthouse on a weekday, even in Shiloh, but there was hardly any movement at all. It was dead.

I pulled into Walt's subdivision, avoiding the house where I had raised Ty and Andi just two doors down. Walt wouldn't be off work and home until around 5 p.m., and I wasn't going to walk into the bank for fear of either being seen or causing a scene. So, I parked a few hundred feet away from his house, and as all the adrenaline of the previous twenty-four hours subsided, I slept. That I slept like a rock would understate it. I was inexperienced with reaction to high stress or trauma, but clearly I had crashed. Only a car door slamming across the street woke me around 4 p.m., as my heightened senses made it sound like gunfire. I shot upright in my seat, half expecting the airbag to have deployed. It was Walt, grabbing bags from his car and heading into his house. He was home early.

"Hey old man! What the hell are you doing here?" Walt smiled as he noticed me, crossing the street with bags in hand. I rolled down the window with a sleepy, uneasy grin of my own. "Catching a few Z's for the road," I hadn't lied yet, "thought maybe I'd catch you and say hey before I head out. You free a while?"

"Anytime for you, T, you know that." He noticed my dirty hands and neck and chuckled, having no thought of mischief. Why would he? "You take up coal mining or something? I know you and manual labor don't mix."

"Was digging through some of Miklos' files at the scrapyard," and so the lies began. "I wouldn't turn down a shower though. Was a long drive back from Pittsburgh."

"Sounds like a plan! C'mon…I have a crazy story for you anyway. You will *NOT* believe!" He had already turned to go. "Gotta put up these groceries, but I'll unlock the basement for you. You know the drill."

Walt's basement was just as I recalled, and still a terrific Shiloh memory. Between his basement and my garage, we had polished off many a workout program. Though we fancied ourselves like Tony Horton, it didn't matter which celebrity. If it was a good workout, we considered it a personal challenge, and we didn't like to lose. Walt still had a cardboard poster of something I'd said years ago, a sample of "old man" motivation we liked to text each other: In the middle of this tornado of a life, it drew a smile. Even better, he still had his work desk and TV above it, a couch and a small fridge along the wall, and a shower around the corner. People joke about men and their beloved man caves, but if ever I deserved to lounge in one, it was now.

Quick shower, towel-dried, and back into sweats. There was no danger here. And I was heading up the stairs when I heard him coming down. "How long can you stay? I can make us dinner." He seemed excited. "And you already know where the beer is."

"Honestly, I've got a few days off, so I'm open to suggestions." I was hinting to at least stay overnight to think. "But I don't want to intrude on your peeps." And now I was hinting to see if we'd be alone.

"It's perfect timing, T. All the kids are already gone back to school from the holiday break, and the missus took a week to go see her mom. Win, win, eh??!" He patted me on the back and tossed me a beer from the fridge.

"You're kinda giddy, aren't you?" Or maybe I was just on edge. "Your story is *that* good?"

"Ah, just the usual Die-Loh Shiloh shit. Another one for our book someday." He leaned back in his chair. "I'm just happy to hang with you."

"In this town, that makes you one of a kind." I was more grateful than sarcastic at this point.

"Well, wait 'til you hear what this town of ours did today…" he started. "You remember the whole Hanji investigation, right? Doctors got off easy in exchange for $500 K, and now Morton is under investigation for it?"

"Sure, I had actually read the article in the paper…this morning, I guess." My mind struggled to find the memory from Dairy Queen that seemed like twelve days, not twelve hours, before.

"Well, apparently, the doctors' kid—Amit—you remember him?"

"Sure, he used to be a social worker or a counselor, right? We had used him on neglect and abuse cases in juvy court." I remembered him as a nice guy, but he always seemed a bit shamed in a small town by his parents' notoriety. Guess I saw a little of myself in him, or worse, a little of my kids as shamed by me.

"That kid…well, he's about thirty now, I guess…wound up dead today, and he will go down as Shiloh's first very own terrorist. No freakin' kidding." Walt wasn't kidding on a whopper of a story, and I was trying to focus from my own head full of terror.

"So, from what I heard," Walt continued, "he was living in his parents' big house up in Big Elk Creek while they're on probation and not allowed to be anywhere in the county as part of the plea deal. Well, unbeknownst to his neighbors and coworkers, he has apparently been building up resentment and planning his parents' revenge. He had set up bombs linked to the cameras on the nature walk trails in Governor Bert Combs Park behind the neighborhood. The cameras are set up with motion detectors to record the wildlife, and one of the bombs went off this morning—killed a small black bear but could've easily been a person."

I had no reply yet. I was trying to wrap my mind around the news. It was surprising, considering my memory of Amit, but I was still like a boxer after taking a haymaker with Paris this morning, trying to bob and weave while regaining enough of my wits to finish a round.

"It gets *so* much better, T." He grabbed another beer. "They were on his house quickly. ATF already had him on their radar because of some suspicious purchases. He had a whole stash of materials in his house. They caught him, interrogated him awhile, and before the feds hauled him off, he agreed to take them up in the woods and point out all the other bombs. But while up there, according to the story I heard, he tried to flee, resisted being retaken, and was shot."

"Guess that explains the cop caravan I heard earlier this morning, eh?" I found it a little odd for all those cops, including the feds, to lose only one guy, and then to need to *shoot* him, but I didn't have my criminal law hat on, nor did I want to put it on.

"Yes, sir. Everyone who walked in the bank either had news about the bomb or wanted to know where everyone was." He recalled dinner. "Hey, let's just order a pizza. Screw cooking, okay?"

I actually laughed. "You know I'll eat anything, man"—and I was truly starving. So far I had held the lie count to just one.

"Alright, I'm on it." He bounded up the stairs to fetch his phone.

But the knock at the door a few minutes later was too soon for the pizza. And even as I saw the flashing police lights through Walt's front door, I still kept walking up the basement stairs, almost like a zombie who was resolved to march forward even as his mates were having their heads blown off by shotguns right in front of them. After all, I had done what I had done, and I'm not a runner. I could never survive like that. I have to be who I am.

Walt let Willie Marr through the door, and I sighed at the sight of a familiar face. Willie and I would always connect through high school football and our later coaching, particularly as our sons came up through the same class. But our day jobs were me as the prosecutor and him as a Kentucky State Police Trooper, a uniform he was still wearing today. And I only needed one guess as to why he was here...I was just glad he was the one who got the call.

"Hey, fellas," he said as he entered, taking off his hat. "I didn't mean to interrupt. Actually just saw Takie's car here and wanted to say hello." Willie was clearly more somber than he was when sharing the usual coaching stories and court jokes we'd shared. "Takie, could I have a word maybe?" He rolled his eyes toward the porch, and I followed him out, ready for handcuffs.

"Takie, you know we go way back. You're like a brother to me...or at least a funny cousin." He attempted a cracked smile. "But I have to handle things like this the same for everyone." I was still the zombie awaiting its fate as he continued. "We got a nine-one-one call about a fire out behind your grandmother's place. It was a couple of hours after everyone went on the hunt for the Hanji kid. I had just gotten to work, so it came my way. Anyway"—his voice trailed—"there's no easy way to say it. We found Paris. It was his truck burning up near your family's graveyard. Somebody shot him, Takie. Shot him in the head and buried him there. Then burned the truck. We had to work the scene, and then I had to talk to Ellen. She's the one who told me you were in town, so I've been looking for you...wanted to tell you the news myself."

Speechless. No idea. None. I just sat down on Walt's porch steps and stared. Tried to think, but was honestly beyond my limit, like when my "A" math skills met calculus. Nothing computed. Nothing made any sense at all. I heard Willie and Walt making small talk, and I'm pretty sure I waved at Willie and thanked him as he got in his car to leave, but after losing my heart this morning, I had now lost my mind.

29

COOKING THE BOOKS

MIDNIGHT

It was a Led Zeppelin night after Willie left, or as Walt and I might have called it, "Dazed and confused." The repeated body blows of the past two days had taken their toll, and even though Walt only had half the story on Paris, he had lost his earlier enthusiasm, too. Color me grateful for his empathy, as he made a little small talk before checking on me one last time and turning in early. But while he left me quiet…he left me without peace.

Instead, I had hypervigilance. A bit of the post-Paris clarity had returned, but I was having trouble harnessing it in any productive direction. I managed a near-perfect count of the eighteen thousand tortuous ticks on Walt's old analog basement clock between 12:30 and 1:00 a.m. I could literally picture my eighth-grade literature teacher doing her rhythmic version of "The Raven." Yes, as Poe had described, I was surely "pondering weak and weary," but I still had no picture of how Paris was found shot with his truck burning. I had buried him myself. That could not be unseen.

Thoughts of Paris reminded me of the money and my hopes of a getaway, and by 1:15, I was quietly checking my trunk in the dark outside, just to make sure the box was still there. I found myself reflexively cautious, even afraid, looking over my shoulder with a roaming eye in search of anything unfamiliar. There were roaming thoughts, too, mostly fear of the cops figuring out what had really happened to Paris *before* his death, and fear of me figuring out what had really happened to Paris *after*. It was possible Vangelis was already local, and if so, he was undoubtedly angry after expecting an answer from me, only to find he'd lost a grandson and a large sum of cash. Was it also possible he had even tried to use a postmortem gunshot and arson to ensure I went to jail for murder? I took a seat in the car, battling an urge to just run now—even at the risk of tipping off the cops with my erratic behavior—or hanging around and risk finding out the hard way that Paris's evil description of Vangelis was legit.

With the key almost in the ignition, my eye caught the ledger in the passenger seat. Strangely, drenched with my mix of insomnia and attention deficits, the idea of something to read or focus upon actually felt like a port in the storm. Best case, I might find a tip or two from Miklos's business records, something that might shed light on Vangelis. After all, I was a lawyer, or so I screamed at myself in my head, still trying to sober or steady my mind. Worst case, maybe the mental exercise would at least help me sleep, which I could use whether I chose flight or fight. So, I grabbed the ledger and crept back inside, still antsy at any lights in the distance, any shadows in nearby windows, or any possible noises from Walt rustling upstairs.

What I found in Miklos's parting gift was a confusing mishmash of a ledger, even by his old-school standards. His entries were strings of numbers and odd lettering, almost Greek or maybe Russian, but not quite…mostly an odd mix of right angles and dots. The handwritten page I had found in the cashbox was unhelpful, a four-line list of the same shapes—perhaps an index or a table of contents—matched with larger numbers. Under the best of circumstances, I'd need an accountant and a translator to track the assets for Miklos's estate. As it was, Mikey had only taught me enough Greek words to verbally survive, if it even was Greek. I surely had no written skills in the language, and only a few hours before the world would swirl again.

What I did have, thankfully, aside from my lifelong expertise in serving people shit with a smile, was a healthy aptitude for brainteasers. In fact, in hindsight, this instance proved yet again that my life might have turned on that skill more than anything else. I had been the kid who aced the puzzles and logic syllogisms on the fifth-grade IQ test, leading to the end of my happy free time of drawing football plays as teachers pushed me toward advanced placement classes, honor societies, and the Kentucky Governor's Scholars Program. And, of course, that same knack for logic puzzles had helped ace the LSAT on a drunken college dare, ending a likely more-fitting path toward coaching while pushing me toward a scholarship, law school, and a career as a round peg in a square hole. While I retained a sliver of doubt that I could be delusional, I still felt that same strange clarity…that this was just another achievable test, complete with the ticking clock on the wall.

Another fortunate piece of this unfolding puzzle was the memory of Jackie Rice, whom I had first met through high school Beta Club, one of those many intellectual activities that had always seemed a waste of time. Jackie, however, proved worthwhile due to her uncanny ability to teleport her way through my life. First there was Beta Club at age seventeen, then sitting together for the bar at twenty-four, then her reappearance to ask for advice on a Social Security case at forty, just after I had jumped to Pittsburgh. Then just last year, in the wake of being kidnapped and physically assaulted by a disgruntled client, she had left her law practice to pursue writing a tell-all book and television pilot on the justice system, and she sought me out for input on any crazy true-crime Rupp County stories that might add to the flavor of her project. Well, if she found me again, Jackie need look no further. I had all the crazy she would ever need.

Jackie's favor back to me was a seed planted way back at our introduction, a day spent as nerds playing around with the pigpen cipher at a Beta Club conference, where other teens chased less noble, but much more entertaining, pursuits. Pigpen splits letters between the corners of an "X" and "+," using the shape of the closest lines to represent the chosen letter. So, the reader sees a lot of "Vs" and "Ls" facing in different directions. It was the encryption of choice among the Freemasons and a common code among many schoolchildren, but I would have never had exposure in Rupp County Public Schools but for Jackie. Using my theory, there were letters now coming into focus. There was the feverish translation of the entries. And there was one laughable, astonished thought in my head: *Miklos literally ran a junkyard...and he used a pigpen code?!* Yes, that was typical Miklos, but could it really be that simple?

It was simple until just past 4 a.m., when exhaustion literally hit—by way of the ledger dropping onto my face while lying on Walt's couch. By then, I had deciphered enough to know that Miklos and/or VPL Enterprises had received regular payments from virtually the entire courthouse. Just initials matched with varying amounts that seemed to rise according to the office held. Barring a flaw in my code or user error, the ledger appeared to show former Sheriff Nathan Grant (NG) and former Judge Paul Runyan (PR), along with a current roll call of county government...Judge-Executive Lee Shipp (LS), Magistrate Rodney Morgan (RM), Commonwealth Attorney Chet Lawson (CL), and Sheriff Lundy Travis, better known as just "LT" (LT). There were many other amounts unassociated with a name...perhaps these were general scrap metal business receipts. And at the end of every month, it looked like two-thirds of the total cashflow was paid out to "VPL," which aligned with Walt's memory of Miklos's bank accounts with monthly installments going to Pittsburgh.

There were payments going out to other people, too, though far less consistently, and there were several people I couldn't quite pin down, no matter how much history I tried to recall. Three more common entries in particular—SD, JB, and BJ—reappeared regularly in the ledger. And those names, along with SB, were linked with much larger numbers as part of the handwritten page from the lockbox. These players, and whatever game they were playing, still remained foggy in my mind as I slept. Had I uncovered a money laundering scheme running through Miklos? And if so, what was the hidden crime? Was Vangelis extorting or bribing the courthouse for political favors? Or were these dues paid for membership in a layered drug or gambling outfit? Or was it all of the above? Or none of the above? Yes, an ounce of me still had hope of another explanation…that Miklos couldn't be involved…that none of this was real.

Around 6 a.m., Walt lightly slammed a kitchen cabinet door upstairs, his polite way of waking me up. I wasn't sure my head had ever pounded more, a combination of two hours of sleep in two days and the riddle I still couldn't get my mind around. Gone was the eager investigator from last night, the one asking, *"Cui bono?"* or "Who benefits?" My mind was now more *"Cui* gives a shit?" I tucked the ledger under a seat cushion and staggered up the steps, trying to remember which parts of my life Walt actually knew about.

"Want some eggs?" Walt was standing at the stove, already dressed for work, flipping a spatula. "You didn't eat much last night."

"Sure, man. Thanks." I kept moving to limit small talk, heading out to the porch to snatch the morning paper. Unwrapping it at the kitchen table, I guess the shock on my face was apparent.

"Yeah, I know. More crazy, eh, T? My phone was blowing up last night, but I figured you'd have plenty of time to catch up." Walt was referring to the front-page headline, "SHERIFF CHARGED WITH MURDER; JUDGE RESIGNS."

I tried to ignore my head splitting in two from back to front so that I could listen to Walt's play-by-play while also digesting the article. Long story short: Sheriff Travis had been arrested and charged with the murder of Amit Hanji, Shiloh's brief walking trail terrorist bomber. Upon actually being cuffed and stuffed, and facing the unfriendly federal prosecutors, "LT" Travis apparently sang like a bird, and also shit like one on Judge Morton in the process. Per the confession, Hanji's escape attempt was a hoax. Travis had volunteered to take Hanji into the woods to identify bomb locations with the intent of killing him at Judge Morton's request. Morton needed Hanji gone, as apparently the infamous $500 K plea bargain "fine" wasn't the only money Morton had wrangled from Hanji's doctor parents in exchange for their sweet probation deal. Amit Hanji had proof of the under-the-table deal, and now, facing his own arrest for the bombing, he would offer any info he could for leniency, thereby posing a threat to Morton.

So, Morton solicited Travis, the kind of outlaw sheriff who would jump at the chance to take down Shiloh's newest and most famous criminal... the chance to take credit for dispensing his own brand of justice by any means necessary. Travis had orchestrated Hanji's chance to flee to justify the shooting, and in exchange for LT's hit, Morton had promised him twenty thousand dollars plus judicial leverage applied to help Travis escape his own ongoing ethics/removal investigation. According to the article, Morton had issued a short statement denying all accusations—he had yet to face any arrest or charges—but he had agreed to resign immediately, citing the inability to effectively administer justice under such a "cloud of lies."

"I gotta get on into work. No one is here for a few days, so just do what you need to do." Walt had carried an entire conversation that I could not remember. All I had were questions I could not ask, all circling in my mind in no particular order. Did any of this news relate to payments in the ledger? Were the cops out there right now circling in on me over Paris? Did Vangelis know what happened at the grave? Or had he even played a role in it? Could I open up and trust Walt to help me with the ledger? Was it even safe to ask him? Or was there anyone else whom I could turn to? And all of these questions were just subsets of the greater conundrum... What did I do now?

The door latching as Walt left shook me to more immediate concerns. Was it even safe to go outside? Did Vangelis have any local assets? What places or people should I avoid? Or was it best to just pretend normalcy? I still needed to extricate myself from Vangelis, that is, get out of town, but without entangling myself with the local authorities over Paris, that is, looking suspicious. Maybe I should just lie low until after Paris's funeral and then quietly fade away. Maybe by then an obvious door would open. Hell, based on the accelerated news cycle of the past forty-eight hours, I guessed anything was possible.

I shook my head with sadness...Paris's funeral...just a week after Miklos'. The thought sobered my hysteria. Yes, the events seemed surreal, but his death was not. There was real danger, real fear, real hurt, and real guilt over my cousin's very real body. And I already knew I'd have to step over that pile of reality today—even if to do only one thing. Of all the texts Walt and I had received overnight as news of Paris spread—some well-wishers and some gossip-seekers—only one was unavoidable. Right or wrong, for better or worse, lies or truth, I'd have to go see Ellen.

30

THE FAMILY FIRST

Her text had just said "*Why don't you come see me? I've got treats!*" Complete with the smiley face attached. Typical Ellen. She buries her husband of forty years, they find her only son murdered less than a week later, and she's making jokes. I sat in her driveway for several minutes with my Spidey sense tingling, but it was all from guilt. I imagined my own son or daughter as Paris, and I tried to imagine his killer at my front door, expressing remorse with me unaware. That was what I was about to do to *her*. I had worried about Vangelis being the devil just two days earlier, but now I think I saw him in my reflection as I got out of the car. What a bastard.

But confession was simply not an option. Not even a passing thought in my head. I had my own kids to protect, and I could best do that alive— and from outside prison. I guess it came down to my definition of "family," and as my options had shrunk since going to Pittsburgh, so had the list of those within the circle of what I could realistically protect. Even as she came to the door, wiping away her tears with a smile, I tried to steady my resolve. Somewhere between Walt's basement and Ellen's driveway, my mission had returned to self-preservation—for me, for Ty, for Andi. When the situation was reframed around them, fear and anxiety faded to the background, and my choices were simpler. What choice did I have?

Coffee or milk, and Chips Ahoy. She always offered the cookies, because she knew them to be my favorite growing up. I wasn't the least bit hungry, but they gave me something to look at and something to occupy my nervous hands. There was small talk, and it was surprisingly comfortable, perhaps because we had just had a similar conversation over Miklos just a few days before. She did stop for tears more often now, though. The second blow had hit harder. Paris was her baby. Still, we found a few memories to laugh about together, and I managed to dodge any landmines (read: *lies*) until we got around to logistics. I assured her I would handle Paris's estate along with Miklos's (*would this be before or after I dropped off the grid?*), then I would make sure all of the business affairs were covered until we could get the business sold (*more like until Vangelis reclaimed what was his*), and when she asked me to do Paris's eulogy, I said, "I'd love to" (*I actually think she knew that one was a lie*).

"I know it's not your favorite thing to do, Takie, and some of the mean spirits around here don't deserve you"—was she actually comforting *me?*—"but you knew him as well as anyone, and you always find exactly the right thing to say. I'm not sure this family could have made it through Mikey, your mom and dad, and then Miklos, without your inspiring words."

"Please don't give it another thought, Ellen." My voice was cracking just a bit. "That's what family is for" (*aside from killing your son, I guess*). But meanwhile, I had plenty of other immediate thoughts about it, first and foremost the possibility of being the next name on the family's list of ghosts if I stuck around for the funeral. Or maybe worse, there was the possibility of missing the funeral from a jail cell awaiting charges and a twenty-year sentence for manslaughter, or even felony murder due to the underlying graveyard theft. And just as I pictured the poetic justice of cops taking me in straight from the church podium, in the middle of the victim's eulogy, there was a perfectly well-timed knock at the door.

I rose to answer and motioned Ellen to rest. I might have killed her son, but the instinctive chivalry and manners engrained by my family remained. Those same manners caused me to muster a smile upon seeing Willie and his state trooper uniform through the screen door. It was either smile at him or run out the back door and jump the fence.

"What's going on, sir?" I spoke casually, as if I was whistling past the graveyard. Ellen had followed me toward the door.

"Hey, Takie... Hello, Ms. Laskaris." He tipped his cap. "I'm actually glad I found you both here together. Mind if I come in?" So, the three of us sat at the kitchen table while he delivered yet another news story that could just have easily come from Mars.

"Look, I just wanted to give you a courtesy heads-up...as the victim's surviving family...it looks like we've got our guy on Paris. They've matched the bullet to a gun registered to Sheriff Travis's personal gun cabinet. He's now been charged with a second murder. I just wanted you to know. It looks like we already have the perp in custody."

"You mean L.T. *Travis*?! Really?! Why on earth would he be involved with Paris?" I had more than a few thoughts swirling around my head, but I was trying to remember first that this was *good* news. If they suspected him, they weren't looking at me.

"We were hoping"—he paused to make sure Ellen was able to proceed with the conversation—"that either of you might be able to help on us understand why. Do you know of any beef between the two of them?"

Ellen was breaking down, offering a needed distraction from the likely words trying to escape my mouth that needed to get back inside my head. Willie and I consoled her, and he relented with his questions, assuring us that we could talk about it later. He left his card in case we thought of anything, and as I walked him out, I told him I'd keep my eyes open for any connections during my upcoming estate work. Still trying to process this new revelation, I mustered a wave and a "Thanks again, man. Really appreciate you telling us," while he drove away.

"Takie," Ellen called from the door. "I forgot to ask you if you would stop by the church this evening. Maybe you could help make sure everything looks nice for Paris. He'd likely throw up to think some stuffy mortician was in charge." She managed a giggle. She was right about Paris, and she knew I'd do what she asked.

"Seven sound about right?" I asked. "I'll bring you dinner. You'll need to eat something." I was backing out as she smiled and waved. And I felt more whole in deciding to help her, almost forgetting that I had caused her pain. Still such a bastard.

Yes, that fact hadn't changed, nor would it, but the axis of the world around me had tilted. Tracing the ledger again in Walt's basement, I could tie Travis to payments to and from Miklos, but I could not find enough bread crumbs to reach the family cemetery where Paris was slain. And even if there was a link, there just wasn't a plausible theory for the killing *after* the killing. Paris had already been buried when I left, period. No matter, though, I could keep refining my thoughts on LT's motives later. For now, I was emboldened with optimism. Without the imminent fear of handcuffs, this was no longer a two-front war. I only needed to make peace with the old man, and that somehow seemed a relief now. Walt would be home from work shortly, and my newly energized self actually pondered asking him for advice.

Walt came in bustling with work files and news of the day I had already heard. He was as amazed at the second Travis murder story, as I was, and like two college roommates procrastinating studying for a final exam, what did we do? We worked out in his basement, managing shortness of breath between sets with our news commentary and conspiracy theories. It felt good to sweat off some stress, it felt good to have a friend, and the discussion of our LT Travis theories segued neatly into what I wanted to share.

"Hey, man," I said while toweling off sweat, "I might need to talk serious for a second, okay?"

"Of course, T. It's easy to see something's on your mind," he replied, "but I was just guessing it's all the grief of the past week."

"Well, that's part of it." I gave it one last thought. "But I've come across some odd stuff in Miklos's business... Was wondering if you might lend your banking or accounting eye. Full disclosure, sir, it actually could be criminal, maybe even related to Travis." After one last pause: "I honestly hesitate to show you, not out of any family pride or shame, but because it is likely dangerous. Not kidding, okay?"

I had barely pulled the ledger from the couch and finished explaining before Walt had spread it across his desk and was pouring through it. At least for the next hour, I had a partner. I gave him my thoughts on what it looked like—a criminal enterprise running through Miklos's scrapyard that might include most of the courthouse—and I pointed him to the unknown initials from my initial review. I neglected the lowdown on the "partner" or parent company in Pittsburgh, which was all Walt knew, and omitted my involvement with Paris the morning before. I didn't want to endanger my friend—or push him away—and at that moment I realized that I sounded an awful lot like Paris had when he'd withheld info and blindsided me with Vangelis. I guess if I hadn't already killed him, I would forgive him.

Walt kicked back in his chair with a whiff of old-school wisdom, and I was happy to let someone else's brain take the lead. "First"—he scratched his chin like King Solomon—"I can solve 'BJ.' That's Ben Browning. 'Ben' is short for 'Benji,' and we all called him 'BJ' when I started over at Mountain

Miners Bank, at least before I walked out." I had known his full name was Benji, and this made total sense after hearing Walt say it. That was one of the names on the handwritten note, across from which was either a payment in or out for thirty thousand dollars.

"Look, T, Miklos is dead, so I'm not breaking any rules or meaning any disrespect here." Walt donned his favorite Steelers cap as if he was getting down to business. "We had suspicions at Black Diamond Bank that Miklos might have been a little dirty—or at least laundering money for those in the dirt—for years. Nothing I could confront with hard evidence, obviously, as his only account with us was—on paper, at least—just that pass-through business expense account. But I know from my earlier time at Mountain Miners, and with all the usual banking gossip afterward, that anyone he referred got preferential treatment...any loan, any rate, any 'project.' And all the top-level shareholders and directors, including BJ as corporate counsel, ended up with fancy cars, houseboats, vacations, and annual cash bonuses. Hell, T, that's mostly why I walked, because I could see the writing on the wall and I wanted no part of that trouble."

"So, you think their game at the bank eventually went sideways," I pondered, "and someone like Ben Browning, or BJ, took the fall."

"EXACTLY! I think they might have pinned the blame on the donkey when needed, similar to what they did with you...no offense. None of this surprises me, T, whether Miklos was paying or getting paid, or whether it was drugs, gambling, or politics. What would surprise me is if it surprises *YOU*."

I had to admit none of this had made my radar. Hell, I had even missed Viola's nonsense during my short stint at the bank. But had I really lived a lifetime of small-town checkers with Miklos playing criminal chess all around me? "One more question...do you think any of these entries on LT Travis tie in to what happened to Paris?"

"Wouldn't shock me, T. His name is more hit-and-miss in the ledger from what I see, but there's more than enough money flowing to or from him to suspect a connection. And we both know Travis was far from a moral man. I could imagine any number of scenarios. I just know this," he finished. "I've never been wealthy, but if I was, I still wouldn't trust a nickel to *any* of them."

I nodded and patted him on the shoulder. "Got mad respect for you, sir. As always. I'll find you later. Gotta get over to the church."

I grabbed drive-thru KFC for Ellen and parked behind the Catholic church, where I sat actually feeling optimistic. The conversation with Walt—just my partial confession and his partial understanding—had lightened my burden, almost to the point of forgetting the task at hand. I needed to console the grieving mother *and* give the eulogy of the cousin I had killed… all while finding a way to settle up with Vangelis, the grandfather who might want to kill me. Yet for some reason, considering my immediate future, I felt good walking into the church. Ellen needed dinner and a smile, and I had both to give.

It was just Ellen and the parish priest, Father Killian, inside. No danger there, just me helping Ellen with a flower arrangement here or a Scripture reading there. About an hour in, around 8:00 p.m., we had done all we could do for the service set to take place the next evening. The three of us were sharing Paris stories in the sanctuary…all the way back to his days as an altar boy. Yes, the longer I stayed, the more I started to worry about spontaneous combustion due my unconfessed, unforgiveable sin, so I offered to run the mile down the road to the Dairy Queen and grab coffee for the group. It would ease my discomfort to get out for a moment and perhaps try to earn an ounce of the ton of penance I needed.

I returned quickly, again entering through the back door into the church's basement reception area. I climbed the steps toward the sanctuary, coffee tray in hand and some drips of optimism still on tap. And that's when things went dark—as in the entire doorway at the top of the steps into the sanctuary was blocked by a dark, hulking figure. It was Maurice.

"Boss Man needs you back downstairs." Maurice's face made it clear his command wasn't optional. We retreated back down the steps. "You should have called him back, Old Timer." The nickname was a slight pleasantry, but not enough to ease the dread. I hit the landing to the reception hall, placing the coffees on a nearby table, and I could see two other figures just inside the back door. The dim lighting made it hard to make out any details, but the one small form, complete with the fedora, was undoubtedly Vangelis. Maybe I should have addressed him as Fate, or the Reaper. Either way, if this was the end, here in the church basement, at least I would have a quick gateway to my likely spot in hell.

31

LAID TO REST

Vangelis hung his hat and cane on the rack just inside the back door with, "Well, hello, Takie, I was hoping to hear from you. Please, take a seat."

First, he actually sounded convinced that I was there by choice. Second, my eyes were glued to Bud...yes, Bud was the second figure, and he had now taken a seat in the corner and crossed his legs, looking as if he only needed popcorn to enjoy the show. I was trying to process his connection, while also noticing that my fear had shifted to a clenched fist.

"I'm fine, sir. Thanks." I remained standing, though I still glanced back at Maurice to make sure it was okay.

"Maurice tells me he knows you, Takie," Vangelis continued, "from your time in Pittsburgh?" Yeah, he knew me, and I knew him enough to know he could break me in half.

"I met him there, too, when he played with the Steelers. I'm a huge fan of the team and one of their largest benefactors. In exchange, I get an occasional dinner with the team, and I get the chance to pick up a player for my employ...when they are finished playing, of course. Maurice was a perfect fit my security detail."

"I understand, sir, but forgive me if I do not feel very 'secure' at the moment."

"Takie, please." Vangelis spoke in a tone as if he wanted me to come sit on Grandpa's knee. "There's no reason to be nervous. The delay in your decision…it's understandable. It's clear that some things have changed since we last spoke, though." I was hoping he meant that Paris's death meant I was now unnecessary to his plan. Maybe he would take all the business back or close up shop. Then again, that could also render me expendable. I began to size up the chances on whether I could clock Maurice with a nearby chair and make it up the stairs behind him.

"My lack of interest hasn't changed." Color me brave for a moment. "If anything, losing Paris eliminates any connection at all for me. I don't care to help with any legal needs in getting everything changed over, though I'm sure Bud can do all that." I shot a visual dagger at him, to see whether he'd flinch, but he remained smug and gleeful, as if I was another *Jerry Springer* redneck at his office looking for his help without a prayer of finding it.

"Takie, my child"—it was a term of endearment that ran all over me— "surely you see how Paris's death…and this thing with the local judge… it all makes you *more* desirable to me? More valuable. You're such a *smart* kid"—spoken in a tone of admiration—"and you're in the driver's seat. You have to know that."

His grandfather act was pissing me off. I had foregone a chair and was now eyeballing a possible chance to grab some cutlery in the reception hall kitchen. "All I know, sir, is that you should likely be in jail, and I want no part of this *family business*." I had thought it through a little, trying to play chess. I had the cash and the ledger, evidence I could perhaps use as insurance if I was threatened.

"Always the chicken*shit*…" Bud's voice from the corner turned our heads. Vangelis, though, still calm and collected, raised both hands toward Bud. "Stop that, please. That's uncalled for." Turning back to me, he went on, "Please forgive him, Takie. He's been consigliere since he took office…as invested in our enterprise as my own sons…invested in you as a brother." And turning back to Bud, he said, "He just doesn't know it yet, and *you* know it."

"Know what?!" I was angry as they discussed me as if I wasn't even in the room…angry at Bud for his obvious animosity, his unexpected years of betrayal. "That you and Miklos were running some kind of criminal racket all these years? Paying off or extorting politicians for protection and bankers to help funnel the money? That you're likely a mass murderer?" The last one brought a long pause from Vangelis…a deep breath as he walked to the front of his table and perched himself on its corner. With the anger, I suddenly didn't care. I was now trying to figure out some way to turn Maurice to my side, or somehow get to the gun inside his coat. If I could get a shot off, I'd start with Bud.

"You really don't know anything, *do* you?" For the first time, Vangelis's voice held venom. "You *think* you know, but you don't have the first damn clue. What have you got? Miklos's ledger? You think you've solved the puzzle with payments to politicians? Well, it's not about the money! And it's not about the *who*! It's about the *why*! And that's to set things up for *YOU!* I've had my nose in your life since it all started, so I'd appreciate just a little respect, if you don't mind."

He recoiled a bit with a smile. "You think your move into the courthouse, for example—the one you pined for—just *appeared* from thin air? That deal with you and Bud, with Miklos...massaging Frank Coxton and the other small-town egos...that was *us*. We moved pieces for you, again, and again. Even the opening itself, good ol' Skinny Don going to prison? Him just giving in at his trial? He was a soldier, Takie. Those clients he took out knew too much, and Don has carried thirty years of weight for us. He's been well-compensated, mind you...legacy payments...but his crime was the severing of an arm to save the patient."

With that, he had just solved the "SD" mystery from the ledger. I knew "Skinny Don's" nickname, but I had just missed it. Vangelis was just getting warmed up.

"Even your first big case with Joe Reznar, remember? You performed splendidly, just as we expected. But Bud and Miklos gave you that. Granted, little Joe Bill. had...how shall we put it...'debts' that had to be dealt with anyway, debts that went back all the way to his thieving father before him, and he helped us out by stealing from his office to pay Miklos. He tied his own noose for us, and he helped you with a big case in the process. Win-win."

And that explained "JB" (Joe Bill) from the ledger. To me, Joe's father had been Bill, but his full name was Joe Bill Reznar. The younger Joe was a junior. I had just forgotten. Vangelis was like John Housman reading Charles Dickens by a fireplace. I was mesmerized. Terrified, yet enjoying it. I didn't want him to stop.

"The same applied to Ben Browning. The alcohol...the gambling. Addictions that even cost him his son. That was all him...but his second round of legal issues was an intolerable risk. He knew too much. We simply leaned on his conscience and helped him see exactly what he needed to see… what he chose to see. He sacrificed himself and took the rap to satisfy the mob, but his remaining family has continued to prosper, and you got the high-profile conviction. Again, Takie, it was a win for him, a win for us, and a win for *you*.

"But you know about Ben Browning from the ledger, right?" He shrugged. "Of course, you do. You see all the angles…always have…and even your friend Walt helped us with that one. How do you think he got his pool? Did you know that's in the book?"

Hold up! Walt was in the ledger? My friend *Walt Isaacs*?

"Now, now…he just helped with some of the needed banking documents to leverage against Browning." He patted down the air with his hands, as if to say *simmer down, son*, while reestablishing himself behind the table. "We needed to test whether or not we could trust him, and it was all unbeknownst to you. You just processed the evidence you had."

I could confront Walt later, but my exasperation at such news helped me speak up now. "With all due respect, sir, I might actually accept your history of events, and simply choose indifference—just say, 'thanks, but no thanks'—but you've yet to justify the *murders*. You've yet to explain your real evil—how killing Deo, or Mikey, or Miklos, and likely many others, was done to help *my* career. You're going to tell me how erasing most of my family heritage was of benefit to *me*?" I was making a leap to the killings based upon Paris's suspicions, but it wasn't a huge one, and he didn't blink, thereby verifying my gut instinct.

"You need not concern yourself with any of that, Takie. No one would attempt to pin any such death on *you*." He took a seat for the first time, and I did the same, astonished at how he thought I would be concerned with any connection to the technical execution of the deaths, as opposed to overwhelming angry over his murder of my grandmother and uncle! Did the old man have no heart at all?! If given the chance, I'd wring his neck.

"Takie," he said with a sigh, "I never ended anything or anyone that wasn't already on the way out, and everyone always received the same loyalty and fairness they gave to me. You can expect the same—always." If you changed the scenery, he could be any accountant, lawyer, or financial advisor, selling you on his trustworthy service. "Deo and Mikey came from *nothing*, and they ended up with many blessings in this life. Miklos, too. Because of me. Because of our business. And they ultimately chose their fates, Deo and Mikey for love and Miklos for money and guilt. Still, from the beginning to the end, it was always their choice and always a fair exchange." He was now speaking just as any contracts professor at any law school, too.

"Anyway, everything is a choice. They made theirs, and now you will make yours. You now have the truth and the ledger, and we would rather you not stand in opposition to the family—that route is bad for everyone—but instead see this as the perfect opportunity. With Morton gone, the circuit judge spot is open again," he said as if it was mine for the taking, "and it is the power and prestige you always wanted, that you always deserved. It rights a lot of wrongs for you personally, and you'll be able to right a lot of wrongs for everyone else in this town. Meanwhile, for the family, you'll provide the ultimate backstage pass…legal access and cover for any of our ventures."

"With me as your puppet, you mean?"

"No, with you as a partner…finally getting the respect and success you deserve. That's all I've *ever* wanted for you, and even now, after all your wayward paths around and away from this position, we've set it up again… just for *you*." He smiled and stroked his chin. "You see it now, right? We cleaned up your Paris situation."

He nodded toward Maurice, who reached around the corner of the kitchen and raised the shovel I had used to bury Paris. Their leverage against me in response to me holding the ledger, I supposed. My mouth fell open.

"They'll soon tie the same gun of Travis's we used on Paris to the famous Gill Blackney murder. Travis knows this. Just like he knows we took out the little terrorist in the woods and left him holding the bag. That's three murders. Hanji, Blackney, Paris. LT is done. But you see, Travis's mix of ambition, vanity, and immorality was always on that path. He was an uncontrollable variable, just like his mentor, Blackney. We tried to pay Blackney, too, but ultimately we had to go the other way—or at least we were going to go that way before your little sheriff's deputy filly did our work for us." And amazingly, he had just cleared the last name, Sheriff Blackney (SB), which was linked to the larger numbers on Miklos's handwritten list.

"Once the Hanji kid's blood was on his hands, we knew a person like Travis would eagerly implicate Morton in that little side deal with the doctors. That would keep Travis off death row, so what choice would he have? And it gives Morton a nice slice of humble pie, which is even more bitter for him considering that Miklos actually instigated the original plea deal with the doctors and even got a piece of that pie for us. The money from that plea—the part that went to line Morton's pocket—was part of our larger negotiation that got Morton to finally cut *your* lawsuit loose. A little personal vindication for you and a deserved result for both of them, wouldn't you agree? Yet again."

I had sunk deeper in my chair, less and less afraid of the moment and more and more lost down a rabbit hole of the ridiculous. I looked over at Maurice, as if to say, *Are you buying all this?* Still standing firm and expressionless, he actually said, "Sounds like you just need to put in your own work around here for a change, Old Timer."

"Something you should've learned a long time ago!" Bud chimed in. "No one *gives* it to you. You have to *take* it at some point."

Vangelis cast his eyes over to Bud, again to calm him down, but there was no scolding this time. "They are right, Takie." He turned back to me. "It is truly *your* time, and there is so little you have to do. All you have to do is be *you*… Use your good name and intentions in the election, and then take your rightful place behind the bench. This is exactly why we kept you clean and unaware all those years…the same reason you won't find Bud in the ledger. Our partners in the legal system must have plausible deniability."

There was a long pause, almost as if he knew that my heart and mind had reached full capacity and he needed the thoughts to soak in. They were goading me…trying to own me by challenging my manhood. The feast was all set, they were saying, and if I had the requisite courage and ambition, I would sit down and eat. They were trying to play the right recording in my head to get me to want exactly what they wanted me to do, as if benefited *me*…the exact thing I had done to countless others over the years. Taking the job would obviously go against good judgment, but what was I to do when all they said—no matter how immoral, how unethical, how illegal, how just plain wrong—was still, when it came to me, exactly right?

"So, it's settled then." I wasn't sure if he thought he had read my mind or was just pushing forward regardless. "You sleep on it, and we will hear from you after the wake tomorrow." He reached for his hat and coat as Bud stepped toward the back door. "An extension of time is clearly warranted after the upheaval of the past two days. Like I said, we only set the stage. You pull your own strings. It is always your choice. I hope you will return to save this town. You can be the hero it has always needed, that it never saw right under its nose. File for the special election, take office by the end of May, and help us run the business we have prepared for you. You can even keep the box of money you dug from the grave. Consider it a signing bonus."

The three of them walked away, appearing as light as they had when they entered, while I slumped further, unable to move. They had left all the weight on me...layers on top of layers to the same life-splitting decision I had debated over the past week...try to shed the weight of my family, of my town, or carry it. Vangelis was right on that point. The choice was still mine.

32

THE OTHER SIDE

SIX MONTHS LATER

I still spent a few minutes every morning in the courtroom, just before the clerk called the first case, reminding myself of all my reasons. The parties and their lawyers would think I was reviewing some last-minute documents or plotting a ruling, but I was rearguing my own case in my head, restating the pros and cons in hopes of convincing myself I had made the right call.

Today, my thoughts had drifted to a scene from my high school graduation, circa 1987. The family had convened at Mikey's for dinner that Sunday afternoon. I was seventeen and had already opened all the gifts. Dinner was just wrapping up, with the men gathered around a basketball game on TV, and the women were cleaning up in the kitchen. It was perhaps a scene from the 1950s, but that's still how our larger family functions operated. I had gone to return dirty dishes to the sink, and my mind paused at the room full of our family's women. I glanced over each face in my mind's eye, pondering the decisions each had made to get where they were in life.

There was Chrissy, only fifteen at the time, already Paris's high school sweetheart and future bride. A product of a rocky relationship with her own mother and sisters, and holding dreams of a life with a better house and a larger wallet—like most kids in Shiloh—she was eager to have a "cool" mother-in-law like Ellen and a kind, hardworking meal ticket like Paris. Perhaps she was so eager that she would have easily opted for the life she had, and pushed Paris to maintain it, even if she knew its criminal source and eventual painful cost.

There were Ellen and my mom, both of whom had married early as the "lucky" girls who got the popular, unique Greek boys in town. As the story went, Miklos and Terez were driving dump trucks and lifting cinder blocks in the scrapyard by the age of thirteen. As a result, they had chiseled arms and expensive vehicles—the result of their hard labor—even in junior high. Add good bone structure and European accents, and the girls would swoon. If Ellen and my mom had *ever* become aware of the family's darker side, they had never shown it. They always seemed happy with their lives, immersed in their children and proud of their men. Maybe they battled the possibilities on some days, or maybe they chose to ignore any suspicions they had. Maybe they loved their men hard enough to never need to ask questions. Ignorance is bliss.

Then, at the end of kitchen counter near the garbage can was Mikey, scraping leftovers in the trash and always eyeballing a possible meal for herself. She loved to cook for the family, but she'd rarely sit down to her own dinner. She was always making sure everyone else had enough, a habit born of her immeasurable love and perhaps the stern demands of her husbands. Instead, she ate at the garbage can, grabbing the occasional leftover bite while washing the dishes. After growing up dirt-poor in Greece and sacrificing any of her own dreams to give her kids a chance for a better life in America— even with the full knowledge of what Vangelis had become—I doubt she knew any other way to live. I hope that made it easier for her, and I hope she knows that someone still carries on her family burden, even if it will never be easy. Funny, even when I'm alone, I still eat standing near the garbage can in the kitchen. True story.

"All rise… The Rupp Circuit Court is now in session, the Honorable Antony Tsegellis presiding." That might be the most pompous thing I've ever heard, just as I had thought when I heard it proclaimed for three prior judges, but I still liked the way he said it. I walked past Edwin the bailiff after his announcement and took my seat. My eyes scanned the gallery as the parties assembled for the weekly criminal motion hour. "Be seated." It was still hard to believe that people had to wait for me to tell them when to sit. Ridiculous.

Only four weeks post-swearing in, and I had already won the battle to learn the job. Twenty-five-plus years post–law school, and I was more than ready to spot and poke holes in all the same arguments and courtroom tactics I had tried myself over the years. Guess that's the point of experience. But I had hardly made any progress toward peace with my decision. I'm the guy who couldn't make big decisions even before law school, remember? And then, after being taught to argue both sides as an attorney, I could struggle for three hours at a store just trying to decide on a pair of shoes…only to have buyer's remorse the moment after I paid for them. Take *that* guy, then show him that his whole life was secretly manufactured by his crime boss grandfather, have him accidentally kill his cousin, put him in fear for the lives of his children, and then ask him to choose between a) life on the run from mobsters, or b) $1 million cash and his dream job, with the catch being it's in the very town and doing the very deeds he hates. Yeah, I think that about sums it up.

The daily grind of my self-assessment comes down to this: We all owe a debt to our families. Some, of course, owe more or less than others, proportionate to the level of blessings received. Per the book of Luke: "To whom much is given, from him much is expected," and in that vein, our ancestors are our demigods. This begs the question: Does the quality or value of my life repay my ancestors in adequate fashion? In other words, in the eyes of those who have gone before, have I earned the life they left behind?

Am I a parent with the strength and devotion of Mikey, who loved and protected her children through war and poverty, through relocation and the unknown, through a tyrant husband and fear? Some might say yes. I'd been through wars if you counted courtroom and career battles. I'd done without and relocated and faced the unknown to keep my kids comfortable. I'd faced my fear of that same tyrant and even swallowed my hatred of him and Shiloh in order to keep my loved ones safe.

Am I a faithful and generous public servant like Miklos, who never flaunted his wealth, never batted an eye at getting dirty alongside his employees, and who was never without a favor for those in need, whether politically or financially? Some might say yes. I'd spent my entire career dodging egos and greed, just wanting to help my hometown and feel some sense of significance. Even after that same town turned its back, and even after I saved myself elsewhere—reaching my own personal salvation—here I was again in the trenches, turning a cheek to Shiloh's ignorance and arrogance while trying to be a source of justice and protection for the locals.

But am I also a small-town organized criminal like my grandfather Vangelis, who bribed politicians for political power, leveraged the weak for financial gain, lied to his family for years, and even killed some of them when he felt justified by his own needs? Well, some might say yes to that, too.

Apparently I'm the grand prize recipient of gifts from a lifetime of organized crime, and apparently I will lie to my children so that they are proud of their father—the judge and not the criminal—and yes, I killed Paris.

So, I keep trying each morning, in those moments on the bench, but as of yet there's no way to clearly sort my mixed bag of history. I console myself with the fact that I'm at least a man who pays his family debt—following my ancestors' footsteps and making them proud—whether good or bad. Still, as I had pondered during Miklos's eulogy, the ancient Egyptians believed that the path to heaven comes with a "yes" to two questions… Did you find joy in your life? And did you give joy to others? Miklos's answers had seemedeasily "yes" to both, but mine remain mixed, both in what I feel inside and what I've given or done to others.

In short, my new life of crime, law, and politics in Shiloh might never lead to redemption or any real significance, but my prior life of running from crime, the law, and politics had never helped me reach those things, either. So, my mind will forever reconsider the move, even though for now it is a weight I choose to carry.

Life usually comes down to what you are prepared to do as you choose daily between what you want and what you might be afraid to lose. For now, I will hold court in Shiloh, manage favors for Vangelis, and perhaps even bury a body when necessary. In exchange, Ty and Andi will be safe and provided for, and my work will allow me to help others on most days. Does that put more good than bad in the columns of my own ledger? That's a tough call, and you know how I struggle with big life decisions.

CPSIA information can be obtained
at www.ICGtesting.com
Printed in the USA
LVHW031306141118
596836LV00008B/155/P